Alex Pine was born and raised on a council estate in south London and left school at sixteen. Before long, he embarked on a career in journalism, which took him all over the world – many of the stories he covered were crime-related. Among his favourite hobbies are hiking and water-based activities, so he and his family have spent lots of holidays in the Lake District. He now lives with his wife on a marina close to the New Forest on the south coast – providing him with the best of both worlds! This is his sixth novel.

By the same author:

The Christmas Killer
The Killer in the Snow
The Winter Killer
The Night Before Christmas
The Killer in the Cold

COLD
BLOODED
KILLER

ALEX PINE

avon.

Published by AVON
A division of HarperCollins*Publishers* Ltd
1 London Bridge Street
London SE1 9GF

www.harpercollins.co.uk

HarperCollins*Publishers*
Macken House, 39/40 Mayor Street Upper
Dublin 1, D01 C9W8, Ireland

A Paperback Original 2025
1

First published in Great Britain by HarperCollins*Publishers* 2025

To my three wonderful daughters – Lyanne, Ellie, and Jodie.
Love you so much.

Introducing DCI Walker and his team

This is the sixth book in the DCI James Walker series.
For those who haven't read *The Christmas Killer*, *The Killer in the Snow*, *The Winter Killer*, *The Night Before Christmas* and *The Killer in the Cold*, here is a brief introduction to the man himself and the key members of his team.

DETECTIVE CHIEF INSPECTOR JAMES WALKER, AGED 44

An officer with the Cumbria Constabulary based in Kendal. He spent twenty years with the Met in London before moving to the quiet village of Kirkby Abbey just over five years ago. He's married to Annie, aged forty, who was born in the village and worked as a teacher. The couple have a daughter, Bella, aged three, and a son, Theo, who is just over eighteen months old.

SUPERINTENDENT JEFF TANNER, AGED 50

Now based at Cumbria Police HQ in Penrith. James took over from him as DCI. He's married with a son.

DETECTIVE INSPECTOR PHIL STEVENS, AGED 42

A no-nonsense detective who moved up the ladder to replace James as DI. He's married with two children.

DETECTIVE SERGEANT JESSICA ABBOTT, AGED 37

A highly respected member of the team and of Irish and East African descent. She's as sharp as a razor, and not afraid to speak her mind. She, too, was promoted to her current position as part of the department shake up. She's married to Sean, a paramedic.

DETECTIVE CONSTABLE CAROLINE FOLEY, AGED 31

The youngest member of the team, she lives with her widowed mother in Kendal. Her three-year relationship with another woman broke down a year ago.

PROLOGUE

It was just after 9 p.m. on Christmas Eve when Gordon Carver stepped out of the pub and onto the wind-lashed street. Snow was still falling, but thankfully not as hard as it had been earlier.

His heart was beating rapidly, and his first instinct was to look around to see if he was being watched. But it was impossible to tell because there were so many people out enjoying the festive atmosphere that had at last consumed the market town of Kendal.

Couples, groups and individuals were making the most of the occasion despite the bad weather that had battered Cumbria for days. The mood was buoyant, but after what he'd just been told, he wasn't able to embrace it. Instead, his body was tight with tension and a ball of anxiety was growing inside him.

This wasn't how he had expected the day to end. Up until now he had been on a high.

This morning he'd had breakfast with his parents at their home in Burneside and they'd given him a £50 Amazon gift voucher as a Christmas present. And then this afternoon he'd managed to spend two hours with the woman who had captured his heart.

But after that came the phone call followed by the revelation that had badly shaken him and left him fearing for his life.

As he headed towards home, he started to give thought to how he should react. He'd faced numerous threats and intimidation during his long journalistic career, but nothing like this. He was therefore convinced that he had no choice but to take it seriously. Doing nothing was not an option. He had to do what was necessary to protect himself.

It was going to take him less than ten minutes to get home, but the further he walked, the more anxious he became. He kept looking over his shoulder to see if he was being followed, gripped by the rising sense of panic.

Only a couple of hundred yards from his house and walking along a path that took him through a small patch of woodland, a rush of blood to his head prompted him to act straight away.

He tugged his mobile from his pocket, and after opening up his contacts, he scrolled down to the last name on the list – Detective Chief Inspector James Walker. He was the Cumbria Constabulary officer with whom Gordon had the closest working relationship. Detective Walker was also the only copper he had ever really trusted, and he was sure that James would offer sound advice on how best to deal with the threat he faced.

He tapped the number, but as it started ringing, he heard the clump of footsteps on the rough gravel behind him.

He started to turn at the same time a hard blow struck the back of his head, sending him tumbling forward onto the ground and into the deep, dark depths of oblivion.

CHAPTER ONE

The kids were at last in bed and fast asleep. It meant that James and Annie could have some quiet time together before turning in themselves.

It was coming up to ten o'clock and they had planned to put the little munchkins down much earlier. But there had been a lot to do in preparation for the big day and so they'd let them stay up and burn off some of their energy.

Three-year-old Bella had been hyperactive because she now knew about Santa and that he would soon be dropping by to deliver her Christmas presents. And her brother Theo, who was almost two, had been loud and lively throughout the day since a howling wind woke everyone at 6 a.m. and brought another lashing of snow to Kirkby Abbey and other parts of Cumbria.

Thankfully the weather had calmed by the time James drove the twenty-five miles from the village to police headquarters in Kendal, where he'd been based for the past five years. He spent the best part of seven hours in the office while Annie took the kids to see the Santa Claus parade in the village square before going to a children's party in the school.

James was pretty sure that his day had been less stressful than his wife's given that, for a change, he'd spent most of it at his desk attending to paperwork and assigning tasks to his team of detectives.

The tasks dealt with three serious incidents: the non-fatal stabbing of a teenage boy in Windermere, an arson attack on a house in Ambleside, and a drunken brawl at a pub in Staveley. They were all straightforward cases and at least no one had been murdered.

As Detective Chief Inspector, James was responsible for overseeing all investigations, formulating strategies, and making the high-level decisions. It was something he was well equipped to do, having served as a copper for over twenty-five years, twenty of them with the Met in London before he and Annie had moved to Cumbria.

Tomorrow, he intended to stay at home with the family, provided that no major crimes were committed on his patch that he'd have to take the lead on.

'I've poured you a whisky and me a gin,' Annie said when James walked into the living room carrying the two sacks of Christmas presents that had been hidden in the wardrobe. 'Come and sit down. We both deserve a break before we sort that lot out,' she said, gesturing to the bags of gifts.

As he perched himself on the sofa next to his wife, she handed him a glass of his favourite whisky.

'Cheers, my love,' she said. 'Here's to a very merry Christmas.'

As they clinked their glasses, James felt a ball of emotion well up inside him. At moments like this it always struck him how lucky he was to have met and married this woman. She was kind and committed, as well as gorgeous, with soft features, bright blue eyes, and long black hair.

'The same to you, sweetheart,' he said before downing a mouthful of whisky that warmed the back of his throat.

The TV was on, but they paid no attention to it as they talked about the following day. The morning was going to be all about ensuring that the kids enjoyed themselves. Then it was the traditional turkey lunch, to which they'd invited Annie's best friend, Janet Dyer. She would otherwise be by herself as her twin sons were spending the festive period with her ex-husband. In the evening, they were hoping to chill out and stream a Christmas movie.

'Are you still glad that we didn't move back to London this year, despite what happened last Christmas?' Annie asked him.

James responded with a smile and a nod. 'Of course I am. And not just because the longer I'm here the more I love the place. It's meant that we've also been able to play a part in helping the village to recover. And it's not as if going back to the Smoke will make us feel any safer.'

Kirkby Abbey had been shaken to the core twelve months ago by the murders of two of its residents, both former police officers. They were killed on Christmas Eve and their bodies were found on Boxing Day within walking distance of James and Annie's four-bedroom cottage.

But it wasn't just those heinous crimes that had made the couple seriously consider upping sticks and returning to London. It was the fact that, since they'd settled in Cumbria five years ago, the county had been blighted by bursts of bloodshed during each successive festive period. It meant that James had been forced to abandon his family at Christmas to investigate no fewer than thirteen murders, and the cases had been among the most disturbing of his career. He'd almost come to accept the rising death toll as a gruesome Christmas tradition.

'We can only hope and pray that this year will be different,' he said, and Annie responded by raising her glass again.

'I'll drink to that,' she replied before leaning over to peck him on the lips. 'And just so you know, I'm also pleased that we stayed here. Sure, we've had more than our fair share of dark days, but I wouldn't want to live anywhere else.'

They enjoyed another drink together before deciding that it was time to wrap the presents and spread them across the floor around the glittering Christmas tree.

But before they got started, they heard the distinctive ringing of James's phone coming from the kitchen. It was where he'd left it when they went upstairs to bathe the kids.

He felt a sharp stab of alarm and instinctively turned to Annie, who rolled her eyes and said, 'Let's just hope that there hasn't been a murder.'

He huffed out a breath before rushing into the kitchen. His phone was on the worktop and as he picked it up, he saw that the name on the screen was that of his boss, Superintendent Jeff Tanner.

'Hello, guv,' he said, his tone sharp. 'I didn't expect to hear from you tonight. What's up?'

'I'm just ringing to wish you a merry Christmas and to let you know that my wife and I have cancelled our trip to Scotland because of the appalling weather there. So, we'll be staying at home.'

James heaved a sigh of relief. 'Thanks for letting me know and a merry Christmas to you, too. I was worried you had some bad news for me.'

Tanner chuckled. 'Thankfully no. It's all quiet on the northern front. And I gather that today was reasonably quiet in the office?'

'That's right. We detained a guy in connection with the stabbing and arrested two men after the pub brawl. Whoever set fire to the house in Ambleside remains a mystery, but thankfully very little damage was done before it was put out.'

'And who will be on duty tomorrow?'

'Detectives Stevens and Abbott. Hopefully they won't be kept busy.'

'Fingers crossed. I'll be back at my desk on Boxing Day now that I'm not going away. What about you?'

'I'm supposed to be off until after the weekend, but we'll see how it goes.'

'Well, I'm due a visit to Kendal so I might pop down on Monday. If I do, we can have a catch-up.'

Tanner had been based at Cumbria HQ in Penrith for three years after moving from Kendal, where he'd been DCI. James was promoted to fill his shoes, and the pair had a good working relationship.

Before hanging up, Tanner added, 'Enjoy your break then, James, and pass on my best wishes to your good wife.'

As he disconnected, James noticed a missed call notification on his home screen. It had come in just under an hour ago, when he was upstairs with the kids, so he hadn't heard it.

The caller was journalist Gordon Carver, who worked for the *Cumbria Gazette* and was one of the very few hacks whom James trusted.

Curiosity compelled him to return the call as he walked back into the living room, but there was no answer.

'Who was it then?' Annie asked him. 'Have you got to go out?'

He shook his head and told her it was Tanner. 'He just wanted me to know that he's not taking his usual Christmas break because of the crap weather in Scotland. And he passed on his best wishes to you.'

'That was nice of him.'

'I missed a call from Gordon Carver,' James noted.

'I'm not surprised we didn't hear it,' she said. 'The noise the kids were making in the bathroom at the time was off the scale.'

James frowned. 'If it was urgent I'm sure he would have called me back by now.'

Annie nodded. 'He probably wanted to pump you for information. That's usually why he calls you.'

She was right, and James saw no point in overthinking it. Instead, he made a mental note to check in with the journalist at some point tomorrow, and decided to spend the rest of the evening relaxing with his wife before chaos once again descended on the Walker household.

CHAPTER TWO
CHRISTMAS DAY

Christmas morning came all too soon for James and Annie. At 6 a.m. Bella wandered into their room and woke them up to ask if Santa had been.

Annie tried to persuade her to go back to bed, but it proved to be a waste of time. She was wide awake, excited, and bursting with energy. It was left to her dad to tell her that they wouldn't know if Santa had been until they ventured downstairs.

'Even if he has, you'll have to wait until your brother is up so that you can go down together,' he said.

As if on cue a sharp cry came from Theo's room, which prompted Annie to roll over and get out of bed.

'I'll bring him in here and he can join me and Bella on the bed,' she said to James. 'You go down and see if Santa's been. If he has, then turn on the fire and kettle, and come and get us.'

James got up and blinked away the tiredness in his eyes. After slipping on his dressing gown, he ruffled his fingers through his daughter's hair, told her to climb onto the bed, and stepped out of the room.

The house was still cold, so once downstairs he upped the temperature on the central heating and turned on the electric fire in the living room, along with the lights.

Next stop was the kitchen where he filled the kettle and switched it on. Then it was into the downstairs bathroom to empty his bladder and rinse his face.

Seeing himself in the mirror made him flinch. He was forty-four, but looked at least five years older. His face was a pale, washed-out colour, and his thick brown hair was now peppered with grey. Not that it bothered him that much. He'd long ago accepted that the stress of the job was bound to leave its mark physically as well as mentally.

He returned to the living room and opened the curtains to check on the weather. It was dark outside, but he could see that more snow had fallen overnight or earlier this morning. It covered the front garden and his car but only by a couple of inches.

After pouring two mugs of tea and preparing drinks for the kids, he went back upstairs to announce that Santa Claus had been and gone.

Bella's face lit up. 'Did he leave some toys for us? Did he, Daddy?' The words spluttered out of her mouth.

James laughed. 'Yes, he did, my darling. So, are you ready to find out what there is?'

The next two hours were fun, chaotic, and memorable, and James made sure to take plenty of photos.

Bella and Theo were delighted with their gifts, which included books, colouring sets, building blocks and a range of other toys. After everything was unwrapped the pair went into manic mode – jumping, clapping, squealing, and flapping their hands.

James and Annie waited until things had quietened down before exchanging their own gifts. She gave him, among other things, an expensive bottle of single malt whisky. And he gave her a bag containing all the items she'd hinted at, including a pair of slippers, a cashmere scarf, and a set of scented candles.

As far as James was concerned, the day had got off to a perfect start and he felt quite emotional.

They tucked into pancakes for breakfast and afterwards he sent goodwill text messages to his parents, who still lived in London, as well as his brother and two sisters.

By nine o'clock, he and Annie were showered and dressed. They were about to share the task of getting the kids ready when James's phone rang. He wasn't expecting anyone to call this early, and so his breath caught, and a hard knot tightened in his throat.

'Don't go into panic mode,' Annie said when he looked at her and pulled a face. 'It's probably just an early rising well-wisher.'

But the caller was Detective Inspector Stevens, and as soon as he started speaking all the festive cheer that had built up inside James evaporated in an instant.

'I'm really sorry to bother you, guv, but something has happened that you need to know about,' he said.

'What is it, Phil?' James asked him with a tremor in his voice.

'There's been a murder here in Kendal. A couple out walking stumbled across a body a short time ago. DC Abbott and I just arrived at the scene, and it turns out the victim is someone we all knew. Gordon Carver, the journalist at the *Gazette*.'

James felt a cold shiver run through him. 'Are you fucking serious?'

'I'm afraid so, guv. It seems he was attacked on a pathway close to his home at some point last night. He received what appears to be a fatal blow to the back of his head.'

James closed his eyes as a heavy weight settled in his stomach.

'There's something you need to know, Phil,' he said after a beat. 'Gordon called me last night just after nine o'clock, but I didn't hear the phone ring. About an hour later I saw I had a missed call and rang him straight back, but he didn't pick up. I suspect that could be because he was already dead by then.'

'Holy shit. Do you know why he wanted to speak to you?'

James blew out a loud breath. 'Not a clue. He usually rang me for info when we were working a big case, but I haven't heard from him in weeks.'

'How do you want to handle it then? Shall we crack on or do you—'

'I'll need to head this one up, so text me the location,' James interrupted. 'You and Jessica stay at the scene and wait for me to get there. I'll be as quick as I can. Have you told anyone else who the victim is?'

'Not yet.'

'Then keep it to yourselves for now. I'll put a call in to the Super. The murder of a high-profile journalist will attract a lot of attention.'

CHAPTER THREE

When James came off the phone his heart was pounding, the beat booming in his ears. He immediately turned to Annie and saw the concern on her face.

'It's bad news, isn't it?' she said, her voice thin and stretched.

He scrunched his brow and nodded. 'I'm sorry, love, but I have to go straight out. Come into the kitchen and I'll explain what's happened.'

They left the kids playing on the floor, oblivious to the fact that it was no longer going to be a merry Christmas for their parents.

When James passed on the news to Annie she gasped as if a punch had taken her breath away.

'I c-can't believe it,' she stammered. 'The poor man.'

Gordon Carver had lived in Kirkby Abbey before moving to Kendal a few years ago, so Annie had met him several times. And his name had frequently cropped up in conversation because he'd reported on every case that James had worked on since joining the Cumbria Constabulary.

James was suddenly reminded of last Boxing Day, when he'd had to break the news to Annie that someone else who she knew had been murdered. Now, once again, he was the bearer of bad news, and was going to have to spend yet another festive occasion away from his family.

'I have to wonder why he phoned me,' he said. 'Could it have been that he knew – or feared – that something was about to happen to him?'

Annie shook her head. 'I very much doubt it. Surely he would have called the three nines rather than you if he'd felt in any way threatened.'

James knew she was probably right, but he still experienced a frisson of guilt for not taking his phone upstairs when they'd bathed the kids. Would Gordon still be alive if he had answered the call and spoken to him? It was a question he would never know the answer to.

'I'd better get going,' he said, glancing at his watch. 'I'm really sorry.'

'Don't be,' Annie told him as she stepped closer to give him a hug. 'You need to do your job. We'll be fine. And I'll make sure that Bella and Theo still have a great day.'

James thanked her, grateful as always that she was so understanding.

A quick change of clothes and James was ready to set off. By then a dark unease had pushed its way into his mind.

'Let me know when to expect you back home,' Annie said as he gave her and the kids farewell kisses.

'You can count on it,' he told her before stepping outside into a bitterly cold Christmas morning.

He felt a strong mixture of emotions as he settled behind the wheel of his Audi. Before starting her up, he placed his mobile on the phone mount and tapped on Superintendent Tanner's number. The boss answered as soon as James pulled off the driveway onto the road.

'Good morning, James,' he said. 'Would I be right in assuming that you're calling to tell me that it looks like we have a murder on our hands?'

'Then you already know,' James replied.

'Control informed me a few minutes ago that a man's body has been found in a woodland on the edge of Kendal. And foul play is suspected.'

'Yes, I just received a call from DI Stevens who's at the scene and it's not good.'

'What more can you tell me then?'

'It looks like the victim received a fatal blow to the back of the head while walking near to his home yesterday evening.'

'Has he been identified?'

'He has, which is why I'm heading there now. It's *Gazette* journalist Gordon Carver.'

Tanner drew a sharp, audible breath. 'Jesus Christ. This is bad. I'll have to alert the Chief Constable.'

'Then you need to tell him that Gordon tried to contact me before he was killed.'

'What do you mean?'

James told him about the missed call.

'It's pretty disturbing because I doubt that he would have wanted to speak to me on Christmas Eve if it wasn't something important, or urgent even. And we don't know if he phoned me seconds or minutes before the attack took place. What we do know is that when I did call him back, he didn't pick up. And the thought that he might already have been dead by then is making me feel more than a little uncomfortable.'

'Update me as soon as you can,' Tanner said. 'I'll speak to the Chief Constable and the press office. It won't be long before Gordon's colleagues in the media get wind of what's happened. Once they do, they'll make sure that everyone knows it's going to be yet another not-so-merry Christmas in Cumbria.'

CHAPTER FOUR

James was familiar with the location of the crime scene, so he didn't need to put it into his satnav.

Being Christmas morning, traffic was light and the roads were clear despite the earlier snowfall. But the sky was an ominous grey and held the promise of more snow to come.

As he drove north towards Kendal, his heartbeat started to ramp up and questions flooded his mind. Among those that would need to be answered quickly was whether Gordon Carver had been the victim of a random or targeted attack.

As a journalist he had no doubt made enemies, so was it possible that one of them had sought revenge against him?

Carver had been a sharp operator and a formidable journalist. He'd had lots of contacts in the Constabulary and was one of the few hacks who had won the trust of the team of detectives.

James first met him five years ago when a serial killer went on the rampage in Kirkby Abbey. It was James's first major case in Cumbria and Carver had approached him outside the village hall to ask him a bunch of questions. Back then the man was in his late twenties, with pointed features and short, reddish hair.

He'd looked much the same when James last had a conversation with him several weeks ago. He was pulling together a feature on the extent of drug trafficking across Cumbria and wanted input from the police.

James knew very little about the man's personal circumstances, except that he wasn't married, had no children, and his parents lived just over two miles from Kendal in the village of Burneside.

They would have to be informed as soon as possible, and James knew that the unenviable task of passing on the devastating news on Christmas Day would fall on him.

The drive to Kendal was fast and uneventful. James arrived just before ten and made his way to the small patch of woodland on the western fringe of the town. Gordon's body had been found on the footpath that ran through it, halfway between a car park and a quiet residential road.

But this morning the road was far from quiet. Several patrol cars were parked on it, along with a forensic van, and officers in reflective yellow jackets were milling about while ensuring that curious residents kept their distance.

A taut ribbon of police tape stretched across the entrance to the gravel path, and just beyond it stood Detective Sergeant Jessica Abbott, who was conversing with a scene of crime officer in a white forensic suit. When she spotted James, she abruptly ended the conversation and signalled for him to step under the tape.

'You got here quickly, guv,' she said.

Abbott was one of his most highly rated officers, and had attended countless crime scenes. She was already a member of the team when James joined.

'The pathway stretches for roughly three hundred yards,' she went on, 'and Gordon's body is about halfway along it. Phil is there now briefing Tony Coppell, who just got here.'

'Has anything new come to light since Phil called me?'

She shook her head. 'Unfortunately, the snow that's been hitting the area severely contaminated the scene. Footprints were wiped out and it's made searching the immediate vicinity more difficult. No likely murder weapon has been found so far.'

'I'm guessing it would have been pitch black here around nine o'clock last night,' James said.

'That's right. But the couple who found the body told me that, even without lighting, the path still gets used after dark as it serves as a shortcut from the town centre to the road. And up until now it's been considered a perfectly safe route.'

'I'll also need to speak to them. Where are they?'

Abbott pointed to a small, detached house directly across the road, in front of which stood a uniformed officer.

'That's where they live. They're both badly shaken and so far we've only spoken to them about how and when they stumbled across the body. Gordon lived two houses along on the left,' she said, pointing to the building, 'and they knew him well. I was on my way to speak to them again just before you pulled up.'

'We'll go together in a minute then. What about Gordon's place? Have you been inside?'

'Not yet, but a couple of uniforms popped in after we found the front-door key in Gordon's pocket. We know he lived alone, but we needed to make sure that the house was empty.'

'And is it?'

'Yes. And nothing is out of place, apparently.'

'Do we know if he was on his way out or going home when he

was attacked?' James asked, in the hope that they had come upon at least one important fact.

But to his disappointment, Abbott shrugged. 'That's yet to be established, guv.'

She then motioned for him to walk with her along the path. It was about twelve feet wide with high trees and bushes on either side. After a hundred yards or so it curved to the right, revealing the crime scene up ahead. The sight of it sent a blast of heat through James's body. And the closer he got to it the faster his heart began to beat in his chest.

'Brace yourself, guv,' Abbott said, as though reading the change in his demeanour. 'This is a tough one to take in.'

CHAPTER FIVE

James and Abbott had to slip on forensic gloves and shoe covers before they approached the crime scene.

SOCOs were busy taking photos and searching for evidence on the path and in the wood. A tent hadn't yet been erected so the victim was clearly visible.

Standing a few yards beyond him were the familiar figures of Detective Inspector Phil Stevens and Chief Forensic Officer Tony Coppell. They both acknowledged James, but said nothing as he stepped up to Gordon Carver's body and stared down at it as dispassionately as he could.

The man was lying on his back and a patch of gravel several inches to the left of his head was heavily stained with blood, suggesting he'd been moved.

His pale features appeared to be frozen – the eyes closed, the mouth open – but he was still easily recognisable as the journalist who James had known and liked.

Carver wore a heavy winter coat over a bright red crew-neck sweater emblazoned with Christmas trees and snowmen, which suggested he'd been embracing the festive spirit before his life was so brutally cut short.

James felt a shudder of unease run through him as he recalled the moment last Boxing Day when he'd stood over the body of another man he had known. Someone who'd been stabbed to death while dressed as Santa Claus.

'I knew you would want to take the lead on this one, guv, bearing in mind who the victim is.'

It was the gravelly voice of DI Stevens that wrenched James out of his thoughts. And as he looked up, he saw that his second-in-command was wearing a mournful expression.

'It was enough of a shock to be told that a body had been found a short walk from police HQ,' Stevens went on. 'I really couldn't believe it when I got here and saw who it was.'

'It's knocked me for six as well,' James replied. 'Especially knowing that Gordon tried to contact me last night. And it could well have been just before the attack took place.'

Stevens nodded. 'That seems highly likely since he didn't pick up when you phoned him back.'

It was Tony Coppell's turn then to step forward and speak. The Chief Forensic Officer had been doing the job for over twenty years and his presence at a crime scene always reassured James.

'It's my considered opinion that he was attacked sometime between nine and midnight,' he said. 'Pam is on her way here and will give us a more accurate assessment.'

Dr Pam Flint was the Forensic Pathologist and had worked alongside James on most of the murder cases he'd run since coming to Cumbria.

'What conclusions have you drawn so far?' James asked.

'Only that he was attacked from behind with a single, fierce blow to the head,' Coppell answered. 'It penetrated the skull and no doubt impacted on his brain. I'm sure he would have died either instantly or within minutes. And no other wounds are visible.'

James took some consolation from the fact that Gordon almost certainly didn't suffer a slow, painful death.

'Any idea what kind of weapon was used?' he asked.

Coppell shrugged. 'It's too soon to say for sure. It could have been anything from a rock to a hammer. It doesn't appear as though the attacker dropped it here at the scene, but the search of the immediate area has only just got underway.'

'I take it the body has been moved?' James said.

'It has. When the couple found him, he was face down. The husband turned him over and wiped the snow from his face.'

James blew out through clenched teeth. 'Then you'd better move him again so that I can see the damage for myself.'

Coppell knelt down and gently turned the body over so that the wound was visible. James knelt down beside Coppell to get a closer look, and as he did so the breath left him with a gasp.

The wound was large and deep, and blood had coagulated inside.

'The snow and low temperatures have slowed down decomposition, which is helpful to us,' Coppell said.

James's thoughts were now burning like a fuse, and his face was tight with tension. It was clear that the journalist had been hit with extreme force, and the extent of the wound raised more questions. Did the attacker mean to kill him? Or was the intention to render him unconscious? And did the attacker leap out of the bushes to surprise him or were they walking together along the path when something sparked a violent confrontation?

As James stood up, he raked a hand through his hair and released a shaky breath.

'What else can you tell me, guys?' he said.

It was Stevens who responded. 'Well, we found his wallet in his jeans pocket, complete with a sum of cash and several bank cards. So, it's an indication that the motive might not have been robbery. However, there's no sign of his mobile phone, which means that it could have been taken, or that we'll eventually find it somewhere around here.'

'Any clue as to which direction the killer fled in?'

Stevens shook his head. 'They could have exited the path at either end or made off through the wood. The only CCTV camera nearby is in the car park and I've asked for it to be checked. I've also requested more uniform backup so we can carry out a door-to-door to see if anyone saw something last night.'

James was thinking fast now, mental gears whirring as he gnawed on his bottom lip.

Turning to DS Abbott, who was standing behind him, he said, 'I'd now like to speak to the couple who found him. After that, you and I will check out Gordon's house.' Turning back to Stevens, he added, 'You continue to oversee things here, Phil. And while you're at it, can you get an address for Gordon's parents in Burneside? They need to be given the bad news before it gets out there.'

CHAPTER SIX

As James followed Abbott along the path, he could feel the pressure forming behind his eyes.

Instinct told him that this case was going to present them with a real challenge. The lack of witnesses and forensic evidence. The contamination of the crime scene. The missed call from the victim. It was surely going to be anything but straightforward.

'What were your plans for today before Phil called you, guv?' Abbott asked him as they approached the road.

He shrugged. 'To stay at home with the kids. I suppose I should be grateful that I at least got to see them open their presents.'

'So will it just be them and Annie for the rest of the day?'

'Her best friend is coming over for lunch and I'm hoping she'll hang around into the evening.'

Abbott gave a thoughtful nod. 'I can appreciate how hard it's been for your wife. Every Christmas since you moved here you've had to leave your family to deal with one or more murders.'

'I know. When was the last time you enjoyed a Christmas break with Sean?' he asked her.

'I can't actually remember. Given Sean's a paramedic we try to make a point of being on duty at the same time, and I'm usually given the Christmas Day shift as we don't have any kids.'

'I'm sure it won't be long before you do,' he responded.

She pushed out a sigh and it made James regret making the comment. 'That's what we keep telling ourselves, guv,' she said. 'I just wish I was still in my twenties instead of my thirties.'

James was well aware that children were a sore subject with his DS. She'd married Sean two years ago, but still hadn't managed to fall pregnant.

Thankfully, the conversation ended abruptly as they exited the path onto the road. Two more patrol cars had arrived and the air was filled with the harsh sounds of police radios and loud voices.

They removed their shoe covers and gloves before crossing over to the house belonging to the couple who found Gordon's body.

'Their names are Erika and Vincent Lynch,' Abbott said. 'They're both retired and in their early seventies.'

The uniformed officer outside the door rang the bell for them and moments later it was opened by a short, bearded man with craggy features.

'Hello again, Mr Lynch,' Abbott said. 'I'm here with my superior officer. Would it be okay to come in so that you can tell him what you told me?'

James quickly introduced himself and Vincent Lynch waved them inside. It was a small, cosy interior and the radiators were blasting out a fierce heat.

They were led into the living room where Mrs Lynch was

sitting on the sofa next to a large, highly decorated Christmas tree.

Her husband introduced James and invited the detectives to sit on the two empty armchairs, before joining his wife on the sofa.

Erika was a small, thin woman with tousled grey hair and eyes that were glazed and haunted. James could tell that she was having a hard time dealing with what she had seen.

'I realise that this is very difficult for you both,' he said, 'but I have to ask you some questions about Mr Carver. Before I do, could you please talk me through what happened earlier, when you found the body?'

The couple glanced at each other and Vincent took his wife's hand before he dragged in a sharp breath and said, 'We make a point of going for a walk most mornings. Today we decided to go along the path towards the town centre. It was snowing, but only lightly by then, and it was no longer dark. There was no one else around and it felt good to get out, but within minutes of leaving the house we saw the snow-covered body in the middle of the path. Naturally it was a horrible shock.

'We didn't realise it was Gordon until I rolled him over. I saw straight away who it was and that he was dead.'

Vincent suddenly squeezed his eyes shut and drew in another lungful of air. His wife picked up where he'd left off.

'I took out my mobile phone and called the emergency services,' she said, her voice unsteady. 'Vincent then told me to come back to the house while he waited for the police to arrive.'

Vincent opened his eyes again and scrunched up his face as though in pain. 'I knew I wouldn't have to wait long because the station is so close, but it was still a terrible experience standing there looking down on the corpse of a man who had been a friend and neighbour.'

'Did you move anything other than the body?' James asked him. 'And did you see anything that might offer up a clue as to what happened?'

A shake of the head. 'I've already explained to your colleague that I didn't touch anything after first moving him. I just stood there shaking and feeling sick.'

'And did anyone else come along the path before the police arrived?'

'No. That didn't surprise me though. Very few people use the path at that time of the morning.'

'And have either of you told friends or neighbours that it's Gordon's body on the path?'

They both shook their heads. 'We thought it best not to,' Vincent said.

James clamped his top lip between his teeth as he considered what they'd been told. Finally, he said, 'We believe that Mr Carver was attacked last night between about nine and twelve, but we don't know if he had just left his house or was returning to it. Can you shed any light on that?'

'I can't. Erika and I went to bed at about seven and watched a film together before going to sleep. But we were planning to knock on his door today, along with our other closest neighbours, to wish them a merry Christmas. It's something we always do.'

'Does that mean you didn't see him at all yesterday?'

'I didn't, but Erika did,' he replied. 'I'd actually forgotten about that.'

James turned back to Erika. 'Did you speak to him, Mrs Lynch?'

'No, I didn't. I just happened to be looking out of the window at about three o'clock when his front door opened and Gordon and a woman stepped out. I was surprised to see them kiss each other quite passionately before she got into a car that was parked at the kerb and drove away.'

'I didn't realise he was in a relationship.'

'Neither did we. That was why I was surprised. He'd never mentioned to us that he was and in all the time he's lived here I've never seen him with a woman. But the way they embraced each other suggested to me that things were pretty serious between them.'

'Can you describe this woman for me?' James asked.

'Not really. She was wearing a headscarf and a long, beige overcoat. I didn't actually see her face.'

'What about the car she got into?'

'I think it was blue or black, but I didn't pay attention to it.'

'Do you know how long it was parked there?'

'Well, I noticed it was there about two hours earlier. Gordon was out himself for most of the morning. He told me the day before that he was going to visit his parents.'

They stayed with the couple for a further fifteen minutes and learned that Gordon Carver had rented his house, but had been planning to buy one elsewhere in Kendal. He'd been regarded by them and the other neighbours as a pleasant individual who got on well with everyone. And they couldn't think of anyone who would want to harm him.

'We realised a while ago that Gordon's job as a journalist meant everything to him,' Erika said as they got to their feet. 'He didn't seem to have much time for an active social life, but he would often invite us over for a drink and a chat. And we never heard a bad word said against him.'

She then broke down in a flood of tears and her husband pulled her close to his chest. Then to James, he said, 'Please find out who did it, detective. Gordon didn't deserve to die in the way he did.'

CHAPTER SEVEN

James had to swallow down his emotion as they left the house. He knew that what Erika and Vincent Lynch had experienced was going to haunt them for the rest of their lives.

At the same time his mind began to process what the couple had said about their dead neighbour. Of particular interest was the revelation that a mystery woman had spent some time with him hours before he was murdered.

'We need to find out who the woman is,' he said to Abbott as they headed along the street to Gordon's house. 'The rough description of her car, and the fact we know she left here about three o'clock yesterday, aren't much to go on, but it's a start.'

'It could be that he struck up a relationship with her very recently and just hadn't got around to mentioning it to his neighbours,' Abbott replied. 'But his parents and colleagues may well know about her.'

James nodded as a frisson of excitement flared in his chest. 'And in turn she might know what he was up to yesterday evening. Hopefully it won't take us long to come up with a name. And CCTV should have picked up the car.'

A uniformed officer was standing outside Gordon's house, and he informed them that SOCOs would soon be carrying out a forensic examination. Gordon's car was on the driveway and another uniform was checking out the inside.

Inevitably they were attracting the attention of neighbours, and a small group had gathered on the pavement across the road.

'I'm sure that by now they'll all be jumping to the right conclusion that it's Gordon's body on the path,' James said. 'And that means the news is probably already spreading like wildfire. So, we need to contact his parents asap.'

'Why don't I head straight to Burneside after we've checked out his house?' Abbott said. 'That way you can take your time sorting things out here.'

James nodded. 'That's a good idea. I'll join you as soon as I can.'

They put fresh forensic gloves and shoe covers on before entering the house. The interior was modern and spacious with a galley kitchen and a combined living/dining area. There were a few Christmas decorations up and about a dozen cards on the mantelpiece, but no tree. The downstairs layout also included a toilet and a small utility room. There was nothing to indicate that the place had been damaged or disturbed by an intruder.

Upstairs there were two bedrooms and a bathroom. A third bedroom had been converted into an office and that was where they came across something that took them both by surprise.

The wall behind the desk was dominated by a large, wood-framed corkboard. Pinned to it were various photographs and newspaper cuttings relating to an investigation that James and Abbott were all too familiar with.

Next to it hung a smaller whiteboard on which a list of notes had been scrawled in black marker pen.

'Bloody hell,' Abbott reacted. 'This looks like a miniature version of a police incident room.'

James was quick to agree.

'I've just remembered something,' he said, as he stepped around the desk to get a closer look at the boards. 'Gordon called me about three weeks ago to tell me he was pulling together another story on Chloe Walsh and wanted to know if we were still looking for her. I told him the investigation was still ongoing, but there had been no new leads and things had therefore stalled.'

'Well, this suggests that he was cracking on with his own investigation, guv,' Abbott said.

James's mind leapt back eight months to when Chloe Walsh disappeared. The twenty-five-year-old local estate agent vanished while walking close to her home near Kendal and hadn't been seen since. The case had continued to play on James's mind and not a day had passed when he hadn't thought about her.

His team interviewed everyone who knew her, including her ex-boyfriend Daniel Porter, who she'd broken up with four months earlier.

His home was searched at the time, but along with all those questioned, he claimed he had no idea what might have happened to her. However, James had never been sure that what he told them was the truth, and to this day he still considered the man a plausible suspect.

Among the photos attached to the corkboard were two of Chloe, one of Porter, two of Porter's home, and one of Chloe's parents. The newspaper cuttings were from the *Cumbria Gazette* and several nationals that had covered the story.

'Gordon clearly suspected Porter of killing Chloe,' Abbott

said, pointing to the notes on the whiteboard, 'and it looks to me as though he was determined to prove it.'

James turned his attention to the whiteboard and felt his throat tighten when he read the notes and questions that Carver had listed.

Did Porter kill or kidnap Chloe on that day?
Where did he hide her body?
Have the police done enough to find her?
Interview parents and friends again.
Arrange something to mark her 26th birthday.
Try to get the BBC interested in producing a documentary.

James chewed on his bottom lip as his mind started leaping in all directions. He recalled the amount of effort that his team had put into the investigation, and the extensive search that was carried out for Chloe.

He also remembered Gordon telling him that he had known her personally because they had attended the same university when he was a postgraduate and stayed in touch afterwards.

Every muscle in James's body was suddenly tense, shoulders rigid, as he turned to Abbott and said, 'If Daniel Porter learned what Gordon was up to, he would not have been happy. It makes sense to treat the guy as our first suspect.'

CHAPTER EIGHT

James used his phone to take photos of the boards on the wall of Gordon's office. What was pinned and scribbled on them had filled his head with disturbing questions.

He now had to seriously consider the possibility that the journalist was murdered because he'd continued to pursue the case of missing person Chloe Walsh. But had he been acting on the instructions of his editor or had it become a personal obsession with him?

The case had attracted a lot of attention eight months ago when Chloe first disappeared after attending a party at a friend's house in Kendal. Those friends claimed she'd left at about ten in the evening and planned to walk the short distance to the home she shared with her parents. They also insisted that although she'd had a few glasses of wine, she was far from drunk.

It wasn't until the following morning that her mother discovered she hadn't returned home. She tried calling Chloe, but her phone was off, so she alerted the police.

James recalled how distressed the poor woman was when

he first met her, and how he'd tried to reassure her by saying that most adults who go missing turn up within days. But despite appeals for information and a widespread search of the area between Chloe's home and where the party was held, her whereabouts remained unknown.

No evidence had emerged to suggest that she was dead, or that her former boyfriend Daniel Porter had been in any way linked to her disappearance. And according to her mother, Chloe had suffered a bout of depression after the break-up with Porter, but there were no serious concerns about her mental health.

As with all long-term missing person cases, it was revived and reviewed after six months, but what had happened to her still remained a mystery. And it was one that the *Cumbria Gazette* reporter had seemed determined to solve.

On top of Carver's desk they found more newspaper cuttings and photos, including several of Porter walking through the town. There was even one of him emerging from his home a couple of miles outside of Kendal.

'These were clearly taken without his knowledge,' Abbott said. 'Gordon must have been stalking the guy at times.'

They were still rummaging through Gordon's office when two SOCOs arrived to start searching the house. With them was Detective Constable Ahmed Sharma, who'd been one of the on-call detectives over Christmas.

James explained what they had found and said he wanted the photos bagged up and taken to headquarters along with Gordon's laptop.

He then tasked Sharma with going through the office filing cabinet to see if it contained anything that was potentially relevant to the case.

'We treat this as our first line of inquiry,' he told his DC. 'If you come up with anything significant, call me right away.'

James and Abbott then left the house and started walking back towards the path. But before they reached it they were approached by a short man with a blunt, square face who they both recognised instantly as Duncan Bishop, a journalist colleague of Gordon Carver at the *Gazette*.

Bishop had also lived in Kendal for some years and was regarded by the Constabulary as another competent and trustworthy reporter.

'I was hoping to catch you, Detective Walker,' he said, and James could see the anxiety etched into his features. 'I need to know if it's true about Gordon. That it's his body lying on the path over there.'

James furrowed his brow. 'Who told you it was?'

'The people I've come into contact with since I arrived here a few minutes ago,' he replied, his tone soft and measured. 'Word has spread along the street, and I can't think why else the police would be going in and out of Gordon's home.'

James hesitated briefly before accepting that there was no point concealing the fact at this stage.

'Well, I can tell you that it is Gordon's body, but I don't want that in the public domain until his parents have been informed,' James said. 'DS Abbott here is going straight to Burneside now to break the news to them.'

Bishop sucked in a breath and shook his head.

'I'll need to break the news to Nadine then,' he said as he struggled to control the emotion in his voice. 'Can you tell me how he was killed? I assume from what's happening that you're treating it as murder.'

Nadine Stone was the *Gazette*'s editor and James had met her several times over the years.

'I can't go into the details about that yet, Mr Bishop,' he said. 'We'll issue a statement later today. But I do intend to speak to Mrs Stone as soon as possible. I can't remember if she lives here in the town.'

'She lives in Oxenholme, but I don't have the address. I do have your number, though, so as soon as I get it, I'll text it to you.'

'Thank you. Do you know if she's at home today?'

Bishop nodded. 'She's there with her family. The reason I'm here is that she was tipped off that a body had been found on the path in suspicious circumstances. She called Gordon because she knew he lived close by, but didn't get an answer. She then called me and asked me to check it out. I live on Windermere Road.'

'Then tell her I'll be dropping by shortly,' James said. 'I need to talk to her about Gordon. And please also tell her that I know his death will come as an awful blow to all his friends and colleagues at the paper. He was a good man.'

CHAPTER NINE

James could feel the adrenaline buzzing through his system as he approached the entrance to the path, which was still a frenzy of activity.

The investigation had only just started, but it was already moving rapidly forward. They had a person of interest in Daniel Porter. A possible motive. And they'd learned that a woman spent several hours in the victim's home shortly before he was attacked, which might well prove significant. James was eager to keep up the pace despite it being Christmas Day.

Before stepping onto the path, he told Abbott to grab a lift in a patrol car to Gordon's parents' home in Burneside.

'I'll make my way there as soon as I can, so text me the address when you have it,' he added. 'I want to finish up here first and then drop in on Gordon's boss to see what she can tell us about his involvement with the Chloe Walsh story.'

'What about Daniel Porter, guv?' Abbott asked.

'I'll call the office now and get someone to go straight to his house. We need to find out where he was last night and if he knew that Gordon was effectively stalking him.'

James made the call as soon as he started walking along the path. By now other members of his team had given up their festive break to report for duty, and as always he fully appreciated how committed they were to their jobs. Among them was Detective Constable Dawn Isaac, who he tasked with questioning Porter after telling her what they'd found in Gordon's house.

'Take a couple of uniforms with you,' he told her. 'He lives just outside of town, off the Sedbergh Road. His address is on file.'

'I know where he lives,' she said. 'I went there with you to speak to him when Chloe disappeared.'

James nodded. 'That's right. So no doubt you'll remember that he's an arrogant bastard.'

'How could I forget? He accused us of being a pair of pathetic plods for suspecting him of killing his ex-girlfriend.'

After hanging up, James took a moment to remind himself of the two occasions he'd spoken to Porter. The guy was an unpleasant individual who had an inflated opinion of himself, despite the fact that he had a somewhat chequered past.

He didn't have a criminal record, but they knew he'd been sacked from two jobs. He spent four years working as a hospital admin assistant, but got the push after he was caught sniffing cocaine while on duty. And then he lost another job working behind the bar in a pub after he punched a customer who swore at him.

After that he moved back in with his parents and set himself up as a freelance web designer. When his parents both died in a car accident three years ago, he inherited the house, and he met Chloe when he hired her firm to value the place. They struck up a relationship and she eventually moved in and lived there with him for six months before she ended it. According to her parents it was because he was controlling and abusive towards her, something that he'd denied when James questioned him about her disappearance.

Back at the crime scene a tent had been erected and DI Stevens told James that Dr Pam Flint, the Forensic Pathologist, was inside examining the body.

'She's arranged for it to be moved to the mortuary within the next half an hour,' Stevens said.

'Has anything turned up?' James asked him.

Stevens shook his head. 'Still no weapon or phone. But as you can see, a few more uniforms are searching the wood.'

James briefed Stevens on his conversation with Mr and Mrs Lynch and described what they'd found in Gordon's house.

'Jessica is on her way to break the news to Gordon's parents,' he said, 'and I've asked Dawn to pay a visit to Daniel Porter, who is now in the frame as a potential suspect.'

'What's your next step, guv?' Stevens asked.

'I'm going to speak to Nadine Stone. One of her other reporters is out there on the road and he's about to send me her address.'

'Is it true that we haven't been able to keep a lid on the victim's ID then?'

'Sadly, it is, but then it was never going to be easy with the crime scene so close to Gordon's home.'

Just then Dr Flint emerged from inside the tent. When she spotted James she removed her face mask and said, 'I was foolish enough to believe that I'd get to spend this Christmas Day with the family. I'm now convinced that it will never happen unless we move away from Cumbria.'

James couldn't help but grin. Dr Flint, who had just turned fifty, had lived in the county all her life, and her husband was a local GP. He didn't believe for a single second that they'd ever go and live elsewhere.

'It's something the wife and I gave serious thought to after last year,' he responded. 'And I don't doubt that it'll be up for discussion again now that another Christmas has been ruined.'

'Well, I hope that if I stay put then so will you, Detective Walker. You, me, and Tony make a bloody good team.'

With the usual banter out of the way, she went on to confirm that Carver had died from a blunt force trauma wound to the head.

'I agree with Tony that it must have happened late last night,' she went on. 'I haven't detected any other injuries, but I won't know for sure until he's on the slab.'

'How soon can you carry out a post-mortem?' James asked.

'Hopefully tomorrow. If there's a problem, I'll let you know.'

James's phone sounded with an incoming text message, and he opened it to find that it was from *Gazette* reporter Duncan Bishop and contained his editor's home address.

Turning to Stevens, James said, 'After I've spoken to Mrs Stone, I'll head to Burneside. Can you start giving some thought as to when we can get the team together for a full briefing, and whether we need to bring anyone else in, bearing in mind it's Christmas Day?'

CHAPTER TEN

The village of Oxenholme was just a few miles south of Kendal and James decided to drive himself there.

It was approaching midday when he set off, and a fierce wind was sending dark clouds across the sky.

It suddenly occurred to him that Annie and the kids would soon be tucking into their Christmas lunch, and he was gutted that he wouldn't be joining them. Yet again he was going to miss out on another very special occasion with his family.

He felt terrible leaving Annie alone with the kids, but at least her friend Janet would be there to keep her company. He made a mental note to call home after his visit to Nadine Stone's house because he knew Annie would want to know what was happening and he was also keen to check that all was well with her.

He then switched his thoughts to the editor of the *Cumbria Gazette*. She had been in the job for seven or eight years and James recalled how she'd made a point of visiting police headquarters to introduce herself to him soon after he arrived from London. He had been struck by her forceful personality and shrewd grey eyes, and knew immediately that she was someone he could get on with.

He also remembered the way she'd praised Gordon over the past few years and said how pleased she was that the reporter had developed such a constructive quid pro quo arrangement with James and his team.

Gordon's murder was going to be big news across the county and was understandably a story that Nadine and her staff were going to find painful to cover.

Nadine lived in a small, detached house close to the railway station. There were already two cars on the driveway so James parked on the road.

Within seconds of him ringing the bell the front door was opened by a stoic, muscular man wearing jeans and a tight T-shirt. He looked to be in his forties, with a shaved head and a stubble-coated jaw.

Before James could introduce himself, the man said, 'You must be Detective Walker. Nadine just received a call from one of her reporters to say that you were coming. I'm Elliott, her husband.'

'Then I take it she knows about Gordon,' James said.

Elliott gave a solemn nod. 'She does. And it's hit her really hard.'

'Is it okay to speak to her?'

'Of course. She's being looked after by our son and daughter.'

Elliott stepped back and motioned for James to come inside. After he closed the door, James followed him along the hall and into the living room.

Nadine was standing in front of a large Christmas tree, her arms crossed, her face stiff and white. She was a tall, slim woman who James knew to be forty-three. She had tightly curled black hair and was wearing a baggy blue jumpsuit.

'Please tell me there's been a mistake, Detective Walker,' she said, her voice low and raspy, 'and that it isn't Gordon's body that's out there.'

James felt the heat rise in his cheeks. 'I wish I could, Nadine, but I can't. I've come straight from the scene and saw for myself that it is him.'

She closed her eyes as a sob erupted from her throat.

Her husband rushed across the room to take her arm and then eased her towards the sofa where she sat down between her two offspring.

The lad, who looked to be in his early twenties, was a small version of his father and wore a dishevelled tracksuit. James recalled that Nadine had once told him that he worked as a local tour guide. His sister had softer features with a sweep of blonde hair, and a button nose that supported a pair of thick-rimmed glasses. She wore a red Santa Claus jumper and a pair of loose pyjama bottoms. James guessed her to be in her late teens.

They each put an arm around their mother and the daughter patted Nadine's knee.

'Do sit down, detective,' Elliott said, gesturing towards an armchair. 'This has come as such a shock to us all. Gordon worked with Nadine, but I met him several times, and so did Ryan and Charlotte.'

A heavy, uncomfortable silence descended on the room and lasted for about fifteen seconds before Nadine recovered her composure and said, 'I couldn't believe it when Duncan told me. And is it true that you think he was murdered?'

James nodded. 'It appears he was struck from behind while walking along the path close to his home last night. Initial

45

findings suggest it happened somewhere between about nine and midnight, but it could possibly have been later.'

She pressed her lips together, igniting deep lines around her eyes.

'A contact within the Constabulary, who shall of course remain anonymous, called to tell me that a body had been found. I phoned Gordon because I knew he lived near to the location, but he didn't answer.'

'Duncan told me,' James replied. 'Gordon was found by two of his neighbours while they were out walking. The path has been cordoned off and a full investigation is underway.'

'He must have been there all night then.'

'It would seem so.'

'Do his parents know yet?'

'An officer is heading there now, but it's possible they've already heard. The news is spreading quite quickly.'

'I'll have to tell his colleagues then,' Nadine said. 'They're going to be devastated. He was well liked by everyone.'

'I don't understand,' her daughter howled suddenly, and phlegm rattled in her throat as the words came out. 'Why would anyone want to kill him?'

Nadine turned to her. 'That's what the police will try to find out, Charlotte. And I'm sure they will.'

The girl's jaw went tight and the tendons in her neck stood out.

'But it's Christmas, for Christ's sake. It makes no fucking sense. People are supposed to be nice to each other.'

'Calm down, love,' her father told her. 'Now is not the time to vent your anger.'

She reacted by jumping to her feet and hurrying out of the room as tears spilled from her eyes.

'I'm sorry about that,' Nadine said to James. 'Like most other teens, my daughter has no filter, and at the same time finds it difficult to deal with bad news of any kind.'

'No need to apologise,' James replied.

He left it a beat before asking her when she last spoke to Gordon.

'It was on Tuesday. All the staff were in the office so we had some pre-Christmas drinks and snacks laid on at the end of the day. A few of us were back in yesterday, but most, including Gordon, had started their festive break.'

'We've been into Gordon's house and it seems that nothing has been disturbed, but I need to ask you about something that we came across in the room he used as an office,' he said. 'There were photos and newspaper cuttings relating to the case of Chloe Walsh. It appears that Gordon was working on—'

She raised a hand to stop him speaking as alarm shivered behind her eyes.

'Oh my god. Something just occurred to me,' she cried out. 'About a week ago Gordon told me that he'd been verbally threatened, and he seemed quite shaken by it.'

James leaned forward, elbows on knees. 'And did he tell you who threatened him?'

'Yes, of course. It was Daniel Porter. Chloe Walsh's former boyfriend. You need to find him.'

CHAPTER ELEVEN

What Nadine had said about Daniel Porter threatening Gordon caused James's body to stiffen.

'It was clear from what we found in Gordon's home office that he'd been stalking Porter, and that he believed Chloe's ex was behind her disappearance.'

'It was a huge story for us at the time and Gordon was desperate to cover it,' Nadine said. 'He made it clear from the start that he'd known the girl for some years, and he didn't try to conceal the fact that he was worried. I gave him free rein to work on it and he had my blessing to provide updates to the national papers and the TV newsrooms.'

'What made him think that her ex had abducted or killed her?' James asked.

'Back then it was what a lot of people thought, including the police, as I remember. You had him in for questioning several times and his home was searched. And then there was the fact that her parents told Gordon that she'd ended things with Porter because he was controlling and abusive. They said he was even physically violent towards her after they moved in together.'

'But Chloe has been missing for eight months,' James said. 'After about six weeks the *Gazette*, along with most other news outlets, rarely gave it a mention. So, why was Gordon still spending so much time on it?'

Nadine blew air out of her mouth through pursed lips. 'Because he became obsessed with the case. I told him there was no point pursuing it so vigorously if there were no new developments, and he accepted that, but he also made it clear that he was going to continue looking into it on his own time. It's no surprise to me that you found all that stuff in his office. Gordon was meticulous in his approach to everything he covered.'

'What did he tell you about Daniel Porter threatening him?' James said. 'What did he say exactly?'

Nadine cleared her throat and wiped a knuckle across the tears that were glistening in her eyes.

'Gordon came to me and asked if we could run an update in the *Gazette* to mark what would have been Chloe's twenty-sixth birthday on December the twenty-ninth, which is next Monday. I gave him the go-ahead, and he started pulling it together. He talked to her parents and friends and was planning to talk to you guys about it. I also said I had no objection to him approaching Porter.'

'And did he?'

She nodded. 'The next day he went to Porter's house. The guy wouldn't let him in, but they had a heated conversation on the doorstep. Gordon told him we were going to carry another story on Chloe, and Porter became angry and started swearing at him. Gordon told him that it sounded like he had something to hide. Porter then warned him not to bring his name up again, but

Gordon said he'd have to. In response, Porter said he was going to make Gordon regret coming to his house to stir things up again and would do all he could to stop the story being published.'

'And that was it?'

'Apparently so. Porter then stepped back into his house and slammed the door. The way the man reacted only reinforced Gordon's belief that he did something to Chloe. I told him that he could have been wrong, and that when he wrote his story, he had to be careful not to accuse the man of something that couldn't be proved.'

Her words prompted her son, Ryan, to speak up for the first time.

'It wouldn't surprise me if it was him who attacked Gordon,' he said. 'A couple of my mates who know him reckon he's a bad apple. And it's common knowledge in the town that he gave Chloe a hard time before she ditched him.'

'Do you know him yourself?' James asked.

'Not personally, but he was pointed out to me in a pub soon after Chloe disappeared. He was drinking by himself, but left in a hurry when two of Chloe's friends came in and started to ask him what he'd done with her.'

'Well, it's only fair to point out that Mr Porter strenuously denied knowing what happened to her, and we haven't come up with any evidence to suggest he lied to us,' James said. 'That said, in view of what your mother has told me, we will need to speak to him about his conversation with Gordon.' Turning to Nadine, he added, 'I would appreciate it if you don't share this information with anyone else. The investigation into Gordon's death has only just begun and I'm sure this will be one of many lines of inquiry. And we have to consider the strong possibility that Gordon was the victim of a random attack carried out by a complete stranger.'

'Don't worry, detective,' Nadine responded. 'I would never say or do anything to make things awkward for you or myself.'

'Can you think of anyone other than Porter who had a problem with Gordon?'

She shrugged. 'On a personal level I find it hard to believe that he had any enemies as he was very popular with everyone. But he was also a journalist for a good number of years and a lot of people would have taken offence at what he wrote about them.'

'Can you provide me with a list of those who kicked up a fuss or complained to the paper in, say, the last six months?'

'I'm sure I can, but I'll have to go through the files.'

'If you could send it to me as soon as you can, that would be a great help. I also wanted to mention that I missed a call from Gordon right around the time he was believed to have been killed last night. Have you any idea why he was trying to reach me?' he asked.

'I haven't a clue,' she said. 'I didn't speak to him yesterday. Perhaps he just wanted to wish you a Merry Christmas.'

James paused there to look at his watch. It was half twelve and he was keen to start his journey to Burneside.

Getting to his feet, he said, 'There's one other question I need to ask you, Nadine, and then I'll be off. It's whether or not you know if Gordon was in a relationship.'

A frown puckered her brow. 'Not to my knowledge. And if he was then I'm sure he would have mentioned it to me and his colleagues. Why do you ask?'

'A neighbour spotted a woman leaving his house yesterday afternoon. She had been there for a couple of hours, apparently, and before driving away they indulged in what the neighbour described as a "passionate" kiss.'

Her frown deepened. 'I can't help you, I'm afraid. As far as I'm aware, Gordon hadn't been involved with anyone for some time. Can't you ask the woman in question?'

'We don't know who she is at this stage. But hopefully we will soon.'

James thanked her and her son before her husband showed him to the door. Once outside he straightened his back to release the tension between his shoulders. What he'd learned about Daniel Porter's threat against Gordon was significant, and he was even more anxious now to speak to the man.

His phone rang as he climbed into his car. It was DC Isaac letting him know that she was outside Daniel Porter's house, but he wasn't at home.

'There's no car here either,' she said, and James felt a sharp tug of disappointment. 'He doesn't have any close neighbours so I can't ask anyone where he is.'

'Do you have his phone number?' James asked.

'I got the office to send it through to me and I just tried to reach him, but I think it's switched off or he's somewhere without a signal. I left a voice message.'

'Okay, head back to HQ and get whoever else is there to help you try to find out where he is. We urgently need to speak to him. I'm about to head to Burneside to see Gordon's parents, but after that I'll join you. Can you start setting things up for a briefing? We need to talk things through before the end of the day.'

CHAPTER TWELVE
ANNIE

Annie had phoned to let Janet know that James would not be joining them for lunch, and she'd been shocked to learn why he'd had to rush off to Kendal.

'It beggars belief that it's happened again,' Janet had said. 'I can only imagine how you must be feeling, hon. Look, I slept in late, so I'll come over as soon as I'm washed and dressed. We can chat while I give you a hand with the kids.'

For Annie it no longer felt like Christmas Day, even though the kids were having a whale of a time playing with their new toys. At least they provided a much-needed distraction and stopped her mind from being overwhelmed by negative thoughts.

She was already tired and stressed out after what had been a busy morning getting Bella and Theo ready and preparing the roast. It had been more of a task than a pleasure, and she was no longer looking forward to the day ahead.

But it wasn't just because her husband had been called to attend the scene of yet another horrendous Christmas crime. It was the other thing, too. The thing he didn't know about because she hadn't told him. And she wasn't going to until after Boxing Day.

Her intention had been to hold back the news so that he could enjoy Christmas, but she should have known that he wouldn't enjoy it anyway because, as in previous years, something bad would happen. This time it was the murder of someone they had both known. Someone who James had regarded as a friend as well as a useful contact.

'When is Daddy coming back, Mummy?'

Bella's loud voice jerked Annie out of herself. She turned away from the sink where she'd been washing some saucepans and saw her daughter standing in the doorway.

'I've already told you, Bella,' she said. 'He's had to go to work and won't be back until later.'

'But he promised he'd spend the day with us. He was going to help me build a castle.'

'I can do that with you after lunch. And Janet will be here to help as well. Daddy said he was sorry, and he'll make it up to you.'

Bella pushed out a sigh. 'Okay. So, when can we eat? I'm starving.'

'As soon as Janet arrives. Now where is your brother? You're supposed to be keeping an eye on him.'

'He's watching the telly. *Paw Patrol* is on.'

Bella then spun around and skipped back into the living room. Annie turned back to the sink and finished cleaning the saucepans as a dull beat started thudding in her chest.

The air suddenly felt heavy around her, and she had to fight the urge to let herself cry. She knew it wouldn't help to give in to self-pity. She had to stay strong … for all their sakes.

James had plenty on his plate now with this latest murder. She didn't want to add to his burden, at least until the investigation was over. And she wasn't going to spoil what was supposed to be such a special day for the kids.

At times like this she wished that she could turn to more people for support. But her parents were no longer alive, and she had no siblings. It was different for James. He still had family living in London. A mum, dad, brother, and two sisters. And they remained close even though he didn't get to see them that often.

Annie felt hot tears threaten as she went to check on the kids, but she managed to stop them breaking free from her eyes.

She entered the living room to see Theo lying on the sofa staring at the television and Bella sitting on the floor dressing her new doll.

They were clearly enjoying themselves and so she left them to it and decided to start laying the table for lunch. But just then she heard her mobile phone ringing and had to dash back into the kitchen to pick it up from the worktop.

It was James calling, and the sound of his voice provided some much-needed comfort.

'Just checking to see if all is well on the home front,' he said. 'Are the little monsters having fun?'

'Of course, but they're missing you,' Annie answered. 'Where are you?'

'On my way to Burneside to speak to Gordon's parents.'

'Do they know what's happened yet?'

'It's possible. Word is spreading quickly around town.'

'I don't suppose you know yet who killed him and why?'

'It's far too soon. There is a suspect, but I can't say more than that.'

'Do you have any idea when you'll be coming home then?'

'Not until much later. There's a lot to get sorted. I just wanted to make sure that all is okay. And to tell you, once again, how sorry I am that I can't be there.'

Annie was sorry, too, but she didn't want to make him feel any worse by putting it into words.

'Don't blame yourself, James,' she said. 'Just find out who killed your friend.'

'I intend to.'

Just then the doorbell rang. 'I think Janet has arrived,' said Annie.

'Then you'd better go and let her in. And try to enjoy lunch. I'll call again later.'

Annie placed her phone back on the worktop and went to answer the door.

'I got here as quickly as I could,' Janet said as she stepped inside. 'How are you holding up?'

Annie shrugged. 'I feel like crying and my head is full of noise. But I suppose things could be worse.'

'Well, I'm here now to help you make the most of what's left of the day. Have you heard from James?'

'He's just phoned and told me he's about to speak to Gordon's parents.'

'That won't be easy for him.'

'I know. It's going to be another tough case.'

'Am I right to assume that he still doesn't know about your problem?'

'Yes, you are. And in view of what's happened, I'm glad I didn't confide in him. He's got enough to worry about.'

Janet pulled Annie into a hug and whispered, 'Well, I'm here for you now, Annie, and with the help of the kids I'll try to put some cheer into your day.'

CHAPTER THIRTEEN

Seconds after coming off the phone to his wife, James received a call from DS Abbott.

'Gordon's parents arrived home fifteen minutes ago, guv,' she said. 'They'd spent the morning with some friends who live close by and returned to prepare lunch. It was lucky I hung around.'

'Were they aware of what's happened?'

'No. I'm afraid I had to break the news to them.'

James felt a blast of relief and said, a tad guiltily, 'That should have been my job, Jess. I'm sorry.'

'Nonsense. We're a team.'

'How did they take it?'

'Badly. Gordon spent Christmas Eve morning with them, and they'd been trying to contact him today. I haven't had a chance to ask them any questions.'

'Then wait for me to get there. I'm on the Burneside Road and it should only take me about ten minutes.'

James may have been spared the task of telling Ruth and Nigel Carver that their son had been murdered, but knowing he was going to have to provide them with the details filled him with dread. He had never met the couple, but it appeared they were a close-knit family. It was therefore quite likely that they knew about Gordon's obsessive interest in the Chloe Walsh case. And perhaps even that Daniel Porter allegedly threatened him just over a week ago because he was writing another story about it.

James had to be careful with how he approached that particular line of inquiry, at least until he'd spoken to Porter. He didn't want Mr and Mrs Carver, or anyone else for that matter, to jump the gun and assume that Porter must be the killer.

He could feel the tension gripping his body as he pulled up outside the couple's semi-detached house. When he rang the bell, it was DS Abbott who answered, and her face was pale against her dark hair.

'They're in the dining room, guv,' she said. 'I'll take you through.'

Ruth and Nigel Carver were sitting next to each other at the table, mugs of steaming tea or coffee in front of them. They were in their sixties and both wore tortured expressions.

Abbott introduced James and it was Nigel who responded with, 'Our hearts are broken, Detective Walker. Gordon was our only son. He was kind and decent, and he should not be dead.'

James felt a flash of heat in his chest. 'I agree, Mr Carver. And I'm so sorry for your loss. I considered your son a friend and I won't rest until I find out who killed him.'

His wife then let out a loud breath and said, 'Your colleague has told us that Gordon was attacked last night while walking through the wood near to where he lived. Is that all you know?'

James nodded. 'At this stage, yes, it is. He suffered a fatal blow to the head. We don't yet know if it was a targeted or random attack, or if he was by himself when it happened.'

Her bloodshot eyes flared with emotion and the words fell from her mouth.

'I hate to think of him lying there all night in the dark and the cold. And we had no idea where he was or what had happened to him.'

She leaned forward and buried her face in her hands, sobbing loudly.

Nigel put an arm around her and said to James, 'When will we be able to see our boy?'

'Later today or tomorrow morning, Mr Carver,' James answered him. 'His body is being taken to the mortuary where a post-mortem will be carried out. He will need to be formally identified but a family liaison officer will be appointed to help you through all of this and keep you informed of what's happening.'

Nigel closed his eyes and squeezed his lips together, and for almost a minute no one spoke. It was James who finally broke the silence.

'I know this is going to be really hard for you both, but I do need to ask some questions,' he said.

They both sat up straight and managed to hold back the tears.

'What is it you want to know?' Nigel said.

'Let's start with yesterday, Christmas Eve,' James said. 'We're sure the attack took place after nine o'clock. Do you know where he'd been or where he was going?'

They shared a glance, and it was Nigel who responded.

'He came here yesterday morning so that we could exchange gifts, and as I recall he said he was planning to stay at home last night. He didn't mention going out anywhere.'

'While he was here, did he express any concerns about anything?'

'Not at all. He was in good spirits. Just like he usually was.'

James had no reason to disbelieve them and drew in a forlorn breath.

'And do you know if he was intending to spend the evening at home by himself?'

Nigel rolled out his bottom lip. 'That's most likely. As you probably know, he was single and had been for some years.'

James told them about the woman seen by a neighbour kissing their son as she left his house yesterday afternoon, and they both reacted with surprise.

'That makes no sense,' Ruth responded as tears continued to creep out between her lashes. 'I specifically asked him if he had started seeing anyone and he said that he hadn't. It was something I always brought up because we both believed he needed to share his life with someone.'

'Is it possible that the neighbour was mistaken?' Nigel asked.

James shook his head. 'I doubt it. In fact, she said that the woman's car was parked outside his house for at least a couple of hours.'

'Well, there was obviously a reason why Gordon didn't tell us about her,' Nigel said. 'Are you going to speak to her?'

'We don't yet know who she is, but we're hoping to find out soon enough.'

'When you do, can you pass her name on to us so that we can speak to her? She might have been the last person to have seen Gordon alive, and she can hopefully tell us how he was.'

'I'll have to get back to you on that, Mr Carver,' James said. 'It might not be possible.'

He moved quickly on to their son's obsession with the Chloe Walsh missing person case. Nigel explained that they were well aware of how much time Gordon spent reporting on it and that he'd become convinced that her ex-boyfriend was responsible for her disappearance.

But it seemed he hadn't told them that he was pulling together yet another article, or that he'd received any kind of threat from Daniel Porter. James therefore decided not to bring it to their attention.

After asking a few more questions, and seeing how hard it was for the couple to answer them, he decided to end the conversation.

Before leaving the house, he called headquarters and arranged for a family liaison officer to be assigned to them. He instructed Abbott to stay with the couple until the FLO arrived.

Handing his card to Nigel, he said, 'Once again I'd like to offer my condolences. What has happened to Gordon is tragic. Please don't hesitate to contact me if you feel I can help in any way, or if you think of something that might lead us to the person who killed your son.'

'When can we go into his house?' Nigel asked. 'We'll need to gather his belongings and there will be things we'll want to keep.'

'The FLO will let you know,' James said, 'but I expect it will be within a day or two.'

CHAPTER FOURTEEN

James exhaled long and hard when he was back in the car, trying to release the tension inside him. After over twenty-five years as a copper, he still wasn't immune to the reactions of those whose loved ones had been murdered.

His heart had gone up a gear, and the blood was storming through his veins. Before starting the engine, he took out his mobile and called Superintendent Tanner to update him.

'I've been hoping to hear from you, James,' the boss said when he picked up. 'What have you got for me?'

'I've just spoken to Gordon's parents and am about to head to HQ for a team briefing,' he said. 'There's very little in the way of forensic evidence on the path because of how long he'd been there. But we know he suffered a single blow to the back of the head and there don't appear to be any defensive wounds.'

'It's just been shared on the system that his phone is missing and there's no sign of a weapon,' Tanner said.

James nodded to himself. 'I also visited the home of Gordon's editor at the *Gazette*, Nadine Stone. As a result of that conversation, we now have a potential suspect in one Daniel Porter.'

'The name rings a bell,' Tanner said.

'That's because he was also a suspect in the case of missing estate agent Chloe Walsh. Porter was her ex-boyfriend.'

'Yes, I remember now. We weren't able to link him to it in the end.'

James filled Tanner in on what they had found in Gordon's house, and what Porter allegedly said to the journalist a week or so ago.

'DC Isaac has been to his home, which is between here and Sedbergh, but he's not there. We're now trying to track him down.'

'I'll pass this on to the Chief Constable then,' Tanner said. 'He wants to be kept in the loop. And the press office is poised to issue a statement as soon as we give the go ahead, although the victim's name is already out there. Is there anything else I should know?'

'There is one other line of inquiry we'll be following up,' James replied. 'Yesterday afternoon a woman spent a couple of hours with Gordon at his home. When she left there a neighbour saw them kissing before she got into a car and drove away.'

'And why is that of interest?'

'Because no one knows who she is. The neighbour, his parents, and his boss have all told me that he wasn't in a relationship. And only yesterday he told his mother that he hadn't started seeing anyone.'

'I'm not convinced we should read too much into it,' Tanner said. 'It could simply be that it was something he wanted to keep secret.'

'Possibly, but it needs checking. I'm hopeful that her car will have been picked up on a road cam so we can identify her. She might well be able to tell us where he'd been or where he was going when he was attacked. Right now, we have no idea.'

'Well, it sounds like you've got off to a promising start,' Tanner said. 'If you need me to go to the office or come to Kendal then I will. Otherwise, I'll continue to monitor the situation from home.'

'That's fine with me,' James responded. 'I'll get back to you soon.'

James checked his watch before pulling away from the kerb. It was approaching two o'clock and he could barely believe that almost five hours had passed since DI Stevens called him at home to tell him that Gordon Carver's body had been found.

It was no wonder his mouth was so dry and his stomach was rumbling. He decided that as soon as he was back in the office, he'd grab something to eat and drink from the vending machine before he kicked off the briefing.

As he drove through Burneside towards Kendal, it felt like his head was stuck in a beehive, with thoughts racing in and out. And then there were the questions nudging at his conscience. *Why did Gordon ring me just before he was murdered? Would he still be alive if I'd answered the call? Did he know he was facing a serious threat?*

James knew it made no sense for him to feel guilty, but he found it hard not to. If only he had kept his phone with him when he went upstairs with the kids. Then he might not be having to investigate Gordon's murder. But when he was with the family, especially on special occasions such as Christmas, he knew he was entitled to switch off from the job, if only for brief periods. No copper could be expected to be fully alert 24/7.

Forcing himself to think about the various other aspects of

the case, he continued to drive into the wind that was growing ever stronger. A light snow had also started to fall, and large flakes were being blown in every direction.

He was just entering the town when his phone rang with a call from DC Isaac, who was eager to pass on a message that caused James's heart to jump a beat.

'Daniel Porter just returned my call, guv,' she said. 'He claims he was out hiking this morning and was in an area with no mobile signal. Anyway, he's back home and I've told him we need to speak to him.'

'What was his reaction?'

'He asked me if it was to do with Gordon Carver's death and claimed that he'd heard about it from a friend. I told him that it was, and he said he was happy to speak to us, but he also made a point of saying that he had nothing to do with it.'

That came as no surprise to James, but of course it didn't mean the guy wasn't lying.

'Are you still in the office, Dawn?' James asked her.

'I am.'

'Then tell the team the briefing needs to be delayed. I'll be there in a few minutes and then we can go to his place together.'

CHAPTER FIFTEEN

When James reached headquarters, he parked his Audi and got a patrol car to ferry him and DC Isaac to Porter's home. Along the way he briefed her on his conversation with Nadine Stone.

'Porter is bound to deny losing his rag with Gordon and it'll be difficult for us to prove that he did,' James said. 'But we need to put him on the spot. Right now, he's our only suspect.'

As the travelled onward they reviewed the details of Porter's chequered past – losing his job as a hospital admin assistant for taking drugs while at work, and getting the sack from his job as a pub barman for assaulting a customer – and Chloe Walsh's claims to her parents that he was controlling, abusive and violent towards her.

'Plus, he may well have killed her as an act of revenge,' Isaac pointed out.

James nodded. 'We've long suspected that he might well have, but we were never really close to proving it. So, perhaps he had nothing to do with her disappearance. Perhaps those people who believe she ran away to start a new life elsewhere are right. It happens often enough, especially with those who have mental health issues. And as we know, Chloe became depressed as a result of what she'd been through.'

Missing person cases often proved to be a challenge as so many factors had to be considered, and far too often families, friends, and sometimes even the police leapt to the wrong conclusion.

James was aware that there were plenty of documented examples of people who had turned up alive and well years after they were believed to have been murdered.

It didn't take them long to reach Porter's home. It was a large, detached house set back from the road and surrounded by fields.

A short driveway led to a paved forecourt on which was parked a black Range Rover SUV.

James asked the driver to stay in the patrol car as he and Isaac approached the front door, which was pulled open before they reached it to reveal Daniel Porter standing there in jeans and a loose hoodie.

He was around six feet tall and in his late twenties, with a square jaw and thin mouth. His thick, dark hair was much shorter than it had been when James last saw him, and it looked as though he'd lost some weight.

He flashed an unfriendly smile at them and said, 'Detectives Walker and Isaac, as I recall. I never thought I'd see the pair of you again.'

'May we come in, Mr Porter?' James said. 'We need to ask you some questions.'

'So I gather. Is it because you suspect me of killing someone else? This time Gordon Carver?'

'You're not officially a suspect, Mr Porter,' James explained, 'but we know that Mr Carver came here to see you a short time ago and we want to hear your version of what transpired.'

Porter started to respond, but stopped himself and stepped back to let them in.

They followed him into the living room, where they were invited to sit on a long leather sofa while he sat facing them. It was a large but gloomy room, and there were no Christmas decorations. Heat was coming from an open fire and the TV was on, but the volume turned low.

'Am I going to need a lawyer?' Porter asked.

'That depends on what you tell us,' James said. 'First, can you confirm where you've spent most of today?'

He released a small sigh. 'I've already told Detective Isaac. I went for a hike with some pals over Cunswick Fell, which is near here. It's a Christmas Day tradition with us. As so often happens, the phone signal was lost, and so I didn't know you were trying to contact me until I got back here.'

'Then how did you know about Mr Carver's body being found?'

'It's all over social media. One of my mates spotted it when he got home and sent me a text. This was just before I heard the message that Detective Isaac left. We set out on the hike early this morning and the guys will confirm that I was with them the whole time. So, there's no way I could have killed that journalist.'

'He wasn't killed this morning,' James said. 'The time of his death hasn't been released yet, but it was actually yesterday evening after nine o'clock.'

Porter was clearly surprised. 'I didn't realise that. But you're still barking up the wrong tree if you think I killed him.'

'Then where were you around that time?' This from Isaac.

Porter sat up straight, a defiant glint in his eyes. 'I didn't go out at all yesterday. I was busy working on a website design that I wanted to get out of the way.'

'Can anyone corroborate that?' Isaac followed up.

He shook his head. 'I was by myself, which is how I've spent most of my evenings since Chloe broke up with me. And I didn't have any visitors. I rarely do these days.'

James experienced a spike of disappointment. There was nothing in Porter's voice or demeanour that suggested he was lying, and he didn't appear at all nervous.

James began to ask another question, but Porter beat him to it. 'You said you came to find out what happened when Carver dropped in on me unexpectedly last week. Is that because I lost my temper and told him to fuck off?'

'He actually told his editor that you threatened him,' James said. 'He claimed that you said he was going to regret coming here to stir things up, and that you'd do everything you could to stop his paper publishing another story about Chloe's disappearance.'

Porter's jaw tightened and bulged, and the breath left him in a gasp.

'That's total bollocks,' he snapped. 'I admit I got angry with him, but that was because he made it clear yet again that he believed I killed my ex, which is ridiculous, as I told you eight months ago. I pleaded with him not to mention me in the story he was going to write, but he insisted that he would have to.'

'So, are you telling us that you didn't threaten him in any way?'

Porter suddenly sat bolt upright and the words exploded out of him.

'That's exactly what I'm saying. He lied, just as Chloe did when she told people that I treated her badly. I didn't. I loved that girl with all my heart. And even though I haven't a fucking clue what happened to her, nobody believes me. I rarely go into town these days because people still point the finger at me, and now they'll probably assume that I've claimed another bloody victim.'

Having got it all off his chest, he rubbed a hand over his face and fixed James with a hard, implacable stare.

'So, what now?' he said. 'I've answered your questions and told you that I did not kill that slippery bastard, although I can't say that I'm sorry he's dead. At least he won't keep coming after me. If you're not going to arrest me then can you please go so that I can get some rest?'

James knew there were no grounds to arrest him or take him in for formal interrogation, but that didn't stop him asking some more questions and getting Porter to give them contact details for his hiking pals.

When they left the house, James photographed the Range Rover's licence plate so they could see if it turned up the night before on street cameras in the town.

Once back in the patrol car, Isaac asked James if he believed what Porter had told them.

'I'm really not sure,' he said, and realised that it was the same answer he'd given eight months ago when she'd asked him if he thought the guy had done something to his ex-girlfriend.

CHAPTER SIXTEEN
ANNIE

It was only the middle of the afternoon and yet Annie was already feeling emotionally drained.

It had been a Christmas like none that had gone before. She'd tried desperately to savour the festive joy for the sake of the kids, but hadn't been able to.

Despite that, the lunch had gone reasonably well, thanks largely to Janet's presence. She had been an absolute godsend and had helped Annie to stay focused and on top of things.

She'd played with Bella and Theo while Annie cleared the table, tidied up, and prepared the supper. And she had engaged her in light conversation throughout, which had stopped Annie from acknowledging the sense of despair that was growing inside her.

'Check this out,' Janet said as Annie walked back into the living room with a tray of cold drinks for everyone.

Her friend was holding up her phone while standing between the kids, who were sprawled on the floor surrounded by their new toys.

'What is it?' Annie asked as she placed the tray on the coffee table.

'It's a news alert on my *Cumbria Gazette* app about what happened in Kendal. And James has got a mention.'

Annie's jaw hardened as she took the phone and looked at the screen. Half of it was filled with a headline that read: BELOVED GAZETTE REPORTER FOUND DEAD.

Below the headline was a short article under the by-line of editor Nadine Stone.

It is with deep regret that I'm having to report on the tragic and untimely death of journalist Gordon Carver, who for years has been a valued member of our editorial team.

His body was found this morning close to his home in Kendal, and police have confirmed that a murder investigation has been launched.

It's believed that he was attacked yesterday evening while walking along a wooded path and suffered a fatal blow to the back of his head.

Gordon, who was aged just thirty-three and single, will be greatly missed by his colleagues here at the Gazette.

We will do all we can to assist the police investigation that is being led by Detective Chief Inspector James Walker. And we will provide further updates as and when we get them.

Beneath the article was a head-and-shoulders photo of Gordon that caused Annie's insides to knot up. She sniffed back tears as she handed the phone back to Janet.

'It didn't seem real until now,' she said. 'And something like this puts my own problems into perspective.'

Janet gave her a sympathetic nod. 'It certainly is shocking, and it sounds like he was the victim of a cold-blooded killer who for all we know is now celebrating Christmas Day without feeling a shred of guilt.'

That thought hit Annie with the force of a slap, and she had to retreat into the kitchen so the kids wouldn't see her cry.

CHAPTER SEVENTEEN

The snow continued to fall as the patrol car carried James and Isaac back into town. It was already stacking up along the sides of the roads, which meant the gritters would soon be out in force.

James was hoping it wouldn't get so bad as to make it difficult, if not impossible, for him to drive home to Kirkby Abbey at the end of the day. He wasn't prepared for an overnight stay in Kendal, and he was pretty sure that there wouldn't be many hotel and B&B rooms available anyway.

His head had begun to ache from the flood of unsettling thoughts running through it following their encounter with Daniel Porter.

He was wondering if they should have spent more time with the guy, putting him under more pressure. But even if they had, it was likely he would have merely stood his ground and continued to insist that he did not kill Gordon Carver.

Sure, the journalist had made an enemy of Porter by seeking to expose him as the person responsible for Chloe Walsh's disappearance. And that could be construed as a clear motive for murder. But there wasn't enough credible evidence to convince James to throw everything at it so early on. Plus, if it turned out that Porter wasn't the killer, they would have lost valuable time.

The first thing the two detectives did when they arrived at HQ was to head for the vending machine. James helped himself to a coffee and a cheese sandwich, and treated Isaac to the same.

After that they entered the open-plan office, where he was surprised to see so many of his team hard at work.

DI Stevens had returned from the crime scene and DS Abbott from the home of Gordon's parents in Burneside. They were busy tapping at their keyboards while DCs Sharma and Foley were laying the finishing touches to a couple of large evidence boards. Also present were three support staff and two uniformed officers.

James let it be known that he'd begin the briefing after he'd spoken to Superintendent Tanner. He made the call from his office after shedding his overcoat and devouring his sandwich.

Tanner was pleased to learn that they had questioned Porter, and agreed with James that there were insufficient grounds to treat him as anything more than a potential suspect.

'A lawyer will tie us in knots if we move too soon on the basis of what we have,' Tanner said.

He went on to say that the Chief Constable had instructed the press office to release a statement confirming that it was *Gazette* journalist Gordon Carver who'd been murdered and include details of where and when it happened.

'There will also be the usual appeal for anyone with information to come forward,' he said. 'Tomorrow, we'll stage a press conference to ramp up interest in the case. Given what's happened over the last several Christmases, I suspect we're bound to be asked if a serial killer could be at large.'

It always seemed to emerge as a genuine concern after a murder was committed in any close-knit community. Fear and suspicion often spread quickly among villagers and townsfolk, and finger pointing could have a detrimental impact on an investigation.

But James had to acknowledge the possibility that despite the plan to issue a message of reassurance to the residents of Kendal, they couldn't be certain that Gordon's killer would not strike again.

The briefing got underway just before four o'clock, after James had drawn up a list of all the issues that needed to be discussed.

He stood between the two evidence boards, one with various notes and the other showing a selection of photographs. These included images of Gordon Carver and Daniel Porter, and shots from the crime scene. There were also several images of the boards pinned to the wall in Gordon's home office.

He began by thanking those who hadn't been rostered on for coming in.

'It's much appreciated,' he said. 'Please let your partners and families know that I'm sorry their Christmas has been spoiled yet again.'

He then told them that the press office was about to issue a statement and acknowledged that he was aware that most of the information was already in the public domain.

'It's a hot topic on social media,' he said. 'The *Cumbria Gazette* has published an online piece that's bound to get people talking and have them focusing on the investigation. If we're not perceived to be doing a good job we'll come in for a barrage of criticism.'

Turning to the crime scene photo on the evidence board, he

said, 'Let's begin here. The spot where Gordon was attacked is less than two hundred yards from his home. What we don't know is if he was returning there or on his way out when it happened. What we do know is that it appears the killer took his phone and made off with the murder weapon.'

He invited Stevens to update them on the forensic work being carried out along the path and in the wood, and the DI explained that the search had been temporarily halted because of the wind and snow that was sweeping across the town.

'I just came from there and conditions are pretty rough,' Stevens said, 'but the forecast says it will ease off in a couple of hours. Hopefully we can then resume the search. Finding Gordon's mobile phone and the murder weapon are priorities.'

Stevens then confirmed that most of Gordon's neighbours had been spoken to and none of them had seen him the previous evening or spotted any suspicious activity in their road. But some of the houses were unoccupied as the owners had gone away for Christmas.

'One other thing to note is that the CCTV camera in the car park at the southern end of the path is out of order and has been for some time,' he added. 'It means there'll be no footage available of anyone entering or leaving the path. But, of course, the killer could have approached through the wood and waited for Gordon to walk past.'

After checking the list he'd made, James moved on to what they had found in Gordon's house.

'He'd been hard at work on another article about the Chloe Walsh case, and was clearly of the view that Daniel Porter had killed her,' James said. 'We spoke to his editor at the *Gazette*, Nadine Stone, who told us that Porter threatened Gordon. What he'd allegedly said was that he would make Gordon regret going to his house to stir things up, and would do whatever it took to stop the article being published. However, Dawn and I have just returned from interviewing Porter, and he denies both threatening and killing Gordon. Neither of us can be sure he wasn't lying, but we have to be careful not to make a snap judgement based on his history. We also can't rule out the possibility that it was a random attack.'

James continued, 'Porter claims he went hiking this morning, but didn't leave his house on Christmas Eve. We therefore need to round up CCTV footage from across the town. He owns a Range Rover SUV and I've taken a picture of the plate. I'm hoping that we'll also spot the car driven by the woman who visited Gordon yesterday afternoon and spent several hours with him.'

The team had already been told about the mystery woman and DC Sharma had taken it upon himself to try to establish her identity. It was still a work in progress, but he did have something interesting to report.

'The SOCOs who checked over Gordon's house found a used condom wrapped in tissue in the bathroom waste bin,' he said. 'I think it's reasonable to assume that he had sex with the woman when she was there, and I'm hopeful that forensics will be able to get a DNA trace from the external surface. I know it's wishful thinking, but there's the remote possibility that at some point in her life she was convicted of a crime and will therefore be on the police database.'

'That would be a result,' James said. 'I remember heading up a case in London where we identified a woman using the same method.'

Next on the agenda was the call James received from Gordon around the time of the attack.

'I know that for the rest of my life I'll regret not hearing the

78

phone ring,' he said. 'It was rare for him to ring me outside of office hours and it's possible it could have been something to do with what was going to happen to him. Perhaps he feared for his life. Or maybe it was just a coincidence. We don't have his phone, but we can check with his service provider to see what other calls he made or received yesterday.'

James listed what needed to be followed up, asking DC Isaac to talk to Porter's friends to confirm that he'd spent this morning hiking with them on Cunswick Fell. DC Foley was allocated the job of securing from Nadine Stone the names of people who had been angered or upset by what Gordon had written about them, going back six months.

'We'll stick with it for another couple of hours,' he said. 'I want to hear your thoughts on what other lines of inquiry we should be following up. And let's set out a plan for tomorrow, starting with how many more team members we'd like to join us.'

CHAPTER EIGHTEEN

James was finally able to leave the office just after seven. He rang Annie to let her know he'd soon be home, and she told him that Janet had left, and she was about to put the kids to bed.

'Have you eaten? Or would you like me to prepare something for you?' she asked.

'It's too late for a meal,' he said. 'Is there any Christmas pudding left from lunch?'

'Quite a bit actually. I can sort it for you along with a drink.'

'Much appreciated, Annie. And I'll be there as soon as I can.'

Thankfully the wind had dropped, and it had stopped snowing, but it was slow going on the slippery roads in the dark, partly because James found it hard to concentrate. His thoughts were spiralling and his eyes were burning.

The briefing had been intense as they'd discussed a number of possible scenarios that might have led to Gordon's murder. But so many questions still needed to be answered, including the whereabouts of the murder weapon and Gordon's mobile. Both could potentially provide them with crucial evidence.

The team's attention had also been drawn to media coverage of the story. It was high up the running orders on the TV news bulletins, but two other stories beat it to the top spot: A young woman stabbed to death in the early hours while returning home from a Christmas Eve drinks party in Manchester, and a police officer shot dead at lunchtime when he tried to arrest a suspected drug dealer in London.

Violent crimes usually spiked over the festive period due to increased alcohol consumption, and there was also an inevitable and tragic surge in the number of domestic-related incidents with families in close proximity for long days. And it seemed that this year was no exception.

Gordon Carver's murder was the only one that had come to light so far this Christmas in Cumbria, and it would be another festive blow to everyone living in the county and in Kendal in particular.

The town had a population of just under thirty thousand and the crime rate was generally extremely low. It was known as 'The Gateway to the Lake District' and attracted huge numbers of tourists throughout the year.

The last thing it needed was for people to start believing that it was no longer a safe place to visit.

James arrived home just after eight and Annie opened the door before he put his key in the lock.

As soon as he stepped over the threshold they fell into each other's arms.

'I bet you've had a hellish day,' she said, her voice soft and scratchy.

'I'm just glad it's over,' he told her. 'And I'm looking forward to a piece of that Christmas pudding.'

She smiled. 'It's waiting for you in the living room, along with a large glass of the single malt whisky I gave you this morning.'

The rest of the evening flew by. They sat together on the sofa and James told her about his day, adhering to protocol by not providing too much detail.

And Annie told him that Bella and Theo had enjoyed themselves and were well behaved throughout.

'It would have been much more of a struggle if Janet hadn't come over,' she said. 'She was really helpful, and the kids had fun with her.'

It struck James that she looked very tired and even somewhat stressed. Her eyes were sunken and shadowed, and she kept closing them as she spoke.

'Are you sure that you're all right?' he asked her. 'It looks like you've got the weight of the world on your shoulders.'

She exhaled an audible sigh and nodded. 'It's just that I'm still struggling to get my head around what's happened. Christmas this year wasn't supposed to be like this.'

'We'll, I'm sure you're going to feel better after a night's sleep,' he said as he fired down a last mouthful of whisky. 'And once again, I'm really sorry that I also won't be spending Boxing Day with you and the kids.'

He felt a lump rise in his throat as he spoke. Apologising for not being with his family during yet another special occasion just didn't seem enough, and the guilt was a weight in his chest. He was just grateful that his wife didn't hold it against him.

She reached across and placed a hand on his shoulder. 'It can't be helped. And besides, there's always next year. And the year after. So, come on. Let's go to bed and hope that despite everything we'll both be able to drop off.'

CHAPTER NINETEEN
BOXING DAY

James had set the alarm for 6 a.m. but he was awake long before then. He'd had a restless night and had managed to sleep for only about four hours.

His mind kept taking him back to the moment he looked down on Gordon's brutalised body on the path. It was an image that he knew was going to frequently surface for a long time to come.

'Are you awake?' Annie whispered beside him.

'Yep, and I have been for a while,' he said.

'Thought so. I can always tell.'

'What about you?'

'I woke up a few minutes ago. It was a rough night.'

'Well, it's coming up to six, so I'll switch off the alarm and get up. I need to give myself plenty of time to get to headquarters because of this bloody weather.'

He had the same routine whenever he had an early start: he'd go and use the downstairs bathroom so as not to wake the kids, and take with him the clothes he'd left out the night before.

'I could make you some breakfast before you go,' Annie mumbled.

He rolled onto his side, put an arm around her, and kissed her forehead. 'No way, my love. I'll make myself a coffee downstairs as usual and then grab something to eat when I get to the office.'

'Are you sure?'

'I am. And tell Bella and Theo that I hope to see them before they go to bed this evening.'

James experienced another blast of guilt as he climbed out of bed and stepped quietly out of the bedroom.

This was meant to have been another day off for him, and he had intended to make the most of it by taking the family out for lunch. But once again he'd been forced to abandon them.

He sensed that Annie was more disappointed than she was letting on. But it didn't surprise him. She had actually been quite subdued this past week, and he'd put it down to the fact that she feared something bad would happen to spoil yet another Christmas, as indeed it had.

He didn't like it when she wasn't her usual bubbly self. He always worried that it was down to him or that there was something she was keeping to herself.

With a conscious effort he managed to push those thoughts from his mind by the time he got downstairs. Before going into the bathroom, he looked out of the window and to his relief saw that very little snow had fallen overnight.

It took him barely twenty minutes to get ready, and once in the kitchen he put the kettle on. As the water boiled, he called the office.

Detective Constable Hall had worked the night shift and informed him that there had been no developments in the case.

'There's a lot of noise on social media, though, guv,' Hall

said. 'Some people have even put up posts saying that Gordon got what he deserved because he was an unscrupulous hack. Naturally, they chose to remain anonymous.'

It didn't surprise James, but it did bother him given that he knew Gordon was a fair and honest journalist. These days vile comments praising the perpetrators and condemning the victims always seemed to be posted after a high-profile murder.

He told Hall to have everything ready for an early briefing and then made himself a coffee. While drinking it he used his phone to check the online news feeds, and as expected, Gordon's murder was getting extensive coverage. But as he scanned the pages, he didn't learn anything that he didn't already know.

Before leaving the house, he checked the weather forecast, which wasn't as bad as he feared it would be. No more snow was expected, but the wind would continue to gust from the north and there'd be a widespread frost. He also noticed that the temperatures across most of Cumbria had dropped overnight to minus ten.

As he set off, just before seven, he was pleased to see that the gritters had been out clearing the roads. And as he drove, adrenaline started to fuel every part of his body.

He was eager to kickstart day two of the investigation, and just hoped that they would begin to make some progress.

More questions were taking shape in his head, and he was making mental notes of the various checks that would need to be carried out.

He was halfway between Kirkby Abbey and Kendal when he got another call from DC Hall.

'I know you're on your way here, guv, but I thought I should flag up that there's been a potential breakthrough,' he said.

'I'm listening,' James said and felt his pulse escalate. 'What is it?'

'Well, a member of the public called Control and was just put through to me. His name is Floyd Nolan, and he says he knew Gordon and bumped into him in a town centre pub on Christmas Eve not long before the murder took place.'

'What pub was this?'

'The Queen's Castle. It's that refurbished place near the bus station, not far from where Gordon lived.'

'Yeah, I know it. Go on.'

'Mr Nolan says he went in there at just after eight and saw Gordon at a table with a man he didn't recognise. He says he and Gordon acknowledged each other, but they didn't speak. Nolan then joined his own pal at the bar.'

'And did he happen to notice when Gordon left there?'

'He did, guv. He reckons it was coming up to nine o'clock. And that's not all. He told me that Gordon was shaking his head as he walked past the bar towards the exit, and looked like he'd just received some bad news.'

James felt a blast of optimism. 'We need to find out who Gordon was meeting with. You're right. This could be a breakthrough.'

'Mr Nolan gave me a rough description of the bloke,' Hall said. 'Mid- to late sixties. Grey hair and quite chubby.'

'The pub is bound to have one or more security cameras and it's highly likely the pair would have been filmed,' James said. 'Find out who owns it and get me a contact number. That will be my first port of call after the morning briefing.'

CHAPTER TWENTY
ANNIE

There was no way she'd be able to go back to sleep. Not with so much going on inside her head.

She was battling with an emotional storm that was making her fearful, confused and anxious. And a growing sense of guilt was adding to the pressure she felt under.

One voice was telling her to open up to her husband because he had a right to know what was happening. But another – stronger – voice was insisting that he didn't need to know, at least not yet.

Not wanting to ruin his Christmas was the reason she initially gave herself for holding back. But now it was because he needed to be fully focused on finding out who murdered Gordon Carver. And he wouldn't be if she unburdened herself on him. It would be a major distraction and cause him to take his eye off the ball.

However, she was well aware that time was running out. She had until 5 January to break the news to him. Just ten days until she expected to find out if her life was about to fall apart. And she needed him to be there with her.

She knew James well enough to be sure that he wouldn't be cross with her, even though she had chosen to confide in her best friend instead of him. He'd understand that she'd been thinking of him when she arrived at that decision.

It didn't make it any easier for her to deal with though. And just lying in bed thinking about it was causing her heart to beat high up in her chest. In fact, it quickly got to the point where she had to bite down on her bottom lip to stop herself crying.

She was able to hold back the tears for another half an hour, which was when she heard Theo cry out to announce that he was awake.

It came as a relief to know that she would now have to switch off the negative thoughts in order to attend to the children. And hopefully they would keep her occupied for the rest of the day and stop her from slipping back into the deep, dark pit of despair.

CHAPTER TWENTY-ONE

It was approaching 8 a.m. when James arrived at headquarters. First stop was the canteen where he got himself a coffee and a bacon sandwich.

The office itself was loud and lively, and he was pleased to see that so many members of the team were in even though, like him, several of them were still meant to be enjoying the festive break.

They had all been made aware by DC Hall of the development in the case, and it had clearly energised them. James started his briefing with it as soon as everyone was gathered.

'We now know that Gordon was walking home from a town-centre pub when he was attacked,' he said. 'He was spotted in the Queen's Castle having a drink with someone, and according to our witness, a Mr Floyd Nolan, he didn't look very happy when he left there just before nine.

'DS Abbott and I will be going to the pub after the briefing to check it out.'

'I've found out that the Queen's Castle is run by a Mr and Mrs

Peston,' DC Hall said. 'It's not open yet, but I've just been given their number.'

'Then ring them,' James told him. 'Ask them if they have security cameras in the bar. If not, I'll still need to talk to them. And can you also arrange for Mr Nolan to provide us with a full statement and detailed description of the man he saw with Gordon?'

There was a lot to get through so James quickly read out a list of all the other issues he wanted addressed, including the media coverage.

'This is a big deal for the papers and especially because Gordon was one of their own,' he said. 'We can expect mounting pressure from them as things progress. If you're contacted by any reporters please refer them to the press office.'

Updates came thick and fast then. The search of the area around where Gordon was found would resume shortly, and it was being widened to take in nearby streets.

'If the killer took off with the murder weapon and Gordon's phone then there's a good chance that they were discarded close to the crime scene,' he said. 'Finding them would give a huge boost to the investigation.'

Daniel Porter's hiking friends had been contacted and had confirmed that he spent most of Christmas Day with them on Cunswick Fell. James had expected that, though it did surprise him that none of them claimed to have seen him on Christmas Eve.

The post-mortem on Gordon's body was due to be carried out later that morning by Dr Pam Flint, and James asked DI Stevens to attend.

Street-camera footage from around the town was coming in, but like everything else the process was slower than usual because it was Christmas. This led to a short discussion about the woman Gordon had spent several hours with on Christmas Eve.

'I think it'd be an idea to go back and speak to Gordon's neighbour, Erika Lynch,' James said. 'It was she and her husband who found his body, but she also saw the woman leaving his house on Christmas Eve. She said she was wearing a beige overcoat and a headscarf, but she might have remembered more to share with us.' Pointing to DC Isaac, he added, 'That'll be your job, Dawn.'

James was then informed that the used condom found in Gordon's bathroom was in the lab undergoing forensic analysis for DNA samples, and they were hoping to have the results back soon. They were also waiting on Gordon's mobile phone data from his service provider and hoping the process wouldn't be held up because it was Boxing Day.

'There's one more thing to touch on before we allocate the various other tasks,' James said, 'and it's the fact that we're still none the wiser as to why Gordon rang me at home on Christmas Eve. Because of the time he made the call it's hard not to believe that it had something to do with what subsequently happened to him. So, it's something we should keep giving thought to.'

Within minutes of the briefing ending DC Hall had managed to speak to the couple who ran the Queen's Castle.

'They do have cameras in the bar,' he told James. 'And they're more than happy to show you the footage from Christmas Eve, which is thankfully still on the system. They themselves don't recall seeing Gordon there, but that was probably because it was quite busy and they didn't know him personally.'

'Are they there now?'

'They live two streets away and will be in a few minutes,' Hall said.

James told Abbott to get ready to go with him to the pub. But before setting out he called Superintendent Tanner to update him, and the boss let it be known that a press conference would take place at Penrith's Carleton Hall HQ this afternoon.

'If you're not tied up you can front it with me,' Tanner said. 'But if you are then I'll do it myself.'

CHAPTER TWENTY-TWO

The Queen's Castle was within walking distance of headquarters, but James opted to go there in a patrol car.

'I'm not being lazy,' he said to Abbott. 'It means we can drive on to another location if necessary.'

It was 9 a.m. and though the sky was still bruised with thick, shapeless clouds, the town was gradually coming to life, and people were taking to the streets despite the bitter wind.

Kendal had become one of James's favourite places since moving to Cumbria, and he hoped the shock of what had happened wouldn't linger for long.

It was a vibrant community and popular tourist hub, with museums, art galleries, and a castle ruin. There were also lots of bars, restaurants, cafes, and quirky shops.

As usual, Kendal had gone all out to embrace the festive spirit, and James recalled bringing the kids here in November to see the tree lights being switched on in the marketplace alongside thousands of people also looking forward to a joyful, peaceful Christmas.

The last thing that anyone had expected back then was for the merrymaking to be marred by a brutal murder.

It took them just minutes to get to the Queen's Castle, which occupied a two-storey limestone building. The place had reopened about nine months ago after a major renovation, and as the patrol car pulled up outside it, Abbott said, 'Sean and I have been meaning to come here, but just haven't got around to it. I wish now we had because it looks really nice, at least from the outside.'

Like many other members of the team, Abbott and her husband lived in the town, and as James turned to her, he noticed for the first time the tired shadows beneath her eyes. He wondered if the fact that the murder had been committed essentially on her doorstep had caused her to have a sleepless night.

'Let's just hope that we're about to see something in there that will take us forward,' he said. 'And that we won't come away disappointed.'

The pub wasn't yet open to the public, but the door was ajar and so they stepped inside.

The interior was large but also cosy, with plenty of comfortable seats, a stone fireplace, and a bar that stretched along one wall.

A couple in their fifties who James assumed to be the owners were standing in front of it and came right over.

'You must be the police officers we were told to expect,' the man said.

He was thick set, with a goatee beard and a prominent beer gut.

James flashed his card. 'I'm Detective Chief Inspector Walker and this is Detective Sergeant Abbott. Thank you for coming in early for us.'

'It's no trouble. We'll soon be opening up anyway,' he said. 'I'm Ron Peston and this is my wife, Sonia.'

She was slim with blonde hair twisted in a knot on top of her head.

'The officer I spoke to on the phone told me why you wanted to pay us a visit,' Peston said, 'so we've checked through the security footage from Christmas Eve and you're in luck. Mr Carver and his drinking companion were caught on camera. We're so sorry that after he left here such a bad thing happened to him.'

He pointed to one of the booths. 'That was where they sat, and they were here for about an hour. If you look over to the left, you'll see the camera that recorded them.'

'Did they arrive together?' James asked him.

'No. Mr Carver got here and paid for two beers at the bar. The other man came in ten or so minutes later. And he stayed for another couple of minutes after Mr Carver left.'

'And you didn't recognise him?'

'No, I didn't. I don't think he'd been in here before. But then I didn't know Mr Carver either. After your officer contacted me, I checked online and saw his photo.'

James nodded. 'I see. Can you show us the recording?'

'Of course. Come this way.'

He led them into the office while his wife stayed in the bar. There was a desk with a laptop resting on top of it and Peston sat down and brought up the video.

They watched as Gordon walked into the pub and over to the bar. The time stamp read 20.02 and the image was surprisingly clear.

Having purchased the two beers, Gordon went and sat in the booth, placing the glasses on the table.

Peston then fast-forwarded the video to the point where a

man wearing a heavy winter coat with the hood up entered the pub and walked straight over to the booth.

It wasn't until he reached it that he pulled down the hood and removed the coat.

His face sent a cold shiver down the length of James's spine.

The man was familiar to him. His name was Michael Frost, but he was also known as Mad Dog Mike because over a number of years he'd built up a fierce reputation as an unpredictable and aggressive career criminal.

'Oh shit,' Abbott whispered in James's ear. 'Is that who I think it is?'

He responded with a slight nod. 'I'm a hundred per cent sure that it is.'

CHAPTER TWENTY-THREE

James and Abbott remained silent as they watched the rest of the video clip play out.

They saw Michael Frost shake Gordon's hand before sitting down opposite him at the table. The pair then had what appeared to be an intense conversation during which they leaned towards each other, presumably so they wouldn't be overheard by the other customers. The time stamp showed that it lasted precisely fifty-five minutes.

When Gordon stood up, he shook Frost's hand again and walked out of the pub. And as Floyd Nolan had said, the expression on his face suggested he'd been given some bad news. As soon as Gordon was gone, they saw Frost take out his mobile phone and make a short call that lasted just twenty seconds. Barely a minute later he got up and exited the pub.

'We need to take a copy of this with us,' James said, and at the same time Abbott produced a USB stick from her shoulder bag.

Handing it to Peston, she said, 'Can you please copy it onto here, Mr Peston?'

She then stood over him as the clip was transferred, while James stepped back out of the office into the bar.

Mrs Peston had been joined by another member of staff and they were busy in the kitchen. When James saw them through the hatch, he moved to the other side of the room and called the office to ask one of the support staff to dig out the file on Michael Frost.

'I want his current address, and I need to know when he was last on our radar,' he said. 'I was under the impression that he'd retired from a life of crime a while ago, but that might not be the case.'

James re-entered the office as Peston completed the transfer of the video clip to the USB stick. He gave it to Abbott and said, 'I hope this proves useful to you, detectives. Do you believe that the man with Mr Carver is the person who killed him? It appears from what I've seen online that it happened soon after they both left here.'

'We have no idea, Mr Peston,' James said. 'And for that reason, I must ask you to delete this segment of footage from the system to ensure that it's not seen by anyone else. If it is, it could compromise our investigation.'

The man curled his lip and nodded. 'We wouldn't allow that to happen, but I can appreciate your concern. And it's not a problem for us anyway because there's memory limitation on the drive we use and all the footage from the past two weeks will be automatically deleted in three days. So, I'm happy to delete it manually now.'

After watching him delete the footage, James asked him not to speak about what he'd seen to anyone.

'It's important at this stage of the investigation that we keep such things to ourselves,' he said.

James thanked the man for his help before he and Abbott left the building.

'So, where to next, guv?' Abbott asked when they got into the patrol car.

'Back to the office to let the team know we have another suspect in Mad Dog Mike,' he answered. 'Then we get his address and head straight there.'

'I can't believe he's resurfaced after so long. It must be over a year since he was released from his last stretch in prison, and I don't think his name has cropped up since then.'

'Or if it did it might not have been brought to our attention. Most of his offences were committed in and around where he lived in Carlisle, and the team there dealt with them. But we did arrest him once about five years ago, shortly after I joined the Constabulary. He came here to Kendal and assaulted a guy who owed him money. As I recall, he was convicted and sentenced to six months.'

'That's right, guv. And then he was put away again, but I can't remember what for.'

'Well, we know he's a repeat offender with a history of violence, now we need to find out if he went on to attack Gordon after they both left the pub.'

'I'm curious to know why they met up,' Abbott said. 'It looked like a heavy conversation, and I didn't see either of them smile once. I suppose it could have been because Gordon was writing a story about him and he'd agreed to be interviewed.'

James shook his head. 'If that were the case then surely Gordon would have made notes, but he didn't. So, the sooner we talk to Frost, the better.'

Back at headquarters James told the patrol car driver to wait outside for them. Once in the office James went straight over to the support officer he'd called from the pub, while Abbott arranged for the video clip to be uploaded onto the system.

'I have Michael Frost's current address for you, sir,' the support officer said. 'He's now living in Staveley. And I've printed off a hard copy of his file, which I've placed on your desk.'

James retrieved the file and as soon as he saw the photos of Frost, he knew for certain that he was the man who'd met Gordon in the pub. He made that clear as soon as he got the team together to brief them. After the video clip was played on the office screens he read from the file.

'Michael Frost, better known as Mad Dog Mike, was released from prison just over a year ago after serving nine months for common assault. But his criminal record goes way back. Two years for GBH. Six months for possession of drugs. Plus, various fines and cautions for offences including burglary and shoplifting.

'The guy is now sixty-seven, but he's been making mischief since his teens. Given what we've just seen, he's now a suspect in Gordon's murder. Jess and I will go and question him, and while we do that, I'd like someone to check street cameras around the Queen's Castle to see if they show where he went when he left there.'

CHAPTER TWENTY-FOUR

James's mind was in overdrive as he and Abbott sped towards Staveley in the patrol car. The case had thrown up yet another surprise.

Michael Frost – or Mad Dog Mike – could well have been the last person to have spoken to Gordon. And whatever he said to the journalist clearly didn't go down well, judging by the look on his face as he left.

'It's tempting to believe that Frost went on to kill Gordon,' he said. 'The guy left the pub just minutes after Gordon did, so he would have had no trouble catching up with him. Or maybe he took a quicker route to the wood and beat him there. Then waited for him to come along.'

'There's also another possible scenario, guv,' Abbott said. 'Before Frost left the pub, we saw him use his mobile to make a quick call. Perhaps he tipped someone off. Told them that Gordon was on his way home. And whoever he spoke to may have gone on to carry out the attack.'

James thought about it and said, 'It would all make perfect

sense but for one thing – the fact that they shook hands both before and after their chat. It suggests to me that it wasn't the first time they'd met, and also that Gordon didn't leave the pub fearing that Frost posed a threat to him.'

'That could just be what Frost wanted him to think?' Abbott responded.

James nodded. 'That's true enough. Let's hope things become clearer when we speak to the guy.'

The village of Staveley was between Kendal and Windermere, and only about four miles from headquarters. Michael Frost lived in a bungalow just off Station Road and according to his file he'd moved there a year ago after being released from prison.

The file also revealed that he'd been married twice, once in his twenties and again in his forties. His first wife died from a hereditary heart condition and the second divorced him after they'd been together for just three years.

James could well remember interviewing Frost almost five years ago. What struck him then was that the man didn't come across as a violent law breaker. He had a friendly disposition, and he'd told James that he didn't believe he deserved the nickname Mad Dog Mike. He did admit to having a short temper, though, and to being a career criminal.

In that sense, he was no different from many of the other felons James had dealt with over the years who had got caught up in a cycle of reoffending.

When Frost opened his front door to them, he was wearing a shabby dressing gown and smoking a cigarette.

James's first impression was that the man had aged considerably since they had last met. He had a tired, sagging face, and blood vessels were bulging out of his neck.

'Good morning, Mr Frost,' James said as he held up his warrant card. 'Do you remember me?'

Frost's eyebrows drew together and he let smoke jet from his nose as he stared at James for several seconds before speaking.

'Of course, I fucking remember you. I never forget the faces of the plods who gave me a hard time. What is it you want and why have you come mob-handed?'

James introduced Abbott and the uniformed officer who had driven them there in the patrol car.

'We need to speak to you, Mr Frost,' he said. 'It can be here, or you can accompany us to the station in Kendal.'

Frost drew on his cigarette before responding. 'Tell me what it's about and I'll tell you if I'm willing to cooperate.'

'Very well,' James said. 'It's about the Christmas Eve murder of local journalist Gordon Carver. His body was found yesterday close to his home in Kendal.'

Frost's features stiffened and his eyes grew wide in their sockets.

'Please tell me it's not true,' he said. 'It can't be.'

'But it is, Mr Frost. I'm a bit surprised you don't yet know as it's been on the news.'

'I didn't watch or listen to any news yesterday, and I've only just got out of bed.'

'Well, the reason we're here is that Gordon was murdered shortly after he spent some time with you in the Queen's Castle pub,' James said. 'We have you both on security camera footage. We therefore want to know what you discussed and whether you went on to kill him when he was walking home from there.'

Frost's face took on a fiery intensity and his whole body started to shake.

'I promise you that I didn't kill Gordon,' he said. 'You have to believe me. He was a friend.' He paused there and flicked his unsteady gaze from James to Abbott and then back to James. He drew air in sharply through his nostrils and added, 'But look, I think I know who may have done it.'

CHAPTER TWENTY-FIVE

Michael Frost invited the two detectives into his bungalow, which was bleak and untidy, and devoid of any Christmas decorations. As the three of them settled on chairs in the tiny living room, he stubbed out what was left of his cigarette and lit another one.

He seemed to be genuinely shocked by the news about Gordon, but James knew it could well be an act.

'I want you to start by telling us about your relationship with Mr Carver,' he said. 'You described him as a friend. What does that mean exactly?'

Frost removed the cigarette from between his lips and a nimbus of smoke swirled around his head.

'Gordon was someone I'd known for years,' he said. He appeared to be struggling to push the words out. 'I used to be mates with his dad when we were teens and living in Carlisle. As a reporter Gordon mostly covered crime-related stories for the *Gazette*, as you obviously know, and it meant he wrote about what I got up to more than a few times.

'After I came out of prison a year ago I let him write a feature about my decision to retire from a life spent on the wrong side of the law.'

'And is that what you did – retired?' James asked him, his tone sceptical.

He nodded. 'You know I did. I made that clear to your lot soon after I came out. I'd had enough, you see, and didn't want to spend any more time in a cell. So, I sold the house in Carlisle because I needed money to help me through retirement, and moved here to Staveley for a quieter life. It meant I had more contact with Gordon. He would often pick my brain about the crime scene across Cumbria.'

'That's interesting, Mr Frost,' James said, and meant it. 'But now let's move on to Christmas Eve. You can surely understand why our suspicions were aroused when we saw the security footage from the pub. When Gordon got up and left, he didn't look very happy. And then, after you made a quick phone call, you followed him out. We believe he was attacked and killed just minutes later while walking through a wood near his home. He received a fatal blow to the back of the head.'

'I didn't follow him, if that's what you think,' Frost said, a note of desperation in his voice. 'The phone call I made was to order a taxi to pick me up. And it did as soon as I stepped out of the pub. The number's still on my mobile so you can check it. And for your information, I was banned from driving six months ago because of poor eyesight. So I have to travel everywhere by cab or bus.'

James shifted restlessly on his chair and exchanged a glance with Abbott. They both knew it would be easy to check what he'd said, which suggested it was probably true.

'So now tell us what you and Gordon discussed and who you think might have murdered him,' James said.

After another drag on his cigarette, Frost said, 'I heard on the grapevine a few days ago about a scumbag who'd just got out of prison as part of the government's latest early release scheme to free up space. His name is Shane O'Brien and he'll be known to you, I'm sure.'

'Shane O'Brien as in the drug dealer?' James said.

'The very same. Anyway, O'Brien made the mistake, after he was told he was going to be released early, of letting a couple of fellow inmates know that he'd drawn up a list of people who he blamed for getting him sent down. He intended to get revenge against them. Well, I was told that Gordon was on that list because he'd helped expose what O'Brien and his gang were up to as part of an investigation carried out by the *Gazette*. I therefore felt I had to warn Gordon and so got him to meet up in the pub. And it really freaked him out. I told him he should let the police know, but not to say that the information came from me.'

'And what was his response to that?'

'Believe it or not, he then mentioned your name, Detective Walker. He said he would probably ring you and ask for advice on what he should do.'

James's breath caught and a hard knot tightened in his throat.

He felt it reasonable to assume that he now knew why he'd received a call from Gordon on Christmas Eve.

CHAPTER TWENTY-SIX

James was of the opinion that Frost's story was too fanciful to have been made up. Nevertheless, he asked to see the call log on his mobile.

It showed that he phoned someone just after nine o'clock on Christmas Eve when he was in the pub. James called the number and learned that it was indeed one of the town's taxi firms. It took them under a minute to confirm that a driver picked Frost up outside the Queen's Castle shortly after he made the call, and that he was taken straight to Staveley.

'I trust that means you no longer suspect me of Gordon's murder,' Frost said. 'As soon as I got back here, I went to bed. So don't waste any more time with me. Go and find Shane O'Brien and see what he's got to say for himself.'

James felt an uncomfortable tightness in his chest. He'd never come across O'Brien because the guy was banged up before he'd moved from London. But his name was among those who were often mentioned when the Constabulary wanted to boast about how it was winning the war against county lines drug gangs operating across Cumbria.

'We'll certainly speak to O'Brien,' James said. 'But I also need you to come to the station so that we can take a formal statement about what you were told about him and about your meeting with Gordon. Will that be a problem?'

Frost's mouth set in a determined line and he shook his head. 'Of course not, considering what's happened. But let's be clear about two things: You need to keep my name out of it, and no way will I tell you who tipped me off about O'Brien's revenge list. If I'm labelled a grass I'll become a target, and that's the last thing I need.'

James assured him that his name would not be shared with anyone and then asked him if he had been given the names of any of the other people on O'Brien's list.

'No, I wasn't. And I have no idea how long the list is.'

James's mouth curled into a half smile. 'I think we can live with that, Mr Frost. We'll take you to town straight away and arrange for you to be given a lift back.'

'I'll get my coat then,' Frost said as he stood up. But before moving away, he added, 'I take it Gordon's parents know about him?'

'They were told yesterday,' James said.

He ran a hand along his jawline and blew out his cheeks. 'Then I'll call them later. I want them to know that I had nothing to do with it.'

On the way back to Kendal James called the office and got someone to check the Police National Computer for the latest information on Shane O'Brien. He wanted to know when he got out of prison, how long he'd spent inside, and where he was now living.

Because Frost was with them in the patrol car, James and Abbott didn't discuss the case between them. But James's mind was busy dissecting what the man had told them.

It was another unsettling development that had opened up a fresh line of inquiry. And if it was true about Shane O'Brien's revenge list, then both their suspects had posed threats to Gordon because of what he'd written or what he was going to write about them.

James knew that it wasn't uncommon for journalists to fall victim to acts of violence because of stories they had written or broadcast. There had always been a risk associated with covering the news, but in recent years those risks had escalated, partly because many social media posts positively encouraged people to seek revenge against those who they believed had wronged them. The range of threats they were confronted with included murder, kidnapping, intimidation, and online and offline harassment. In fact, the United Nations now regarded journalism as one of the world's most dangerous professions.

James was reminded of a case he was involved in while with the Met in which a tabloid reporter was stabbed to death in his home. His killer was arrested days later and at his trial admitted to murdering the journalist because he'd exposed him in a front-page article as a serial fraudster who'd preyed on vulnerable women through various dating agencies.

The man had pretended he was someone he wasn't and conned twelve of them out of a total of over a hundred thousand pounds. He was sentenced to life in prison for the murder, but told the jury he didn't regret what he'd done.

Revenge, as James well knew, was one of the most powerful

motivators for murder, and could turn otherwise good people into cold-blooded killers.

But it was too soon to conclude that Gordon Carver was attacked by someone seeking retribution. The investigation had only just got started and god only knew where it was going to take them next.

CHAPTER TWENTY-SEVEN

They were back at headquarters by one o'clock. Just before they arrived James had sent a text to Superintendent Tanner to let him know that he would have to front the press conference by himself as James was too busy to come to Penrith. He knew that it wouldn't be a problem for Tanner. The boss was more than capable of facing the media by himself, and he was well aware that James hated pressers.

Once inside the building James asked Abbott to escort Frost to an interview room and take down his statement.

'Detective Sergeant Abbott will have a few more questions for you,' James said to Frost, 'and as soon as she's done, you'll be taken home. If there's anything you haven't told us that could prove helpful then now's your chance.'

'I'm not holding anything back,' Frost replied. 'And I haven't lied. Gordon was a friend and the reason I got him to meet me on Christmas Eve was to warn him of a potential threat. If he was followed from the pub by someone who knew he was there then it wasn't my fault.'

James grabbed a coffee and a snack bar before going to the office. He had no appetite for anything more substantial and planned to be on the move again as soon as he had an address for Shane O'Brien.

But before then he needed to bring the team up to date along with the boss. He also intended to call *Cumbria Gazette* editor Nadine Stone. He wanted to know what she could tell him about the paper's investigation that led to O'Brien's arrest and conviction, and how big a part Gordon played in it.

There were fewer team members present because DI Stevens was attending Gordon's post-mortem and DC Isaac was having another conversation with his neighbour Erika Lynch about the woman she saw leaving his house on Christmas Eve afternoon.

It was DC Foley who approached him first as he entered the office.

'I've pulled up the file you asked for on Shane O'Brien, guv,' she said. 'I've also spoken to the probation officer who was assigned to him upon his early release from prison two weeks ago. He's apparently been on his best behaviour, and she last spoke to him four days ago. So, are you going to tell me what he's got to do with anything?'

'I will soon,' he told her. 'Where is he living now?'

'According to the officer, an address in Milnthorpe. It's his widowed father's house apparently.'

'That's good. After I've briefed everyone and made a couple of calls, I want you to go there with me along with a uniformed unit.' He took the file from her and added, 'Can you get everyone together while I remind myself exactly what the guy went down for?'

It took him just seconds to take in the relevant information. Shane Timothy O'Brien, aged twenty-eight and unmarried, was one of the leading figures in a drugs gang that was smashed by Cumbria's Organised Crime Unit four years ago. He was jailed for seven years on a number of charges including supplying class A drugs, money laundering, and possessing an offensive weapon. But like many before him he was released early as part of the government's bid to reduce prison overcrowding.

There was also a photo of him that James remembered seeing before. He was a big man with a fleshy face, sunken eyes, and a crooked nose.

James relayed the information to the team along with what Michael Frost had told them.

'At least one mystery appears to have been solved,' he said. 'Gordon told Frost that he might call me for advice on what he should do in response to the threat from O'Brien. So, that's likely what he did as he was walking home from the pub. It could be he was attacked while he waited for me to answer, or very soon after he'd hung up.'

Once again, he felt a pang of guilt as he wondered if things would have turned out differently if he'd heard the phone ringing.

'I'll go to Milnthorpe with Caroline and some uniforms after this,' he went on. 'If the guy did draw up a revenge list with Gordon's name on it, then we need to question him.'

He went on to say that DS Abbott was taking down Frost's statement, which prompted one of the support officers to confirm that the man was caught on a CCTV camera getting into a taxi outside the pub after his meeting with Gordon on Christmas Eve. The same camera showed Gordon leaving the pub a few minutes earlier and crossing the road in the direction of his home.

'This doesn't rule Mad Dog Mike out entirely,' James said. 'Since we don't know the precise time of Gordon's death, it's possible that after being dropped off in Staveley, he returned to

Kendal in order to carry out the attack. I know he claims he's been banned from driving because of poor eyesight, but even if that's true, it doesn't mean he no longer gets behind the wheel. So, he remains a suspect.'

James instructed DC Sharma to find out from Gordon's parents if their son did form a friendship with Frost, and also if O'Brien's name had ever come up in their discussions with their son.

Finally, he got Foley to gather a uniformed unit while he put in a call to Tanner.

The Super listened to his update and they agreed between them what information would be released at the press conference, which was due to take place at two o'clock.

'There's now a lot more for you and the team to get your heads around,' the Superintendent said, 'and if Shane O'Brien did draw up a list of people who he wanted to seek revenge against, then it certainly raises the stakes. It might have been a kill list, and if so, more bodies might soon turn up.'

The thought of it sent James's pulse racing and caused the acid to churn in his stomach.

CHAPTER TWENTY-EIGHT

James couldn't get what the Super had said about a so-called 'kill list' out of his head.

He knew that there were numerous cases on record where convicted murderers were found to be in possession of such lists.

One high-profile case he recalled had involved a female killer who drew up a list of almost a hundred future targets. And more recently a man who murdered a woman in Southampton in 2024 was found in possession of a list of seven other people whose lives he wanted to end.

James therefore had to consider that it was entirely possible that, during the four years he spent behind bars, Shane O'Brien did what many other inmates do and entertained all sorts of revenge fantasies, the most extreme being to murder those he blamed for putting him away.

James called Nadine Stone on her mobile. When she answered she told him that she was in her office at the *Gazette* and asked if there had been any developments in the case.

'I take it you know about the press conference that will soon be taking place at Carleton Hall?' he said.

'Yes, and we'll have a reporter there.'

'Superintendent Tanner will be fronting it, and he'll explain where we are with the investigation.'

'But I assume it hasn't been discovered who killed Gordon?'

'I'm afraid we still don't know.'

'Then what can I do for you, Detective Walker?'

'I need to ask you about something and it's strictly off the record for now.'

'I'm intrigued. Fire away.'

'It concerns a man named Shane O'Brien,' James said. 'He was a drug dealer who was jailed some four years ago.'

'I know who he is,' Nadine replied. 'He and his cohorts were the subject of an investigation that my paper carried out. It was just before you came to Cumbria.'

'And I gather it was partly instrumental in bringing them down.'

'That's right. We were given information that we shared with the police. In fact, it was Gordon who …'

She stopped suddenly and James heard her catch her breath.

'Oh god, are you thinking that O'Brien may have killed Gordon? I don't know why it didn't occur to me. We even carried the story of his early release a couple of weeks ago.'

'Right now, he's only a person of interest,' James pointed out. 'And that's why you have to keep this to yourself, Nadine. But can you tell me how involved Gordon was with what you published back then?'

After clearing her throat, she said, 'It was Gordon who convinced me that we should launch the investigation. At the time everyone knew that there was a county lines drug gang operating between

Carlisle and Penrith. Gordon's underworld contacts fed him the names of some of the key players and O'Brien was among them.

'Gordon was fully focused on it for weeks and pulled together a wealth of information on the gang members and how they were operating. Whenever he came up with something interesting, he passed it on to his contact inside the Organised Crime Unit. Then one day he got a tip about a drugs exchange that was going to take place in a Carlisle car park. He let the OCU know and they staked it out. That was when O'Brien and two others were caught handing over bags of crack cocaine in exchange for cash. It was the beginning of the end for the gang, and we ran major features before and after the trial.'

'And did O'Brien or any of the other gang members threaten Gordon or anyone else at the *Gazette*?' James asked.

'If they did, I wasn't made aware of it. But it wouldn't surprise me if O'Brien bore a grudge. After all, without Gordon's input the OCU might not have been able to do what they did.'

James thanked Nadine and stressed again that their conversation was off the record.

'We will be speaking to O'Brien as soon as possible,' he said. 'It's far too early to assume that he was the person responsible for Gordon's death, but information has come to light that makes it necessary for us to question him.'

After the call, James and Foley climbed into a patrol car and headed towards Milnthorpe. They were followed by a van carrying four uniformed officers.

The village was just seven miles south of Kendal, and on the way James was told that O'Brien's father, Edward, had lived there for most of his life. He was a retired electrical engineer, and his wife had died three years ago.

The wind continued unabated during the short drive, but thankfully the snow held off.

It didn't take them long to find O'Brien's address, just off the A6, which passed through the village. It was a small, detached, stone cottage in a secluded spot, with the nearest neighbour several hundred yards away. There was an old Vauxhall Corsa on the driveway and James snapped a picture of it on his phone.

He and Foley approached the front door followed by the uniforms. He rang the bell, but there was no response, and he felt a spike of irritation.

After trying the handle and discovering the door was locked, he rushed around to the back of the cottage where there was a patio area and a spectacular view of the distant fells.

There were also large, sliding glass doors that allowed him to see into the living room. But the sight that greeted him snatched his breath away.

The room was a mess and looked as though it had been vandalised. A Christmas tree had toppled over, a chair had been upended, and a broken glass lay on the coffee table.

But most shocking of all was the figure of a man stretched out on the floor. He was on his back and James could see that his face was smeared with what looked like blood.

CHAPTER TWENTY-NINE

The sliding doors were locked so James instructed the uniforms to force open the front door.

It took them mere seconds using a battering ram, and when he stepped inside he saw a set of keys on the mat, which suggested to him that they'd been dropped through the letterbox by someone exiting the cottage.

James called out to announce their presence, and when there was no response he headed along the hall towards the living room, telling the uniforms to check the other rooms on the ground floor and upstairs.

A cold dread flowed through his lungs as he approached what he feared was the scene of another murder.

The man was lying between the coffee table and a long leather sofa. He was wearing jeans and a dark T-shirt and was as still as a statue.

It wasn't until James got closer that he realised he was looking down on Shane O'Brien. Despite the blood that was smeared across his forehead and mouth, it was clearly the same face James had seen in the photograph back at headquarters.

Two distinct wounds were immediately visible – a gash across his forehead and another above his top lip.

James dropped onto the floor next to him and instinctively looked for signs of life. Much to his surprise, he discovered that the man wasn't dead. His chest was rising and falling ever so slightly, and he was breathing softly through his open mouth.

'Call an ambulance,' James yelled to Foley. 'He's alive.'

Foley took out her phone and tapped at the keypad.

Turning back to O'Brien, James nudged his shoulder and said, 'Can you hear me, Mr O'Brien? Are you awake?'

No response.

James leaned forward and studied the man's wounds more closely. It certainly looked as though he'd been hit with a hard object rather than a fist. And there were no blood stains on his T-shirt, but there may well have been bruises beneath it.

'Ambulance is on its way, guv,' Foley said. 'Is that Shane O'Brien?'

James nodded. 'Most definitely. Looks like he was severely beaten by one or more people. I suspect the blow to the forehead was what rendered him unconscious. We can only hope that there's no brain damage.'

Foley knelt down next to him and pointed to O'Brien's left wrist.

'Take a look at that,' she said. 'The glass on his watch face is smashed. And it stopped working at twelve. That was just under two hours ago.'

'Then we have to assume that it was damaged when he was

attacked. He may well have lost consciousness long after that but hadn't been able to get up.'

Just then a uniformed officer entered the room to tell them that the rest of the house was empty, and it appeared that everything was in order.

'We'll need to get forensics here,' James said as he stood up. 'The place needs to be thoroughly searched.'

He looked around and his eyes alighted on a framed photo on a shelf above the television. It was of a couple who he assumed were O'Brien's parents.

He drew Foley's attention to it. 'That reminds me. This cottage belongs to O'Brien's dad. So where is he?'

'It's Boxing Day, guv. He may be visiting someone.'

'Let's hope so. But we can't ignore the possibility that the man was also attacked or even that he attacked his own son.'

This prompted James to tell the uniforms to check the back garden and the area surrounding the cottage.

Turning back to O'Brien, he tried again to get a response from him, but failed.

'At least he's breathing,' he said. 'With luck the paramedics will work their magic when they get here, and he'll regain consciousness.'

The ambulance arrived within fifteen minutes and James explained to the paramedics that they had come to the cottage to question O'Brien and broke in when they saw him on the floor. He also pointed to the man's broken watch and said that it was likely the attack took place at twelve.

James asked Foley to go in the ambulance to the A&E department at the Royal Lancaster Infirmary, and provide an update on O'Brien's condition as soon as the medics had carried out an assessment.

After the ambulance set off again, James called headquarters to let his colleagues know what had happened and ask for a forensics team to be sent to the cottage. He also told them to see if they could locate O'Brien's father, and said the probation service would have his contact details.

He then rang Superintendent Tanner, and when the call didn't go through he sent a text asking him to call back as soon as he could.

James took a moment to get his mind around what had happened. The last thing he'd expected was to find Shane O'Brien lying unconscious having been beaten.

It filled his head with more questions. Who was responsible? Was it linked in any way to what happened to Gordon? And was O'Brien targeted by someone he himself had planned to seek revenge against?

The case was certainly becoming more complicated as it veered off in different directions. And now the man who only hours ago had become a suspect in Gordon's murder was seriously injured and on his way to hospital. It was yet another bolt from the blue and James just didn't know what to make of it.

He decided to have a look around the cottage, but before doing so he pulled on a pair of latex gloves and called the uniformed officers into the living room.

He was told that nothing of interest had been found in the back garden or the immediate area.

'We need to search all the rooms for potential clues and look out for any electronic devices. We don't have a warrant, but these count as special circumstances as this is the scene of a crime,' he said. 'We're especially interested in a list of names. I have no idea how long the list is or if it even exists. But if it does, we need to find it.'

As soon as they began the search, James received a call back from Tanner.

'The press conference just finished,' the boss said. 'Did you ring me to find out how it went?'

'No, boss. There's been another development, and it won't make things any easier for us.'

After James told him about O'Brien, Tanner said, 'Do you think whoever did it also killed Gordon?'

'That's not what my gut is telling me,' James answered.

'Well, at least he's not dead and will hopefully recover enough to tell us what happened.'

'We should know soon enough. If he's not already at the hospital then it won't be long before he is. DC Foley went with him in the ambulance, and she'll call me as soon as there's an update. Meanwhile, how did the presser go?'

'Pretty much as expected,' Tanner said. 'There were a lot of questions I couldn't answer, and a lot of compliments were paid to Gordon. I let it be known that we were throwing everything at the investigation and would provide them with another update tomorrow. Let's hope we'll have something positive to pass on to them.'

After the call ended, James joined in the search of the house. There were two bedrooms and he focused on the one that was obviously being used by Shane O'Brien.

The man didn't have much in the way of personal belongings, which was hardly a surprise since he'd spent the past four years in prison, but he did have a laptop and a mobile phone, and a drawer full of paperwork that included documents relating to his probation and a bank savings account, which showed a balance of several thousand pounds.

There was also an old leather wallet lying on the bedside table and that was where James found what he'd been looking for. It was a lined page from a notebook that had been folded and concealed in the wallet's zipper pouch.

Three names had been written on the page with a biro, including Gordon Carver's.

James felt his stomach tighten as he wondered if what he was looking at was in fact O'Brien's very own 'kill list.'

CHAPTER THIRTY

James stared at the list of names on the piece of paper he'd found in O'Brien's wallet.

Jack Delaney
Gordon Carver
Toby McGrath

Gordon's was the only one he recognised, but that was probably because he himself hadn't been part of the investigation that resulted in O'Brien and the other drug dealers being imprisoned. What he now needed to establish was whether those other two men had played a part, as Gordon did, in bringing O'Brien to justice.

And if O'Brien did murder Gordon, then was he also planning to murder the other two? Or had he already done so and their bodies were waiting somewhere to be discovered?

It was also possible that Jack Delaney and/or Toby McGrath had learned about O'Brien's list via the underworld grapevine, just as Michael Frost had. Had one or both of them decided to come here to O'Brien's home and attack him before he went after them? Or was the attack completely unrelated to the list he'd drawn up?

Another question that needed answering was whether the assailant had fled the scene believing that O'Brien was dead. Or had they known he was still breathing when they left the cottage and locked the front door behind them?

James stood in the bedroom grinding his teeth for almost a minute as he tried to make sense of it all. When he realised that he wasn't able to, he slid the list into a clear plastic evidence bag and called headquarters.

He passed on the two other names from O'Brien's list to a support officer and asked him to find out who they were.

'I'll be heading back after the forensic team arrives,' he said. 'I'll want everyone together for the final briefing of the day. And can you let the press office know what's happened here, but tell them that they're not to answer any questions that come in about O'Brien without speaking to me first?'

He had to wait another half an hour before the scene of crime officers arrived and he used the time to have another look around the cottage. But neither he nor the uniformed officers came up with any other evidence linking O'Brien to Gordon's murder.

Before leaving the cottage, he spoke to the SOCOs whose primary focus would be on finding clues that would help them identify O'Brien's attacker. He gave them the set of keys that had been left on the doormat and showed them photos he'd taken on his phone of O'Brien lying on the living-room floor.

It was starting to get dark by the time he set off back to Kendal in the patrol car, and it suddenly occurred to him that he hadn't spoken to Annie all day. He took out his mobile and called her.

'Apologies for not phoning earlier,' he said. 'Things have been really hectic.'

'Don't worry, my love,' she replied. 'It's actually been quite peaceful here. Janet came over again and we took the kids for a walk in the snow, which they really enjoyed. I don't suppose you'll be back to see them before bedtime?'

'I very much doubt it. I've been to Milnthorpe and am now on the way back to the office. Not sure how long I'll be there.'

'Have you made any progress?'

'Some, but I fear the case is still a long way from being solved.'

'That's such a shame,' she said. 'I hate to think what Gordon's parents must be going through.'

James ended the call after telling her that he would let her know when he was on his way home. He couldn't give her a time because there was so much going on, and it caused the guilt to resurface in his mind. He managed to push it down after a few seconds and switched his thoughts back to the case. As he made notes of all the issues he intended to raise with the team before Boxing Day came to an end, he was forced to accept that things were becoming more challenging with every passing hour.

CHAPTER THIRTY-ONE

James's body was rigid with tension by the time he was dropped off back at headquarters.

The case was really getting to him now. Things were moving at a startling pace, but not in a straight line. Whenever that happened it increased the risk of mistakes being made. Officers were distracted, resources got diverted, and the unwelcome element of confusion tended to slow things down.

James was determined that it wasn't going to happen with this investigation. It meant staying focused on their primary objective, which was to find out who murdered one of Cumbria's most respected journalists.

Just before he entered the office his phone rang, and as he swiped it from his pocket, he saw DC Foley's name on the screen.

'What have you got for me, Caroline?' he said when he answered.

'Just to let you know that O'Brien is in intensive care, guv,' she replied. 'He's been evaluated, and I'm told he's comatose, but responding to stimuli. The only wounds are those to his head and face. He'll be having a brain scan and blood tests, but the medics believe he'd be in a much worse state if we hadn't got to him when we did. And they're confident that he could regain consciousness fairly soon if there's no internal damage.'

'That's good,' James said. 'Are you okay to stay there until I arrange for a local uniform to take your place?'

'Of course, guv. No problem.'

'Then, when you're relieved, you should go straight home. I'll keep an ear out and if I don't hear anything else this evening, I'll assume that there's been no change to his condition.'

The team were waiting anxiously to hear what he had to tell them. He shrugged off his coat and brought them up to date, beginning with what Foley had just told him about O'Brien's condition.

'So, it turns out that it may be thanks to us that he's still alive,' he said. 'If he had lain there in the cottage for much longer, his condition would likely have deteriorated. Unless, of course, his father had returned home from wherever he's been.'

'That wouldn't have happened, boss,' DC Sharma said. 'I got the dad's number from the probation service and called him. He's actually spent Christmas in Belfast. It's where his brother lives, and he flew there on the twenty-third. I told him what's happened to his son and he's flying back first thing in the morning. He says he tried to persuade Shane to go with him, but he didn't want to. He also said he has no idea who carried out the attack, but he's in no doubt that Shane had enemies.'

'Well, at least we can rule his dad out as a suspect,' James said.

Turning to one of the support staff, he added, 'I need you to arrange for a uniformed officer to take over from Foley at the hospital.'

The woman nodded and James moved swiftly on to the names

on O'Brien's list. It was DI Stevens who'd taken it upon himself to check them out.

'Before I get started, I should tell you that the post-mortem on Gordon didn't throw up any surprises,' Stevens said. 'Dr Flint is confident that he died from brain damage caused by blunt force trauma to the head. The weapon could have been a rock or a brick. And she noted that there were no defence wounds or bruises to his body.'

'That's about what we expected,' James said. 'Now what about the names on the list?'

Stevens flipped open his notebook. 'It took us just minutes to place them. First there's Jack Delaney. He was the Crown prosecutor at O'Brien's trial, and he's living in Ulverston. I called him a short time ago and though it came as a shock that his name was on the list, he said it's not the first time he's faced threats from people he got convicted. Anyway, he and his wife are going to stay with friends until we can assure him that he's not in any danger.'

'Did you mention that Gordon was also on the list?'

Stevens shook his head. 'No way. That would have really spooked him.'

'What about Toby McGrath?'

'Well, he was part of the same gang as O'Brien, but they fell out big time over money issues about five years ago and O'Brien kicked him out of the gang. McGrath then moved to Manchester where he set up his own outfit, which is apparently still going strong. By all accounts he's a pretty violent character. He spent two years inside for attacking a man with a club hammer – the victim, who owed him money, spent two months in hospital with serious head and chest injuries. And then he got six months for threatening behaviour towards a woman who accused him of groping her. According to the files a hammer is McGrath's weapon of choice, and he carries one around with him most of the time.

'I also have it on good authority that when he learned that the Organised Crime Unit was closing in on O'Brien's lot, he provided the team there with some incriminating information that helped them to smash the gang. It was his way of getting back at O'Brien.'

'Have you spoken to him?' James asked.

'Not yet. Manchester CID haven't been able to contact him.'

'Then I suppose it's possible he came up from Manchester to settle an old score after he found out that O'Brien had been released early from prison. Or he may even have been told about O'Brien's list and decided to get in first.'

Stevens shrugged. 'Or maybe O'Brien had already paid him a visit before moving on to Gordon. And his body has yet to be found.'

There was a lot more to discuss before James was prepared to call it a day. So, he told everyone to take a break and grab something to eat and drink.

He got himself a strong, black coffee because he needed a caffeine jolt, and before reconvening the briefing, he rang Superintendent Tanner to tell him about the list he'd found in O'Brien's bedroom.

'This case is becoming more interesting by the hour,' the boss said. 'I think I need to be closer to the action for a spell, so I'll come down to Kendal tomorrow. We can discuss how much to release to the media.'

As James stood before the team again, he let loose a long breath and felt the muscles around his eyes tighten. He was ready to go home now. To wind down. Have a drink. Go to bed. He had no doubt that tomorrow was going to be another energy-sapping day.

'Okay, listen up, everyone,' he said. 'I know we're about to enter the weekend, but I'll expect you all to come in unless you have a good reason not to. I'm hoping that more CCTV footage will become available, and more people will return to their homes near to where Gordon was murdered as it means we might be able to gain access to more door-camera video recordings. The first thing I intend to do tomorrow is speak to Shane O'Brien's father to see if there's anything else he can tell us. And if we're lucky his son will have regained consciousness.'

James invited updates and first up was DC Sharma who said he had spoken to Gordon's parents about Michael Frost.

'His dad confirmed that he used to hang out with Frost when they were teenagers, but said they haven't been in touch for years,' Sharma said. 'But he was aware that Gordon had a good relationship with the man, and used him as an underworld source of information.'

Next came DC Isaac who had been to see the couple who had found Gordon's body on the path.

'You asked me to find out if Mrs Lynch could recall any more details about the woman she saw coming out of Gordon's house on Christmas Eve,' she said. 'Well, it turns out there was something she remembered. The woman was apparently wearing a pair of distinctive red winter boots. And she's pretty sure that there was a red pattern of some kind in the scarf she had on.'

'It's not much, but it's something,' James said, before turning to DS Abbott. 'Did Michael Frost give anything else away in the interview room?'

'Nothing at all, guv,' she said. 'I took down his statement and the more it sank in that Gordon had been murdered, the more emotional he became. And I'm finding it hard not to believe what he's told us.'

James carried on throwing ideas around and assigning tasks for another hour. By then he was surrounded by a lot of tired eyes and pale faces.

'Let's end it there then,' he said as he stroked the stubble on his chin. 'Thankfully we've made some progress, and we at least have two strong suspects in the frame in Daniel Porter and Shane O'Brien. I believe either one of them could be our killer, but we're a long way from proving it so we need to work harder and faster. So, try to get a good night's sleep and be back here by eight tomorrow morning.'

CHAPTER THIRTY-TWO
ANNIE

James phoned just after six to tell her that he was about to head home.

'In that case I'll let the kids stay up so that you can spend a bit of time with them,' she said. 'I made a stew with what was left of the turkey so it can be warmed up if you want it,' she added before they said their goodbyes.

She was looking forward to seeing her husband, but knew that as soon as he walked through the door, she was going to feel uncomfortable.

It was becoming increasingly difficult to keep her secret. Janet had tried to convince her that she'd been right to hold back. That telling James before she had to might actually make it harder for her to control her emotions.

He would worry and want to talk about it. And it might even prove such a distraction that he'd fail to solve the mystery of Gordon's murder. And if that happened, Annie would never forgive herself. After all, it might turn out to be all right in the end, and it'd be panic over. She could then stop fearing the worst and get her life back on track.

'I think Theo is asleep, Mummy,' Bella said.

He was lying across Annie's lap as she sat on the sofa, and she hadn't realised that he'd dropped off. It wasn't a problem, though. She had already bathed him and put him in his pyjamas.

'You stay here while I take him up and put him to bed,' she said to Bella. 'Daddy will be here soon.'

There was no point in keeping Theo up. He was shattered and unlikely to stay awake for long even if she did.

His eyes remained closed and he didn't make a sound as she gently placed him on the bed and pulled the cover over him.

Back downstairs she left Bella on the living-room floor playing with her dolls and went into the kitchen to put the kettle on. And just as she was pouring hot water onto a tea bag, James arrived home.

His face was drawn, and he looked tired, but he managed a broad smile as soon as he saw her.

They kissed and cuddled before he shed his overcoat and jacket and went to join Bella on the living-room floor. He stayed playing with her for almost half an hour before taking her up to bed while Annie put a bowl of stew in the microwave for him.

She sat with him while he ate it and if he hadn't appeared so unsettled she might have opened up to him. But she decided not to since he was clearly under enormous pressure and she didn't want to add to it. She was glad that he didn't ask her how she was because it might well have prompted her to let loose and say too much.

Instead, she asked him how the investigation was going, and he told her more than he was probably supposed to.

It was a lot to take in. Gordon's meeting in the pub with a man called Mad Dog Mike shortly before he was murdered. Discovering the battered body of a convicted drug dealer who was now clinging to life in hospital. And then the list of men it was believed the man had intended to harm or even kill.

Not for the first time Annie wondered how James coped with the stress of the job. She was full of admiration for him.

Most of the time he managed to switch off when he came home, but some cases really got to him, and she could tell that this was proving to be one of them.

All the more reason not to tell him about the threat that she herself was facing. It could wait a few more days, by which time he would hopefully have identified the callous bastard who had murdered Gordon Carver.

CHAPTER THIRTY-THREE

James was up and dressed by seven on Saturday morning. It had been another restless night, but after Annie joined him for a breakfast of coffee and toast, he felt ready to face the day ahead.

She planned to spend it with the kids at a festive fête that was going to take place in the village square. Fortunately, the forecast was for a cold day with strong winds but no snow. If James hadn't had to answer the call of duty he would have gone along with them. That had been the original plan, so inevitably he felt another twinge of guilt.

Before setting off, he called the office for an update. DC Hall had worked the graveyard shift again and told him that Shane O'Brien remained in a coma while Toby McGrath, O'Brien's former gang mate, still hadn't surfaced.

'We've just had it confirmed that O'Brien's father will soon be arriving at Manchester airport from Belfast, guv,' Hall said. 'He'll then be driving himself to the Royal Lancaster Infirmary to see his son.'

'I want to talk to the guy so I might as well go there before coming to headquarters,' James said. 'Tell the rest of the team to get started on whatever needs to be done and to keep me posted.'

James was well used to travelling to the Royal Lancaster Infirmary. Many of the victims of crimes he had investigated had ended up there in the A&E department or the critical care unit. The hospital was about twenty miles south of Kirkby Abbey, and he'd be taking the M6 to get there.

It was another quiet morning on the roads, but he expected it to get much busier later when those people who'd stayed at home over Christmas decided to venture out to shop or visit friends. They'd have to put up with a dreary grey sky, though, and the wind that continued to batter the county.

As he drove, he chewed over the many questions in his mind, wondering when the various strands would start coming together. Two days had passed since Gordon's body had been found, and it was concerning that there was still so much that they didn't know.

Was the motive revenge? Had Shane O'Brien killed Gordon because his investigation for the *Cumbria Gazette* into the county lines drugs racket helped get him convicted?

Or was the perpetrator Daniel Porter, who was desperate to stop Gordon from writing another piece about missing estate agent Chloe Walsh?

Two other scenarios also had to be considered. That Gordon was murdered by someone else for an entirely different reason. And that he was the victim of a random attack by a violent psycho who needed to satisfy a desperate urge to spill some blood on Christmas Eve.

*

James got to the hospital before Edward O'Brien and took the opportunity to speak to the consultant taking care of Shane.

He learned that Shane's condition remained stable, but he had yet to emerge from the coma, which came as a huge disappointment.

'However, there's good reason for optimism,' the consultant said. 'The brain scan was clear and nothing bad showed up in his bloods. In cases like this the patient often wakes up suddenly and goes on to make a full recovery.'

James spoke to the uniformed officer who had been stationed outside the room during the night, and was told that no suspicious characters had turned up.

Edward O'Brien arrived just after nine and was escorted to the unit by a member of the hospital staff. Before the consultant took him in to see his son, James introduced himself.

'I was the officer who found Shane, Mr O'Brien,' he said. 'It was lucky for him that we turned up when we did. After you've seen him, I'll explain why we went to your house, and I also need to ask you some questions.'

The man was in his late sixties or early seventies with a face that was drawn and sallow.

'Do you know who attacked him?' he asked, his voice unsteady.

James shook his head. 'We're hoping he'll eventually be able to tell us, Mr O'Brien.'

The man spent the best part of twenty minutes at his son's bedside. When he came out of the room James suggested they have a coffee in the canteen.

'I feel guilty because I wasn't at home with him on Christmas Eve,' Edward said when they were seated at a table. 'I wish to god I hadn't gone to Ireland.'

'Was it a trip you'd had planned before Shane's release?' James asked.

He nodded. 'My brother lives there. I hadn't seen him in over a year and he's been having a rough time with his health. I arranged to go before I knew that Shane was being released early from prison, and I told my son I'd cancel it and spend Christmas with him, but he wouldn't let me. I then tried to get him to go with me, but he insisted he had people to see and places to go.'

'Did he tell you who he was going to see?'

'I didn't ask him. I just assumed that after four years banged up, he had a lot of catching up to do.'

Edward's face was pinched with concern and his voice rasped in his throat as he spoke.

'So, tell us what happened yesterday,' he said. 'All I know is that you went to my house and saw him through the window lying on the living-room floor. Then you had to force the front door open to get to him.'

James pulled out his notebook and placed it on the table before responding.

'Let me start by asking you a question,' he said. 'Were you aware that he held three men directly responsible for getting him sent to prison? He even made a list of their names and told a couple of his fellow inmates that when released he would be seeking revenge against them.'

The man's face registered alarm. 'I don't know what you're talking about.'

'Well, I found the list in his wallet when we were in your house. The names on it were Jack Delaney, Gordon Carver, and Toby McGrath. Are they familiar to you?'

'Two of them are. McGrath used to work alongside Shane before he moved away. And Gordon Carver is the journalist who helped expose him as a drug dealer. I'm not sure who the other bloke is.'

141

'Jack Delaney was the lawyer who presented the case for the prosecution at Shane's trial.'

He nodded. 'Yeah, I remember now.'

'Can I take it that you're not aware that one of the three men, Gordon Carver, was murdered close to his home in Kendal on Christmas Eve, and his body was found on Christmas Day?'

His face paled and his eyes widened.

'Oh shit. Please don't tell me that you think Shane did it.'

'We don't yet know who was responsible,' James said. 'But your son became a suspect after we heard about his list. And it does seem odd that the murder took place just weeks after Shane walked free.'

'But my son is not a murderer,' Edward snapped, attracting the attention of the people at the other tables. 'He was so glad and grateful to be out. He couldn't believe his luck. There's no way he would have done something, anything, that would have put him at risk of going back inside.'

'Then he didn't tell you that he wanted to seek revenge against those men?'

'Of course not, because that wasn't ever his intention. He's not a fucking serial killer if that's what you're thinking. I paid him lots of visits during the four years he was banged up and he never once suggested getting his own back on anyone. My son made a big mistake getting involved with drugs, but he isn't crazy enough to go on a killing spree. And anyway, I'm not interested in who murdered that reporter. I want to know who tried to kill Shane.'

'I was coming to that, Mr O'Brien,' James said. 'Did he mention to you that he felt threatened? Or perhaps even name someone he had a problem with?'

'No to both. Since coming out he's been upbeat. He's talked

142

endlessly about the future, of staying on the straight and narrow from now on.'

'Well, the fact that he was attacked in your living room suggests that he knew the assailant and let them into the cottage. There was no sign of a break-in.'

'Then it sounds to me like whoever it was thought Shane was dead before leaving him there.'

'That is possible. And that's why there will be an officer standing outside his room here until we're sure that he's not at risk of another attack.'

James stayed talking to Edward for another fifteen minutes before deciding there wasn't much more that the man could tell him.

He walked with him back to the critical care unit where he handed him his card and said, 'I'll be alerted the moment your son regains consciousness, Mr O'Brien. And I'll come straight back here to get him to tell me what he knows. In the meantime, if you can think of anything that will help our investigation then please call me. Oh, and there's one other question I need to ask. The Vauxhall Corsa on your driveway. Does it belong to your son?'

He nodded. 'He had it before he went inside and so I kept it for him. It still works a treat.'

CHAPTER THIRTY-FOUR

Before leaving the infirmary James let O'Brien's consultant know that as well as being an attack victim, the man was also a suspect in the Christmas Eve murder of journalist Gordon Carver in Kendal.

'You need to inform your staff and step up security,' he said, and a shocked expression froze on the consultant's face. 'I'll arrange for at least one more police officer to come here. And the patient's father can't be allowed to see him again unless I give the go ahead.'

James briefed the uniformed officer and told him to arrange for another officer to join him.

'I want at least two of you here around the clock,' he said. 'Get your boss to contact me in Kendal if it's a problem.'

Another question played on James's mind as he drove back to HQ, and it was whether Edward O'Brien had told them the truth.

Did he really not know that his son had drawn up a list of three men he allegedly intended to seek revenge against? He'd certainly seemed shocked to hear about Gordon's murder, but that might well have been an act. Perhaps he'd even made a point of going to Ireland so that he wouldn't be around when the killing took place.

Other thoughts were humming like high voltage electricity through James's head. The attack on Shane O'Brien was brutal, but was it a case of attempted murder? And was it carried out by his former gang mate Toby McGrath, who appeared to have dropped off the radar?

Or could DI Stevens have been right when he suggested that O'Brien might have gone after McGrath before attacking Gordon? And McGrath was now lying dead somewhere?

But if that was what happened, then who the hell had battered O'Brien to within an inch of his life?

This latest development had certainly created more work for the team and would stretch their limited resources. And every minute focused on trying to find O'Brien's attacker would be less time spent searching for Gordon's killer.

James released a frustrated sigh before calling the office on the hands-free. It was DS Abbott who picked up and he told her that he was on his way to headquarters from Lancaster.

'There's still no change in O'Brien's condition,' he said. 'I spoke to his father and he's claiming he has no idea who attacked his son and refuses to believe that he murdered Gordon.'

'Well, no other suspects have emerged so far this morning, guv,' Abbott said. 'But more CCTV footage from Christmas Eve is now coming in, along with forensic results. It will all be pulled together by the time you get here.'

'And as soon as I do, we'll have a briefing,' he said.

It took James forty-five minutes to get to Kendal, and he arrived at half eleven.

He was already feeling tired due to lack of sleep, and blood was pounding through his head. But as he entered the office, he experienced a shudder of anticipation. The place was buzzing and the team were going at full pelt on their phones and computers. Even Superintendent Tanner was busy making notes of whatever DI Stevens was telling him.

James caught Tanner's eye and signalled for him to join him in his office when he was done. It had been weeks since the boss had travelled south to Kendal from his base in Penrith and James was always pleased to see him.

Tanner was a thick-set man in his fifties and had the respect of all the detectives. He was also one of the rising stars in the Cumbria Constabulary and tipped to be a future chief constable.

'I've been told about your meeting with Shane O'Brien's dad,' he said to James. 'I gather it wasn't very helpful.'

James shrugged. 'He claims not to know what his son was up to or who attacked him, but I'm not convinced he was completely honest with me.'

Tanner lifted his brow. 'Then it's an added complication to a case that's already bloody complicated. That's why I'm not sure what we should release to the media.'

James nodded. 'I know what you mean. For now, I think it's best if we don't reveal why O'Brien's a suspect. As soon as the hacks know about the list he drew up it will generate an avalanche of unhelpful speculation, including claims that it must have been a kill list.'

'I agree, although we're going to have to give them something. I don't intend to stage another presser today, but I do want to issue a statement.'

'Then let's pull something together after the briefing.'

Before addressing the troops, James cast his eyes over the two updated evidence boards. Photos of Shane O'Brien and Toby McGrath had been added to them, along with images of the latest crime scene. There were also more scribbled notes and questions, plus a copy of O'Brien's list of names.

He began the briefing by relaying his conversation with Edward O'Brien and made clear that O'Brien's ex-drug dealer son was now one of their prime suspects.

'It's a plausible hypothesis that he targeted Gordon out of revenge for the investigation the *Gazette* carried out that helped get him convicted,' he said. 'There's his list of three names and the fact that he made his intentions clear to fellow prison inmates. However, we don't know if his aim was to kill or merely harm Gordon and the other two on the list. And we also can't be sure that we're not barking up the wrong tree entirely and the guy had nothing to do with it.

'That's why we need to keep an open mind and come up with more suspects and likely motives. So, for now, let's put aside today's attack on Shane O'Brien and focus on what happened to Gordon. Where are we with CCTV footage and forensics from Christmas Eve?'

DS Abbott was the first to speak. 'We've heard back from the lab regarding the DNA profiles from the used condom found in Gordon's bathroom bin, guv. Unsurprisingly, it was his semen on the inside, but the sample from the outside doesn't match anything on the database.'

James knew that the odds had been against coming up with a result, but it was nevertheless yet another disappointment.

'Also, officers have resumed the search for the weapon used to inflict the fatal blow on Gordon, and though his phone still hasn't been found, we expect his service provider to get back to us in the coming hours with his mobile call data,' Abbott added.

DC Sharma then gave an update on footage from the CCTV cameras around the town.

'More has been made available, but nothing significant has turned up,' he said. 'And Christmas Eve was extra busy in town so there were far more vehicles than usual. However, we might be getting some positive news soon. DC Isaac just sent me a text to say that she's on her way back here having secured some video footage from a front-door camera on Gordon's road.'

'What does it show?' James asked.

'The car that was driven by the woman who visited Gordon's house hours before he was murdered. It should help us identify who she is.'

They only had to wait a few minutes for DC Isaac to turn up, during which a level of excitement built up among the team.

The briefing was paused while Isaac explained that she'd spent the morning checking properties that had been unoccupied on Christmas Eve.

'The house in question is about fifty yards from Gordon's place and on the other side of the road,' she said. 'The couple who live there returned last night after staying with relatives on Christmas Day. Anyway, their door cam has a clear view along the road and because they were going away, they enabled the continuous record setting. So, after rewinding to Christmas Eve we saw the car, a Volkswagen Polo, draw up outside Gordon's house in the afternoon. A woman got out and went up to the door and was let in. She was too far away to see her face, but you could tell she was wearing an overcoat and scarf, plus red boots, which confirmed what the neighbour told us about her.

'She stayed there for about two hours. Then two people emerged from the house and embraced before the woman climbed back into the car. She drove towards the camera, enabling me to read the car's number plate.'

'Have you run it through the system?' James asked her.

'Not yet. I'll do that now while the footage I've got on a memory stick is uploaded onto the system.'

Isaac was still waiting to hear who the car was registered to when the footage appeared on the monitors. It was grainy, which unfortunately meant that they were not able to see the face of the person behind the wheel as the car was driven past the camera.

But that didn't matter because moments later Isaac was given the name of the registered owner.

When she told the rest of the team there was a collective gasp, and the shock of it tore through James like a bullet.

CHAPTER THIRTY-FIVE

'Does this mean that Gordon was screwing his married boss?' Superintendent Tanner asked.

It was the question on everyone's lips after DC Isaac revealed that the car that arrived at the journalist's house on Christmas Eve belonged to none other than Nadine Stone, editor of the *Cumbria Gazette*.

'Well, I can't imagine it was a different woman who drove the car there and spent a couple of hours with him,' DI Stevens responded. 'And it clearly wasn't just a platonic visit when you consider the used condom in the bathroom and the fact that the neighbour saw them snogging.'

James shook his head as his mind churned with unwelcome thoughts and images. And he started to wonder if he should have spotted the connection earlier when he spoke to Nadine in her home.

'She told me that she had no idea who the woman was and that she wasn't aware that Gordon was in a relationship,' he said. 'But it doesn't surprise me that she chose to lie given that her husband and kids were in the room at the time.'

'It does raise the possibility that it's not the only thing she's keeping from us, though,' Stevens said. 'And it also opens up a new line of inquiry. Infidelity has proven to be a significant factor in some homicide cases, the jealousy and rage of the betrayal provoking crimes of passion, so it's potentially not insignificant that Gordon was attacked only a matter of hours after spending time with Nadine. What if her husband found out and went looking for him? And when he saw him on the path, he lost control and clobbered him.'

James nodded. 'That is a possibility. We need to speak to both Nadine and her husband. Get them to account for their movements on Christmas Eve.' Turning to DS Abbott, he added, 'Can you call the *Gazette*'s office, Jess, and find out if she's there today? If she isn't then you and I will go straight to their place in Oxenholme.'

James warned the team that they couldn't allow this latest twist to distract them from the other lines of inquiry. To ensure they remained focused, he dished out more instructions.

'As yet we don't know where Shane O'Brien was on Christmas Eve,' he said, 'but we do know now that his car is a Vauxhall Corsa. So, let's check to see if it's on any of the town's CCTV footage. We should also pass on our increasing concerns to Manchester CID about Toby McGrath, who was on O'Brien's revenge list. Tell them we need to track him down, but also make them aware that we can't be sure he isn't dead.'

As James got ready to hit the road again, he felt an uneasy turn in the pit of his stomach. He wasn't looking forward to confronting Nadine with what they had found. It was a real turn up for the books and could conceivably have a huge impact on the woman's family as well as the investigation.

But she had intentionally withheld information from the police in order to protect herself. And now she was going to have to provide an explanation.

CHAPTER THIRTY-SIX

When DS Abbott got through to the *Cumbria Gazette*, she was told that Nadine wouldn't be in the office until Monday.

'Let's go straight to Oxenholme then,' James said.

As soon as they were in the patrol car, he took out his notebook and started listing all the latest questions that needed answering.

Were Gordon and Nadine having an affair? If so, then how long had it been going on? Or was their Christmas Eve tryst a one-off? And did Nadine's husband find out about it and go on to kill Gordon to bring it to an abrupt end?

'This case is certainly full of surprises, guv,' Abbott said. 'You have to wonder where it will take us next.'

James had to agree. It'd been a while since he'd headed up an investigation with so many strands to it, and this latest revelation had completely thrown him.

He wouldn't have guessed that Nadine was cheating on her husband or that Gordon was having sex with his editor. But then he knew very little about Nadine and had never asked Gordon what he got up to in his private life.

When they reached the small, detached house in Oxenholme village, the first thing James noticed was that there was only one vehicle on the driveway, a Peugeot van.

'Nadine may not be home,' he said. 'Her Volkswagen isn't here. The van must belong to her husband.'

'So how do we raise the issue with him?' Abbott asked. 'We need to find out where he was on Christmas Eve around the time Gordon was killed, but should we ask him if he knows what his wife was up to that afternoon?'

James twisted his lips in thought. 'It's a tricky one. I think we should play it by ear.'

It wasn't Elliott Stone who answered the door to them. It was his son, Ryan, and he was clearly shocked to see them again.

'Hello, Ryan,' James said. 'I assume you remember me. Detective Walker. This is Detective Abbott.'

Ryan nodded. 'Of course. Have you come here with some news? Do you know who murdered Gordon?'

James shook his head. 'Not yet we don't, but I'm hoping that we soon will. We've actually come to speak to your mother. Is she in?'

'No. She and my dad went to pay their respects to Gordon's parents in Burneside. But they should be back any minute. You can come in and wait if you want to. And I can phone them to let them know that you're here.'

'That's kind of you.'

'Not at all. They're both keen to know what progress you're making.'

He waved them through the door and told them to go into the living room while he retrieved his phone from the kitchen and called his dad.

'Charlotte is in there so brace yourselves,' he said. 'She's bound to bombard you with questions. She can't get what's happened out of her head and she's driving us all crazy.'

Ryan's younger sister was slouched on an armchair playing a game on her phone. When they entered, she sat up straight and wrinkled her brow.

'The police have come to see Mum,' Ryan told her. 'I said they could wait here. I'll call Dad so can you make them comfortable?'

As Charlotte invited them to sit on the sofa, James's mind flicked back to Christmas Day and how she'd reacted after he'd come to tell them what had happened to Gordon. She yelled angrily that it made no sense because people were supposed to be nice to one another at Christmas, then started crying before rushing out of the room.

'Have you caught the killer?' she asked them.

'Not yet, I'm afraid,' James replied.

Her jaw tensed. 'Why is it taking so long? This is a small town. There can't be that many suspects.'

'These things take time, Charlotte.'

'But they make it look so easy on the telly. And quick. They shouldn't be allowed to mislead us like that. It's not right.'

Anxious to change the subject, James said, 'So when is your Christmas break over?'

She pulled her lips tight. 'I'm back to work on Monday.'

'And where do you work?'

'A grocery store in the village. And to be honest I can't wait. This Christmas has been a total fucking disaster. The worst ever. First Mum and Dad had a blazing row and then we were told about Gordon. I've not enjoyed it one bit.'

James and Abbott shared a look, and it was his DS who got in first with a question.

'We're sorry to hear that,' Abbott said. 'When did your parents fall out?'

Charlotte didn't need to think about it. 'On Christmas Eve. They suddenly started shouting at each other after we had our tea. I didn't know what it was about, and I still don't. Dad was so pissed off he left the house and went for a drive, and Mum went upstairs to have a sulk. I was left on my own for a couple of hours at least. Dad didn't get back until after nine and when he did, it kicked off again upstairs. When I asked what it was about, they told me it wasn't serious, but I could tell that it was.'

'Where was Ryan?' James asked.

Charlotte shrugged. 'He wasn't due here until Christmas morning. He lives with his girlfriend in town, but she's been spending a few days with her own parents who live over the border in Scotland. Mum and Dad were speaking again by the time he arrived, but they were both still in a rotten mood.'

Just then Ryan walked into the room. Eyes blazing, he stabbed a finger at his sister.

'I heard you from the kitchen,' he snapped. 'How many times have you been told not to spout to other people about what goes on in the family? It's no one else's business.'

Charlotte's body stiffened. 'Oh, leave it out, bruv. I was asked a question and I answered it. Isn't that what you're supposed to do? It's called being polite.'

'No, Charlotte,' Ryan hit back. 'It's called being indiscreet. The police are not here to talk about our parents' marriage. Their only concern is who killed Gordon Carver.'

Charlotte twisted her mouth, searching for words, but before any came out her attention was suddenly drawn to the window.

James followed her gaze and through it he saw her mother's Volkswagen pulling onto the driveway.

'They're back,' Charlotte said to her brother in a hurried, tearful voice. 'Now you can fucking leave me alone.'

Ryan pulled a face and shook his head before hurrying to the front door.

As Charlotte slumped back on the armchair and clenched her eyes shut, James couldn't help but feel sorry for her.

At the same time, though, he was glad she'd told them what had happened on Christmas Eve. They now knew that her parents had had what sounded like a fierce argument shortly before Gordon was murdered.

They therefore needed to find out if the row was about what Nadine had got up to that afternoon. And where her husband drove to after he stormed out of the house.

CHAPTER THIRTY-SEVEN

James and DS Abbott stood up from the sofa when they heard the front door open and close. But it was some thirty seconds before Nadine and her husband entered the living room.

'Ryan has told us what his sister has been saying,' Nadine said. 'Sorry about that. I'm sure you're not interested in a family squabble.'

'You don't have to apologise,' James replied. 'She was merely making conversation.'

As Nadine crossed the room to where her daughter was sitting, James noticed she was wearing dark red ankle boots, and he immediately assumed they were the same pair she'd had on when she was seen leaving Gordon's house on Christmas Eve.

'I think you should go upstairs, Charlotte, while your dad and I speak to the officers,' Nadine said.

Her daughter took a deep breath, clearing her voice of tears. 'I'm not a bloody child, Mum. I'm staying here so that I can listen to what they have to say. I'm as interested as you are. But don't worry. I'll keep quiet.'

Elliott stepped further into the room then and spoke just as his wife was about to.

'Best leave her be, Nadine,' he said. 'We don't want to set her off.'

He then turned to James. 'If we'd known you were coming here, we would have been waiting for you, Detective Walker. I'm sure the kids have told you told you where we went this morning.'

James nodded. 'Ryan did, yes. How are Gordon's parents?'

'Still struggling to come to terms with his death. I'm not sure they ever will.'

James quickly introduced Abbott to both of them, but with all the family in the room he was suddenly unsure how best to get to the point of their visit. It was going to be hard to prevent Nadine's secret from getting out.

'Sit yourselves down,' she said. 'Would you like a tea or coffee?'

'Not for me,' James replied, and Abbott gave a polite shake of the head.

Nadine then sat on the empty armchair while her husband and son stood next to it, both with their arms folded.

There was an awkward silence that lasted about five seconds before James said, 'We came here to ask you some questions, Nadine, in relation to information that has come to light about Gordon. It's of a sensitive nature and I'd like to suggest we speak to you in private.'

Her jaw dropped in shock and James suspected it was because she knew what she was going to be confronted with.

But before she could respond, Elliott spoke up. 'You have got to be joking. Whatever you're going to say, detective, you can say in front of the rest of us.' He snapped his head towards his wife. 'Have you got any idea what this is about?'

She shook her head as her face suddenly lost all of its colour. 'No, I haven't,' she muttered unconvincingly.

Turning back to James, Elliott said, 'So, come on then. What is it that's come to light?'

James knew he had no choice but to get on with it. The circumstances were such that it would be wrong, and pointless even, to hold back.

Switching his gaze back to Nadine, he said, 'Why didn't you tell us that you were the woman who went to Gordon's house on Christmas Eve afternoon and spent roughly two hours there? We know it was you because we have your car on door-cam footage, and a description from Gordon's neighbour of the very boots you're now wearing.'

Silence descended on the room like a heavy weight. For several long seconds no one spoke, and Nadine just sat there staring at James, her mouth open, her body as rigid as a tent peg.

'Well, answer the question, Mum,' Charlotte said. 'Why didn't you tell him it was you? I don't understand.'

Nadine cleared her throat to find her voice and as she spoke her blinking became more rapid.

'I just paid him a visit to discuss the Chloe Walsh story,' she said. 'That was all. He wanted to know what I thought about—'

She didn't get to finish the sentence because Elliott stepped in front of her, his face contorted with anger.

'Don't take us for fools, Nadine,' he growled. 'You're forgetting that the neighbour saw you snogging the bastard when you left there. The detective told us that when he first came to see us. He said the neighbour described it as a passionate kiss. So, you obviously didn't go there just to discuss work. Which means I was right to be suspicious.'

Nadine swallowed hard and shook her head. 'But the neighbour was mistaken. We didn't snog. We just wished each

159

other a happy Christmas with a light kiss and a friendly hug. There was nothing passionate about it.'

'If that's true then why didn't you say so when Detective Walker asked you about the woman seen leaving the house?'

'Because I knew you'd jump to the wrong conclusion, and I didn't want to re-ignite the row. It was stupid, I know. I should have been honest with the police and with you.'

Elliott clearly wasn't convinced. He continued to stare at his wife, judgement clear in his eyes.

'Look, I acted impulsively and I'm sorry,' Nadine went on. 'But I knew instinctively that if I admitted it was me then you'd have lost the plot. I just thought it best not to feed the narrative that was, and still is, raging inside your head.'

A bout of trembling gripped her then and tears welled in her eyes.

'I need a minute by myself,' she said as she shot to her feet. 'And I'll leave it to you to explain to these officers what the hell this is all about.'

As she stepped towards the door, her daughter also jumped up and said to her father, 'I believe Mum even if you don't. She would never be unfaithful. It's all in your bloody head, Dad.'

Charlotte then followed her mum out of the room and slammed the door shut behind her.

CHAPTER THIRTY-EIGHT

'That was uncalled for, Dad,' Ryan said. 'You can't blame Mum for doing what she felt she had to in order to keep the peace. And surely you don't believe she's been cheating on you with Gordon.'

Elliott puffed out a loud breath before dropping onto the armchair vacated by his wife.

'I don't know what to believe,' he said. 'But I do know that she lied to me about where she was on Christmas Eve. And she shouldn't have.'

James had heard enough. He gave a little cough and said, 'We still have some questions, Mr Stone. But first can you do what your wife asked you to and tell us what this is all about? We have to determine whether it's in any way relevant to our investigation.'

'But that's ridiculous,' Elliott reacted sharply. 'How can it be? Nadine and I had an argument. So what? And although she went to Gordon's house that afternoon, she was back here in the evening when he was attacked.'

'What exactly did you argue about?' James asked. 'And what was the lie she told?'

Elliott muttered a curse and then contrived a weak smile.

'I suppose I'll have to tell you even though it's got nothing to do with anyone but us,' he said, and as he spoke his son stood next to him and placed a hand on his shoulder.

'Our marriage has been going through a rough patch. Things started to become strained between us about a year ago. For my part, I felt she'd lost interest in me, and I started to suspect she might be seeing someone else. It didn't help that we were both so wrapped up in our jobs that we neglected each other.

'I work as a construction manager, which means I'm often away for days at a time. And Nadine puts her all into that fucking paper. I started getting suspicious because of the sheer number of times she came home late. And too often I couldn't reach her on the phone while I was working away. That's what led to the row on Christmas Eve. I spent the night before in Preston and before heading home I called her, but she didn't answer the phone. So, I called her office, and they told me she'd taken the afternoon off. When she got home, I asked her where she'd been, and she said she went shopping in town and left her phone in the car by mistake. But I wasn't convinced she was being honest with me and told her so. She then got all defensive and accused me of trying to control her. It sparked a shouting match and I had to go out for a drive to clear my head.'

'And where did you go?' This from Abbott.

It suddenly dawned on the man where this was leading, and a flash of panic passed over his face.

'This is getting more absurd by the minute,' he said. 'Are you seriously suggesting that I'm a suspect? I wasn't even aware until just now that Nadine went to Gordon's house. Or that anything might have been going on between them.'

'Nevertheless, you're clearly very angry about things and for elimination purposes we need to establish where you were when he was attacked, particularly as it happened shortly after you went out and only hours after your wife visited him.'

'This is not fair,' Ryan blurted out. 'There's no way my dad would have killed anyone. And I can't see how Gordon's murder would have had anything to do with my mum's visit to his house.'

'It's okay, son,' Elliott told him. 'I've got nothing to hide, and they're the ones who will come out of this looking bad as the longer they spend wasting time with us the less likely it is they'll find whoever did murder Gordon.

'I left the house around seven p.m. on Christmas Eve and drove south along the A65 for about three miles. There's a hotel called the Majestic. I went there and had a couple of drinks at the bar. I'm a regular and they know me, so you can check that I'm telling the truth. I stayed until just about half eight and then came straight back home. Charlotte was here and will confirm that. I would have stayed longer in the pub, but I didn't want to go over the limit.'

James was satisfied with that since it would be easy enough to check.

'Well, I think we'll leave it at that for now,' he said and rose to his feet, followed by Abbott. 'But before we go, I would like another word with Nadine.'

'I'll go and tell her,' Ryan said as he swiftly left the room.

'I'm sorry that our visit has caused such a stir,' James said to Elliott. 'And I hope that you and your wife can sort things out between you.'

Elliott stayed sitting on the armchair and dropped his face into his hands as the two detectives exited the room.

They were approaching the front door when Nadine stepped out of the kitchen.

'Ryan said that you want to speak to me again before you go,' she said. 'And he also told me that you think Elliott might have killed Gordon, which is preposterous.'

James shook his head. 'Given what we just learned about events on Christmas Eve, we had to ask him where he went after he left here.'

'I know where he went. For a drink. He told me.'

'He told us, too. But look, would you mind coming outside with us? There's something I'd like to ask you.'

She looked back over her shoulder to where her son and daughter were standing behind the breakfast bar.

'Stay here, guys. I won't be long.'

Nadine slipped on an overcoat and pushed her feet into a pair of slippers.

Once outside, James said, 'I'm sorry that I didn't get to speak to you in private about the door-cam footage that showed it was you who visited Gordon that day.'

'It was my fault,' she responded. 'I should have been truthful with you. It was a big mistake.'

'Indeed, it was, and it could be construed as perverting the course of justice. It's something we'll have to consider, and I'll get back to you when a decision has been taken. But now I want to ask you another question, and before you answer you need to know that we found something in Gordon's house that suggests to us that you just told your husband yet another lie.'

Her eyes popped out on stalks. 'What do you mean?'

James kept his voice low. 'We found a used condom in the bathroom bin, and we've taken DNA swabs from it. My question is this – if we take a DNA sample from you, will it be a match?'

She threw a glance over her shoulder to make sure the front door was still closed. As she looked back at James, he could see the glittering shine of emotion in her eyes.

'It seems that I've got little choice but to confess,' she said in a voice that was raw with pain. 'It will be my DNA. And yes, we did have sex, and not for the first time. And I can assure you that Elliott didn't know about it. Nobody did. We kept it secret for obvious reasons.'

'So how did it all start?' James asked.

'We began getting together about once or twice a week some four months ago. It was just a bit of fun. And for me a distraction from my marital woes.

'Elliott and I just weren't getting on and our love life was non-existent. It really pissed me off the way he kept assuming I was being unfaithful – I actually thought that *he* might have been cheating on *me* – and I eventually decided that I might as well be. Gordon and I got on well and I'd always quite fancied him. So, one day when Elliott was away dealing with some building project, I invited him for an after-work drink. It was a really nice evening. We both flirted, got a bit tipsy, and then ended up in his bed. That's why his death has really hit me, and it's been such a struggle to keep my feelings bottled up.'

By now tears were streaming down her cheeks and her body was shaking.

'Thanks, Nadine,' James said. 'I can quite understand why you don't want Elliott, Ryan and Charlotte to know about it, but it won't be an easy secret to keep. So, why don't you go back inside and talk to your husband about where you go from here?'

CHAPTER THIRTY-NINE

Once they were back in the patrol car, James told the driver to head south along the A65.

'We'll go to the Majestic Hotel and kill two birds with one stone,' he said. 'I'll buy you both some lunch and we can check out Elliott Stone's claim that he went there on Christmas Eve.'

Along the way James and Abbott discussed their encounter with the Stone family, agreeing that it had been a real eye-opener.

'It's the son and daughter I feel sorry for,' Abbott said. 'I'm sure that life is not going to be easy for them going forward, even if their dad had nothing to do with Gordon's murder, and even if Nadine can convince him that she wasn't having an affair. I can't see the marriage surviving for long.'

James nodded. 'You're probably right about that. But did you believe him when he said he wasn't aware that Nadine had been cheating on him with Gordon?'

'I'm not sure. He did seem shocked when it came out, but that could have been put on for our benefit.'

'Exactly. An affair would be pretty difficult to conceal if your partner already suspected you of cheating. But then … it seems they didn't really try to. It wasn't very sensible to kiss each other like that in front of Gordon's house.'

The Majestic Hotel occupied a small, white-fronted building on the main road. James had passed it many times, but had never been inside.

He was impressed with what he saw when they entered. The place was warm and cosy, and while he spoke to the manager, Abbott and the driver headed for the restaurant.

Luckily there were security cameras in the car park, reception area, and bar, and the manager let him see the recorded footage from Christmas Eve. And, sure enough, Elliott Stone's story held up. He arrived soon after seven and stayed for an hour and a half in the bar by himself before driving off.

James joined the others in the restaurant and after they'd ordered drinks and sandwiches, they discussed whether Stone should be ruled out as a suspect.

'The timeline works in his favour,' James said. 'We know that Gordon was attacked after nine o'clock because that's when he left the pub. What we don't know is if he headed straight home or went somewhere else before making his way along the path through the wood. But we now have video footage of Elliott leaving here at half eight and he reckons he arrived home soon after nine.'

Abbott shrugged. 'I suppose he could have popped into town and killed Gordon first. It would have only taken him minutes to get to the location.'

James considered it. 'That's quite possible. But he would have had to know that Gordon was in the Queen's Castle.'

'Someone could have tipped him off,' Abbott said. 'Perhaps someone who followed Gordon there.'

James nodded. 'That's certainly conceivable, I suppose, but I can't think who would have done that or why.'

It was a quick lunch, and they were back at headquarters by 3 p.m.

Before James called the team together for a briefing, he was shown the press statement that was about to be released. It didn't include any of the latest developments, but made clear that progress was being made and the Force was committed to finding Gordon Carver's killer.

James okayed the wording before it was passed back to Superintendent Tanner at Penrith. He then began the briefing with an account of his and Abbott's meeting with the Stone family and their visit to the Majestic Hotel.

'As it stands, Elliott Stone has to be considered a low-level suspect,' he said. 'We haven't placed him at the crime scene and that's something we need to work on. And he could be lying to us about being unaware of his wife's infidelity with Gordon, which would have given him a strong motive for murder. So, let's check to see if his van shows up on any road-cam footage in the town centre after he left the hotel. If it does then we'll know for sure that he lied to us.'

Various updates were then provided by team members, but James didn't find them very encouraging.

Shane O'Brien remained in a coma and Toby McGrath still hadn't turned up.

Digital forensics had managed to access O'Brien's laptop, and it showed that after he was released from prison he'd spent time Google searching the three men he blamed for his downfall, gathering information on where they were and what they were up to.

Gordon's mobile service provider had sent through the call

data from his missing phone. It showed that the last call he made was to James at just after 9 p.m. on Christmas Eve, shortly before he was murdered.

'There are also numerous calls to and from Nadine Stone's phone number,' DC Sharma pointed out. 'That's no surprise since she was his boss, but I think we can now assume that more than a few were to arrange after-work get-togethers.'

Meanwhile, no useful forensic evidence had been discovered inside O'Brien's house, and the man's Vauxhall Corsa hadn't been spotted on CCTV cameras on Christmas Eve in or around the town.

'This is all rather disappointing,' James said. 'We need to be making more headway. In respect of Gordon's murder we have no witnesses and no firm forensics. Plus, we still haven't found his phone or the murder weapon. And we can't even be sure of the murder motive. What we do have is a strong suspect in Shane O'Brien, and if I was a betting man, I'd have to put my money on him as the killer. But there's a chance he'll never regain consciousness and we won't get to question him.'

The team spent the next hour reviewing all the information that had been gathered and the conversations they'd had with Daniel Porter, Mad Dog Mike, Elliott Stone, and Gordon's parents.

At the same time several officers continued to stare at their computer screens as they monitored the incoming footage from CCTV and security cameras.

Eventually DC Isaac spotted something. It was a short clip proving that someone else had told a blatant lie about where they were on Christmas Eve.

CHAPTER FORTY

'Daniel Porter told me that he didn't leave his house on Christmas Eve,' James said, 'but now we know that the bastard lied.'

The CCTV footage showed Porter's Range Rover in a stream of traffic moving slowly along a road on the western edge of Kendal, then pulling up to the kerb in front of a general store. Porter got out of the vehicle and went inside. He emerged five minutes later with a carrier bag and drove off.

'You did well to spot him, Dawn,' James said.

'I got lucky, guv,' DC Isaac replied. 'The footage from this particular camera only just came in. I was scrolling forward to the evening when the Range Rover caught my eye. The time stamp is for five p.m. though, which is at least four hours before we believe Gordon was murdered.'

'Porter could have hung around in town or gone back home and returned in the evening,' James said.

Issac lifted her brow. 'But the Range Rover hasn't shown up on any of the other footage we've seen.'

'Well, let's review it all. You can start by checking to see if we can find out where he went after leaving the store.'

'Do we pay him another visit then, boss?' This from DI Stevens.

James twisted his lips in thought before coming to a decision.

'I think we should bring him in for an interview under caution,' he said. 'We need to apply a degree of pressure and take the opportunity to ask him again about the threat he allegedly made against Gordon.

'Stevens and Foley, I want you to go straight to Porter's place. He's an arrogant and unpleasant individual who is likely to kick up a fuss, so make it clear to him that it will be in his own interest to cooperate and to come in voluntarily,' he said. 'And if he refuses, then I reckon we have enough grounds to place him under arrest.'

After Stevens and Foley left, James put the duty solicitor on stand by as he thought it likely that Porter would insist on legal representation during the interview.

He then went and got himself a strong coffee in the hope it would help him to remain focused and alert.

This was a promising development, and as was so often the case, it had come about as a result of CCTV footage. It never ceased to amaze him that so many people either didn't realise or didn't care that what they were doing was being recorded on one or more of the millions of cameras keeping a watchful eye on Britain's streets, shopping centres, and public spaces.

Nadine Stone and Daniel Porter had already been rumbled after being caught on camera, and James had to wonder if others would follow.

'You might want to see this, guv,' one of the support officers said. 'The BBC News channel is about to run something on the murder.'

James perched himself on the edge of a desk in front of one of the monitors. What the BBC ran was more of a feature than a news report, and it focused on Gordon himself rather than the hunt for his killer.

The reporter began with a piece to camera outside Gordon's home describing what happened to him in the wood across the road. There followed emotional sound bites from his colleagues at the *Cumbria Gazette*, including Nadine, who described him as one of the best reporters she had ever worked with.

Attention was also drawn to some of the big stories he'd covered during his career, among them the disappearance of Chloe Walsh and the investigation into the county lines drug gang that helped to put the ringleaders behind bars.

His distraught parents were also interviewed and his mother talked about the last time they saw their son on Christmas Eve morning.

'We gave him an Amazon gift card,' she said between sobs, 'and because of what has happened we intend to frame it rather than spend it.'

The piece lasted four minutes and by the end of it, James was feeling the blood stir inside him. He was moved by what he'd seen and heard, and it made him even more determined to find and bring to justice the bastard who had caused so much pain and anguish to so many people.

CHAPTER FORTY-ONE
ANNIE

Annie had switched on the TV to catch up with the news and now she wished she hadn't. Tears blurred her vision, and a lump had formed in her throat.

The BBC bulletin feature on Gordon Carver had triggered a strong emotional response, in particular the tributes paid to him by his parents and fellow journalists.

Throughout the day she had forced herself not to think about what had happened so that she could give all her attention to Bella and Theo. And it had helped to ensure they had a great time at the festive fête in the village, which was followed by a visit to the children's play area at the White Hart pub.

But now the murder was back at the forefront of her mind, alongside the crisis in her own life.

Thankfully the kids were too young to realise that this Christmas had been so horrendous. Since returning home they'd played on the living-room floor and their screams and laughter had lifted her spirits.

She was now watching them from the sofa and wondering if

James would return from Kendal early enough to spend some time with them before they were put to bed. He hadn't seen Theo since Christmas morning and had spent barely half an hour with Bella yesterday.

Annie felt sorry for both him and the kids, and it didn't appear that things were going to change any time soon. From the sound of it his team were struggling to resolve the case. She wasn't sure why, but suspected it was partly because Gordon had made enemies of more than a few unsavoury characters through his work as a reporter.

She herself had only met him three or four times, but he'd always come across as a decent and friendly guy. And it hadn't surprised her that over the years James had come to like and trust the man.

She realised suddenly that tears were spilling from her eyes, and she didn't want the kids to see them. Getting up from the sofa, she shuffled into the kitchen.

After wiping her face, she decided to start preparing the tea, but just as she opened the fridge her phone rang. She picked it up from the worktop, and when she saw who was ringing, she felt her heart jump a beat.

'Hi, Fi,' she said. 'How are you?'

'I'm fine, Annie,' came the reply. 'I got your message and I'm so sorry I missed your call earlier. I was driving and couldn't get to my phone.'

'That's not a problem. Did you have a nice Christmas?'

'We did, thanks; Mum and Dad came over. But I gather that you spent most of yours alone with the children again.'

'That's right. And James will likely be working through the weekend as well.'

'Then let my brother know that we're all thinking about him,'

174

Fiona said. 'Now, you asked me to call you back because you had something important to tell me. And it's the first time I've heard my sister-in-law sound so anxious. Worried, even. So, what's up, my love?'

A wave of heat rolled up Annie's neck and as she spoke her lips trembled over the words.

'I want to confide in you, Fi, because I might be about to go through what you yourself went through seventeen months ago,' Annie said. 'I know we've spoken about it before, but now I have a whole pile of new questions I need to ask.'

She heard Fiona draw a sharp breath.

'Oh, Jesus, Annie. I'm so sorry. Does James know?'

'He doesn't. I kept it to myself so as not to spoil his Christmas, but it was spoiled anyway. And now he's got the murder case to deal with. But I will have to tell him soon.'

'I completely understand. I was in the same position, so I know how hard and confusing it all is for you.'

'Then you don't mind if I pick your brain?'

'Of course not. I'm here for you. James will be too when he knows. So, come on. Tell me what stage things are at and how you're coping.'

Annie inhaled deeply, trying to control her racing heart, and went on to tell Fiona about the pit of despair she'd been thrown into.

CHAPTER FORTY-TWO

It was coming up to five when James received a call from DI Stevens to tell him that they were on their way back to headquarters with Daniel Porter.

'He's not happy, guv, but we didn't have to arrest him,' Stevens said. 'I told him we have information that suggests he wasn't completely truthful with us when we last spoke to him, but I didn't say what it was.'

'Does he know it'll be an interview under caution?'

'He does, and he wants us to lay on a solicitor.'

'I expected that. There's one on standby.'

Fifty minutes later James and Stevens entered the interview room together. Porter was already sitting at the table next to Graham Bond, the duty solicitor who had been given time to brief his client.

Bond was a sharply dressed man in his forties with a narrow face and short black hair. James knew him to be a formidable, no-nonsense lawyer with a solid reputation.

He was the first to speak when the two detectives were seated at the table.

'Mr Porter has informed me that he hasn't been told why he was brought here to the station to be interviewed under caution,' he said. 'Perhaps you could begin by telling him.'

James nodded. 'We'll get to that. First you need to know, Mr Porter, that this conversation will be recorded. You do not have to say anything, but it may harm your defence if you do not mention, when questioned, something which you later rely on in court. Anything you do say may be given in evidence. Do you understand?'

Porter gave James a cold stare from below a jutted forehead. 'I'm familiar with the process, detective. Now, can you please just get on with it?'

James took out his phone. He'd already brought up the video clip of Porter arriving at the store and he pressed 'play' as he placed it on the table.

'You made a point of telling us when we spoke to you on Christmas Day that you did not leave your house on Christmas Eve,' he said. 'But this CCTV footage shows that you did. You actually drove into the centre of town only a matter of hours before Gordon Carver was murdered. So, why did you lie to us?'

Porter was clearly taken aback. He rearranged his weight on the chair and sucked in a breath before responding.

'It was a genuine mistake,' he said. 'I forgot that I'd popped out to get some drink.'

James tutted. 'And do you really expect us to believe that?'

Porter gave a tight grimace. 'You're going to have to because it's the truth.'

'But it seems highly unlikely that you wouldn't have remembered. And how can we be sure that you didn't hang around in town or go back later in order to carry out your threat against Mr Carver?'

Porter jabbed an accusing finger at James and his tone grew sharper. 'I've already told you that I didn't threaten him. He made it up. We had words and I asked him not to bring me into any more stories he wrote about Chloe. He was on a fucking mission to make people think that I killed her.'

James leaned forward and screwed up his brow. 'Then surely that would have provided you with a very strong motive for wanting him dead.'

Porter's eyes started dancing in their sockets and he squeezed his hands into fists on top of the table.

'I did not fucking kill him,' he shouted. 'Just as I didn't kill Chloe. There's no way I should be a suspect.'

'Mr Porter has a point,' Bond cut in. 'You seem to be suggesting that after he drove away from the convenience store, he went to another location in town and waited several hours before attacking Mr Carver. That strikes me as a rather far-fetched assumption, Detective Walker. Do you have any evidence to back it up?'

'We're in the process of trawling through CCTV footage,' James replied.

'Well, you're wasting your time,' Porter said. 'When I left the store, I went straight home. And I didn't go out again after that. I swear to god that I stayed in all evening.'

'But I'm guessing there's no one who can corroborate that?'

Porter thrust out his jaw and bared his teeth. 'Just as there's no way that you can prove that I'm lying, which is why I shouldn't be having to listen to this crap.'

After asking a few more questions and getting nowhere, James was forced to concede that there was no point continuing with the interview. For now, they had to accept that Porter did simply forget that he went out on Christmas Eve when asked. And as yet they had no evidence to prove that he'd stayed in town after leaving the store, or that he went back in the evening around the time Gordon was murdered.

'We'll leave it at that for now,' he said, and told Porter that he was free to go.

'I still think that Porter could be our killer,' James told the team when he was back in the office. 'He had motive, and he's known to be a violent person. He was sacked from his job as a barman for assaulting a customer and was allegedly physically abusive towards Chloe Walsh when they were together. But as of this moment we can't place him at or near the murder scene that evening. And we can't rely on finding what we need in the CCTV footage. Not every street in the town is covered, and someone who knows where the cameras are can easily avoid them.'

They carried on discussing the case for another half an hour, but during that time no more updates came in. James called a halt to proceedings at half six and after every one of them said they'd be reporting for duty on Sunday morning, he told them to go home.

He himself then spent a further hour dealing with the backlog of emails and paperwork. Before knocking off, he let Annie know that he was about to leave and called Superintendent Tanner to bring him fully up to date.

The drive to Kirkby Abbey was pretty unpleasant. A heavy frost had begun turning road surfaces to ice, and the settled snow was being whipped up by ferocious winds.

James could feel the tiredness surging through him and he was mightily relieved when he made it home just after eight.

The kids were in bed by then, but Annie was there to give him a warm welcome. He had asked her to put a jacket potato in the oven and that was ready and waiting by the time he'd changed into his pyjamas and dressing gown.

While he ate it, she told him about her day spent with Bella and Theo at the festive fête and children's play area. She made it sound like she'd really enjoyed it, but he wasn't convinced. He sensed that she was trying to appear upbeat for his benefit.

They didn't stay up for long after that. James could tell that Annie wasn't keen on a long conversation and neither was he. So, after sharing half a bottle of wine, they went to bed and within minutes of his head hitting the pillow James was fast asleep.

CHAPTER FORTY-THREE

It was Sunday, but taking the day off was not an option for James.

He couldn't afford to take a break. There was too much at stake. Too many things that might be missed if he didn't stay on top of things.

He was lucky that he had an understanding wife in Annie. She was always fully supportive, no matter how much time he was forced to commit to the job, or how many special occasions were spoiled because of it.

She had nothing planned for the day, so she stayed in bed when James got up at seven. Before he left the house, he checked on the kids. They were out cold, so he didn't disturb them.

It was another grim day with low, menacing clouds and a light falling of snow. But the drive to Kendal was without incident and he arrived at half eight.

Most of the team were already in, but while he waited for the rest to clock on he spoke to DC Hall and learned that there had been no new developments overnight.

He then checked the Sunday papers and saw that Gordon's

murder was receiving much less coverage. It was an inside page lead in the *Mail* under the headline: CUMBRIA KILLER STILL AT LARGE. But in the other tabloids it warranted only a few paragraphs.

James was about to begin the briefing when he got a call from Superintendent Tanner.

'I know it's early in the day, James,' he said, 'but have you got some good news for me?'

'Not yet, boss,' James replied. 'We're still where we were at the end of play yesterday.'

'Just what I feared. I have a Zoom call with the Chief Constable in an hour, and I was hoping to tell him that we'd made some progress.'

'We're chasing up some promising leads, but I really don't think we're on the brink of a breakthrough.'

'Are you in the office?'

'Just arrived and about to start the briefing. Where will you be today?'

'I'll be staying at home, but I can go straight to Penrith or Kendal if you need me. And I'll continue to oversee our response to media inquiries.'

'That suits me, boss. I'll make sure to keep you up to speed.'

The briefing offered up very little that was new, much to James's disappointment. Shane O'Brien hadn't come out of his coma and Toby McGrath was still unaccounted for. Plus, Daniel Porter's Range Rover had been caught on another CCTV camera soon after he left the store on Christmas Eve, and it showed him heading out of town in the direction of his home.

'This probably means that he didn't hang around in order to attack Gordon,' James said. 'But it doesn't mean that he didn't return that evening and made sure to use roads that are not covered by cameras.'

James was handing out assignments when he was told that Nadine Stone had turned up at the station and wanted to speak to him.

He arranged for her to be taken to an interview room and when he got there, he saw that she wasn't by herself. Her son, Ryan, was sitting next to her at the table.

'I wasn't expecting to see you today, Nadine,' James said when he sat down opposite them. 'And good morning to you, too, Ryan.'

'I have the information you requested,' Nadine said. 'And there's a question I need to ask.'

She placed her handbag on the table and took a sheet of paper from it.

'You wanted me to provide you with a list of names of people who complained about something that Gordon wrote for the *Gazette* over the past six months,' she said. 'It's taken me a while to go through the files, but here are the names of five individuals who contacted the office or him directly to express their anger. They include a man who was fired from his job after we exposed him as an illegal immigrant with a criminal record, and a female councillor whom Gordon discovered had blatantly lied about being a solicitor on her CV. Now, I very much doubt that any of them decided to seek such a brutal revenge by killing him, but it's the information you wanted.'

'Thank you, I'm very grateful to have it,' James said, 'and we'll check each of them out. But you could have emailed it to me. You didn't have to come into town.'

'I was already here. You see, things got really difficult between me and my husband after your visit yesterday. I thought it best if we spent some time apart, so I stayed at Ryan's flat last night. It's only a short walk from here and his girlfriend isn't back from Scotland yet.'

'I'm sorry to hear that, Nadine,' James said. 'Hopefully you and Elliott can sort things out between you.'

Her face remained firm, stoic, but her voice was gruff with emotion.

'That's what I'm hoping, Detective Walker. For all our sakes.'

James gave a thoughtful nod. 'You said you also had a question to ask me.'

She nodded. 'That's right. It concerns Shane O'Brien. You told me he was a person of interest and not to reveal that to anyone. Well, we've received information that he's in hospital after being attacked. Is that true?'

James wasn't at all surprised that the news had got out, but at least she hadn't mentioned O'Brien's 'revenge' or 'kill' list.

'It is true that he was the victim of a serious assault,' he responded, 'but as yet we don't know who was responsible because he's in a coma and we haven't been able to speak to him.'

'And do you think the attack might have had something to do with Gordon's murder?'

James shrugged. 'We're keeping an open mind as regards motive. The man only just got out of prison as part of an early release scheme, so one or more of his enemies may well have seized the opportunity to pay him back for something he did to them before he was locked up.'

She was about to ask a follow-up question when her son got in first.

'So where are you with Gordon's murder?' Ryan asked in a low, gravelly voice. 'Can we take it that you no longer think my dad had anything to do with it?'

'I'm in no position to answer that question, Ryan. The investigation is ongoing and we're pursuing numerous lines of inquiry.'

Ryan drew a hand through his hair and his eyes turned small and fierce.

'Well maybe things would move more quickly if you stopped wasting time harassing innocent people,' he said.

His mother was quick to react. She grabbed his arm and got to her feet, pulling him up with her.

'There's no need for that, Ryan,' she snapped. 'The police are only doing their job. You're being rude and it's uncalled for. I want you to apologise to Detective Walker before we go.'

Ryan turned back to James, his eyes glittering with suppressed anger.

'Okay, I'm sorry,' he muttered, but clearly didn't mean it if his expression was anything to go by. 'I'll keep my thoughts to myself from now on.'

Before leading him out of the room, Nadine rolled her eyes at James and mouthed her own apology.

James had a degree of sympathy for Ryan Stone. He was struggling to handle the fact that his own father was a suspect in a murder investigation. It had been an understandable shock to his system, along with the brutal realisation that his parents might be on the verge of splitting up.

For that reason, James wasn't angry with the guy. Just glad that his mother had seen fit to whisk him away before he was able to continue his rant.

Once back in the office, James passed on to the team the list that Nadine had given him.

'These are the names of five people who complained about what Gordon wrote about them during the past six months,' he explained. 'Let's check each of them out. If they don't have an alibi for Christmas Eve, bring them in for questioning.'

He then let it be known that the attack on Shane O'Brien was now public knowledge.

'We can expect the local media to soon be all over it. And it might only be a matter of time before they get wind of the list he wrote and establish the link between him and Gordon.'

James spent the next two hours going over everything they had on their victim and the suspects. He moved between his office and the evidence boards, making notes and seeking answers to the questions that were piling up in his mind.

It wasn't until early afternoon that he received a call that made him believe they were about to make some progress. It was from the Royal Lancashire Infirmary, and it was to let him know that Shane O'Brien had at last regained consciousness.

CHAPTER FORTY-FOUR

James felt a flare of excitement sweep through him as he passed on the news to the team about O'Brien.

'I'll go straight to the hospital,' he told them. 'He came out of the coma several hours ago, but is only now aware of where he is and able to speak. He apparently remembers what happened to him and has made it known that he wants to talk to the police.'

'And if we're lucky he might also confess to killing Gordon Carver,' DI Stevens said with a grin on his face.

James chose DS Abbott to go with him and told the rest of the team to continue following up the other leads.

He and Abbott then travelled south in a patrol car. Snow was falling like confetti, but there was no longer a wind to speak of.

James sat in silence for much of the way, his features taut with anticipation. Shane O'Brien coming out of the coma was a real result. They'd be able to ask the convicted drug dealer where he was on Christmas Eve, as well as who attacked him in his father's house. And they'd confront him with the list of the three men he allegedly intended to seek revenge against.

'I have a friend who was in a coma for several weeks after suffering a severe head injury during a car accident,' Abbott said. 'No one, including the hospital surgeons, expected her to come out of it. But when she suddenly did, she didn't stop talking and had no memory loss whatsoever.'

'Then let's hope that O'Brien is equally fully cognitive,' James replied. 'I don't expect him to confess to anything, but it will make our job easier if he can answer at least some of the outstanding questions.'

They were approaching Lancaster on the M6 when James's phone rang, and his chest tightened when he saw that the caller was his sister Fiona.

'Well, this is a pleasant surprise, sis,' he said when he answered. 'Is everything okay?'

'All good at my end,' she answered. 'It just occurred to me that I haven't seen you and Annie for ages, and I wondered when might be a good time to pay you a visit. Dave and I can come next week for a couple of days if you'll have us.'

James was surprised, but pleased. 'That'd be great. I'll talk to Annie and we can agree on a date. But you need to know that I'm heavily involved in a big case right now and I'm not sure how long it will go on.'

'Yeah, I heard about it. But we can spend time with Annie and the little ones while you're out chasing killers. How is your good wife, by the way?'

'She's trying to pretend that she's her usual cheery self, but our Christmas was ruined again, and it's clearly knocked her for six.'

'Oh, bless her. Well, tell her I asked after her and let me know when we can head north.'

They spoke for another minute or so before James realised that they were approaching the hospital and was forced to end the call.

'Well, that was totally unexpected,' he said to Abbott. 'It's not often that I hear from either of my sisters and Fiona has only visited us once since we moved here.'

'Is she the one who had serious health problems?' Abbott asked.

'Yes, she is. It was breast cancer. She had to have a double mastectomy.'

Abbott nodded. 'I remember. You were really worried for her. And you went to London to see her after she was diagnosed.'

James felt his pulse quicken. 'It was a terrible time. We thought we were going to lose her. Thankfully the cancer was spotted early enough. And the reconstruction surgery went well, too.'

'I myself got into a panic a few years ago when I felt a lump in my right breast,' Abbott said. 'It turned out to be a non-cancerous tumour.'

'You were lucky then,' James said. 'Breast cancer is more common than I realised, and I just pray that it doesn't strike any more of my family and friends.'

CHAPTER FORTY-FIVE

Just before they arrived at the hospital James sent a text message to Annie telling her that Fiona was keen to visit them next week.

He was sure she'd be pleased as she got on well with both his younger sisters and hadn't spoken to them in quite a while.

He then switched his phone to silent and turned his thoughts back to Shane O'Brien.

Two uniformed officers were stationed outside the man's room when they got there, and a consultant was also on hand to provide them with an update.

'The patient is making excellent progress,' he said. 'As soon as he was able to speak, he told me that he wanted to pass on information to the police about the person who was responsible for his injury. And just so you know, the hospital has just informed his father that he's conscious and he'll undoubtedly soon be making his way here.'

O'Brien was sitting up in the bed when James and Abbott entered the room. The top of his head was encased in a thick bandage, a plaster covered the gash below his nose, and tubes were going into his arms.

But he seemed wide awake. His face was grey, the skin tight, and his eyes shifted towards them as they approached the bed.

It was the consultant who told him who they were before he retreated from the room at James's request.

'I was the person who found you when we called at your father's house, Mr O'Brien,' James said. 'I'll explain in a moment why we went there, but first please tell us who attacked you and why.'

O'Brien responded immediately, his voice low and slurred. 'The bastard is known to the police. His name's McGrath. Toby McGrath.' His breath was coming in short gasps and his lips were trembling. 'He left me for dead and you need to find him and bang him up for the rest of his fucking life.'

James felt his pulse escalate. The revelation was a big step forward.

'Can you tell us what happened, Mr O'Brien?' he asked. 'Start with how the man gained access to the house.'

After a pause, O'Brien said, 'He turned up unexpectedly because he'd heard that I'd been let out of prison early. He said he wanted to talk to me, and I was stupid enough to let him in. As soon as I did, he asked me if I was alone. When I told him I was he started yelling at me. He accused me of stitching him up back when we were partners in crime. Things turned violent pretty quickly. He kicked over my dad's Christmas tree and threw a chair across the room. Then, as I went for him, he punched me in the face. Before I could regain my balance, he pulled a fucking club hammer from his pocket and hit me with it. I'd forgotten he's always tooled up. Anyway, that was the last thing I remember. But it's clear that he came to kill me and he obviously thought he had.'

James was minded to believe O'Brien given that his description

191

of what had happened was consistent with what they'd found at the crime scene.

'You should know that we have been trying to trace Toby McGrath,' James said. 'But he appears to have disappeared.'

'Does he know that I'm alive?' O'Brien asked.

'We can't be sure, but the media are now aware of what happened to you, and so it's likely that he does, too.'

O'Brien offered a lifeless smile. 'Then he's running scared because he knows I'll be telling you what happened and he's fucked.'

James cleared his throat. 'That's all very helpful, and I can assure you that we'll continue searching for McGrath, but I should now tell you why we came to your father's house to speak to you.'

'I'm assuming it was a routine check following my release.'

'No, it wasn't. It was to question you about the murder of Cumbria journalist Gordon Carver. You see, we heard about the list you drew up containing the names of the three men you held responsible for your conviction and prison sentence. And before you tell me that you didn't draw up the list you should know that I found it in your wallet when I searched your bedroom. We also know that you boasted about it to your fellow inmates.'

O'Brien's face froze and he took a moment to digest what he'd been told. Finally, he said, 'I didn't know Carver was dead and I didn't kill him. And I didn't intend to kill him either. Or those other two.'

'So, it wasn't a kill list you drew up?'

'Of course it bloody wasn't.'

James shook his head. 'You need to convince me of that, Mr O'Brien. Because given what you've told us, I'm inclined to believe that Toby McGrath found out about your list as well, and when he heard that you'd been released, he panicked and decided to go after you before you went after him.

'Gordon Carver wasn't so lucky. We know for a fact that he'd learned that you were going to seek revenge against him for helping to expose your drug dealing. But he was attacked while walking home before he could do anything about it.'

O'Brien responded by closing his eyes and moving his head slowly from side to side.

'It wasn't me who did it,' he said. 'I admit I wanted to hurt him, but I'm not a murderer.'

'Then convince us of that,' James said. 'Because right now you are our prime suspect.'

CHAPTER FORTY-SIX

'Fine. I did make a list of the three men I intended to punish for the parts they played in getting me sent to prison. The first mistake I made was to tell my cellmate,' O'Brien said. As he spoke the muscles flexed in his jaw. 'The bastard told another couple of inmates and so I'm not surprised that word got out. Then I made another mistake by writing the names down on paper, but I did it because I wanted to keep reminding myself what they did to me.

'I was locked up for four years and from the start I promised myself that I wouldn't let those three get away with it. During the trial the prosecuting lawyer, Jack Delaney, made my crimes appear far worse than they were. Gordon Carver gathered information that he passed on to the police and then he wrote stuff that painted me as the world's worst villain. Then, about a year ago, I was told that McGrath was your snitch and he told you about what me and the other guys were doing to get his own back on me for kicking him out of the gang.

'So, can you blame me for wanting to hurt them? It gave me something to look forward to. But I never planned to murder them. My intention was to beat them to a pulp and to make sure they didn't know who it was. I was going to wear a balaclava and strike when they least expected it. And to make sure that each time I had a concrete alibi.'

He paused as his breath faltered and for several seconds his eyes seemed to go out of focus.

When he continued, his voice was little more than a whisper.

'The thing is … I didn't expect to be released, so I hadn't come up with a detailed plan. It meant that I had to do some research to find out where those three gits were and what they were up to. That's what I was doing on Christmas Day when McGrath showed up at my dad's house and told me that he'd heard what I was planning to do. You know what happened after that.'

James shook his head. 'There's one thing we don't know, and that's where you were when Gordon Carver was murdered.'

O'Brien screwed his face into a frown. 'I don't even know when it happened. You said it was on Christmas Eve. But when exactly?'

'At some point after nine p.m.'

'And where did it happen?'

'On a woodland path close to his home in Kendal.'

'Well, I was nowhere near there that evening. In fact, I was a fair way from Kendal.'

'Then where were you?' James asked.

O'Brien raised his eyes to the ceiling. 'If you must know, I was in Penrith and spent the evening doing what I'd been wanting to do for the past four years.'

'And what was that?'

O'Brien curled his lips into something resembling a smile.

'I was getting my end away with an old flame and loving every fucking minute of it.'

O'Brien thankfully cut back on the crudity as he continued to tell them what he was apparently getting up to when Gordon was murdered.

He claimed he drove to the home of a former girlfriend in Penrith at 5 p.m. on Christmas Eve. It was the reason he didn't want to travel to Ireland with his dad.

The woman cooked him a meal before they had sex, and he then stayed the night in her flat before returning to his father's house on Christmas morning. Soon after he arrived Toby McGrath turned up and battered him with the hammer.

He gave the woman's name as Carla Whittiker and DS Abbott made a note of her address and phone number.

'We were seeing each other before I got banged up,' he said. 'It wasn't serious, but it might have gone on to be. We exchanged letters over the past four years, and she came to visit me a few times. I did want to go and see her before Christmas Eve, but I had a lot to sort out and she was busy with her business.'

'And what is her business?' James asked.

'She runs an escort agency,' O'Brien said. 'When I met her, she was one of the employees, but now she's the boss.'

James was going to ask another question, but O'Brien suddenly developed a loud coughing fit and his face reddened dramatically.

Abbott alerted the consultant who'd been waiting outside in the hall, and he rushed in to tend to his patient.

James and Abbott left him to it and stepped out of the room. When the consultant emerged a few minutes later he told them that the coughing had stopped.

'But I really think that Mr O'Brien needs to rest now,' he added. 'It seems he got over-excited and it affected his breathing.'

'We're done here anyway,' James said. 'But please keep us informed if there are any dramatic changes to his condition.'

'And are you happy for his father to see him when he arrives?'

James nodded. 'Yes, that's no longer a problem, but we'd like the uniformed officers to remain here for the time being.'

CHAPTER FORTY-SEVEN

Before leaving the hospital the two detectives went to the canteen to grab a lunchtime snack.

As they sat down to eat, James called the office and spoke to DI Stevens. He told him what they'd got from O'Brien and said he wanted the man's alibi checked out.

'Get someone from Carleton Hall to visit Carla Whittiker's flat,' he instructed. 'If she's not in we'll have to establish her whereabouts. And let's check road-cam footage between there and Milnthorpe on Christmas Eve after five p.m. That's when O'Brien claims he left his father's house.'

After he came off the phone, Abbott said, 'Let's assume for now that he's told us the truth, guv, and that he was with that woman when Gordon's murder took place. Will we still pursue charges against him for planning to harm Gordon and the other two on his list?'

'Almost certainly,' James said. 'Making threats is a serious offence, but I'm not sure we can believe his claim that his aim wasn't to kill them.'

Abbott nodded. 'That's a good point, but even if it was, I don't suppose there's any way we'll be able to prove it.'

James knew that to be the case. He also knew that if O'Brien had told the truth, then they were going to lose their prime suspect. The thought of it played on his mind during the drive back to Kendal and by the time they got there he was feeling a throbbing in his temples.

Too many roads were leading nowhere, and he was becoming increasingly concerned about that. It was now four days since Gordon had been murdered on the path and three days since his body was found. James was worried that the investigation was set to drag on, as so many of them do, and the leads would dry up. He'd worked on quite a few cases that at the start he had expected to solve within days, but which lasted for weeks. And then there were those from years ago that remained unsolved to this day.

He tried not to sound too downbeat when he got the team together, but he could tell from their expressions that they were all struggling to conceal their irritation.

'We won't rule Shane O'Brien out just yet,' he told them. 'And I'm not prepared to take this Carla Whittiker's word either. I want concrete proof that he was with her on Christmas Eve. For all we know, she may have agreed to provide him with an alibi as a favour. That's why we need to trawl CCTV to see if his car turns up on footage in Penrith.'

The woman's name had already been put through the system, and it turned out she was a known sex worker who had a conviction from five years ago for soliciting in a public place.

James was then told that online news sites were now reporting the attack on O'Brien, and it would doubtless feature in tomorrow's papers, but so far there had been no mention of

199

Toby McGrath being the alleged attacker or the list of names drawn up by O'Brien.

'It's becoming a headline-grabber because the guy was among the latest batch of convicts to be released early from prison,' DC Sharma pointed out. 'And there's growing criticism about the policy itself.'

DC Foley had been assigned the task of checking out the five names given to them by Nadine Stone. One of them resided in Kendal and the other four lived elsewhere in Cumbria.

'Mrs Stone provided very few details so I'm in the process of gathering information on each individual before we approach them,' she said.

The team did not have to wait long before they heard back from Penrith. Carla Whittiker was at home when detectives called at her flat and she was said to be shocked to learn that O'Brien was in hospital having been attacked.

She did go on to provide him with his alibi for Christmas Eve, claiming that he arrived about six and stayed overnight.

'That's pretty much what we expected to hear,' James said. 'But unless we get CCTV footage showing him arriving and leaving Penrith when he reckoned that he did, then he remains a suspect.'

Much to everyone's disappointment, footage from several traffic cameras was made available two hours later that showed O'Brien's Vauxhall Corsa heading north on the M6 at 5.30 p.m., and shortly after on two roads in the town centre. On one of them, which was close to Carla Whittiker's address, he could clearly be seen at the wheel. He was then caught on the same cameras leaving Penrith on Christmas morning.

'This almost certainly proves that O'Brien did not kill Gordon,' James said. 'But it doesn't mean that he didn't arrange for someone to do it on his behalf. After all, we know for certain that he intended to go after the man, as he's admitted it to us. So, we keep him in our sights for now and think carefully about where we go next with it.'

James hadn't realised how quickly the time had passed until he checked his watch and saw that it was approaching six o'clock. It prompted him to tell the team to put things on hold and prepare for another full day tomorrow.

'Just keep telling yourselves that we'll get there in the end,' he said. 'It's just taking longer than we hoped it would.'

Before leaving the office, he emailed a full update to Superintendent Tanner and told the officers working the night shift to let him know if there were any developments, regardless of the time.

CHAPTER FORTY-EIGHT

James couldn't wait to get home. He needed to unwind before the inevitable onset of one of his tension headaches.

It had been a long, disappointing day, and he was looking forward to relaxing for a couple of hours with Annie.

He'd sent her a text earlier to let her know that he didn't expect to be home until much later, so hopefully it would come as a pleasant surprise when he rolled up earlier.

The kids were bound to be in bed, but he had made up his mind not to leave home in the morning until he'd at least proved to them that he was still part of their lives.

It was another slow drive to Kirkby Abbey because the wind had picked up and the snow was heavier. With his mind raging in all directions, he found it hard to concentrate on the road ahead. At the same time, his eyes felt heavy and gritty, and a wave of tiredness crashed over him.

It didn't help that Gordon Carver's face kept pushing itself into his thoughts. Each time it stirred up a riot of emotions from guilt to frustration, and piled on the pressure that was growing by the hour.

This was to be expected, of course, since he had known the man. It was always more challenging heading up a murder investigation when the victim wasn't a total stranger.

He breathed a sigh of relief when he finally pulled onto their driveway. He switched off the engine, grabbed his briefcase, and got out of the car.

The front door was pulled open as he approached it and he expected to see Annie standing there. But instead the familiar figure of Janet Dyer appeared.

'Hello, Janet,' he said, as she stepped outside.

His voice startled her. 'Oh, my Lord, you made me jump.'

He grinned. 'I'm sorry. I just pulled up. And I'm guessing you're just leaving.'

'That's right.'

Annie then appeared in the doorway behind Janet.

'I thought you were going to be home later than this,' she said.

He nodded. 'So did I, but things didn't work out as I'd hoped they would, and so I decided to call it a day.'

'I dropped by for a drink and a bite to eat with your good wife,' Janet said. 'I get the boys back from my ex tomorrow and it'll be a return to the same old routine.'

'Well, it's good to see you, Janet, and thanks for keeping Annie company. I know she appreciates it, especially when I have to leave her at Christmastime.'

'It was my pleasure, as always,' she replied as she wiped away the snow that had fallen on her head and face. 'I'd better be off before I get drenched.'

James offered to walk her home, but she told him not to be silly. 'I live barely a hundred yards away and I'm sure I'll be perfectly safe.'

After watching her walk away, he stepped inside and planted a kiss on Annie's forehead.

'Are you hungry?' she asked him.

'I fancy some nibbles and a drink rather than a meal.'

'Then there's plenty of rubbish for you to munch on,' she said, closing the door behind them. 'Come and get stuck in and tell me about your day.'

He dropped his briefcase, took off his coat, and followed her into the kitchen. And that was when the harsh ceiling light showed him that her eyes were inflamed and bloodshot.

'Are you all right?' he asked, his voice heavy with concern.

'Why wouldn't I be?'

He gave a little shrug. 'It's just that you look as though you've been crying. Have you?'

'Of course not. I'm just exhausted. And I think I might be coming down with something. I've been sneezing a lot.'

She turned away from him and pulled open the cupboard containing all the biscuits and crisps.

He suspected that she wasn't being totally honest with him, and he wondered if yet another ruined Christmas had finally got to her. He decided to wait until they were together in the living room before he pressed her on it.

'Are you up for sharing a bottle of wine with me?' he asked.

She took a couple of bags of crisps from the cupboard and dropped them onto the worktop.

'There's a bottle of white already open in the fridge,' she replied. 'I had one glass with Janet, but I could do with a few more.'

'Has it been a tough day?'

'Not really. A bit boring actually. The kids were good and they were both so tired I put them to bed not long after six.'

He took the bottle of wine from the fridge while she poured some of the crisps into a bowl.

'Is this going to be enough for you?' she asked him.

'More than enough. I'm not that hungry.'

He went into the living room and placed the bottle of wine on the coffee table. As he moved towards the sideboard to get two glasses, he saw that the TV was on and tuned in to the YouTube app. The screen was showing the search history list above two videos that were ready and waiting to be played.

As soon as the subject matter registered with him, he cast his eyes down the search list and what he read both shocked and confused him.

Breast Cancer Treatment
Don't ignore breast lumps
Symptoms of breast cancer
My breast cancer diagnosis

He turned away from the screen the moment he heard Annie enter the room behind him, and he saw a shadow pass over her features as her eyes moved quickly between him and the TV.

'I forgot I left it on,' she said before swallowing hard. 'We were browsing YouTube because there was nothing worth watching and—'

He raised a hand to stop her speaking. 'Annie, I'm not stupid. I can't imagine why anyone would look for information on breast cancer just to pass the time. Be honest with me. Has Janet got a problem? Is that why she came here? To talk about it with you?'

She stared at him for several seconds as if trying to decide how to respond, and the look on her face sent a chill flushing through his body.

'What is it, Annie?' he said. 'You're scaring me.'

A sob exploded in her throat and the words that came out of her mouth sliced through him like a rotor blade.

'It's me, James,' she said in a small, pitiful voice. 'There's a chance I've got what your sister had. I won't know for sure until I have the tests.'

CHAPTER FORTY-NINE

James recoiled in shock at what Annie had told him. He didn't want to believe it, but he knew it had to be true.

His first instinct was to rush forward and pull her into an embrace.

'Oh, my love, how long have you known? And why haven't you told me?'

She had to clear her throat before responding. 'I went to see the GP last Monday after I felt a lump in my left breast. He referred me to a clinic for a bunch of tests because he says they need to rule out cancer, but the earliest they can fit me in is eight days from now, on January the fifth.'

Stepping back, James cupped her face in his hands. 'I can't believe you kept it to yourself. Why, for heaven's sake?'

'I told Janet and Fiona,' she replied, 'but I held back from telling you at first because I didn't want to spoil your Christmas. I knew how much you'd worry. And then came Gordon's murder and I decided it wouldn't be fair to open up to you while you had to deal with that.'

Tears pooled in her eyes and his heart went out to her.

'You should have been thinking about yourself and not me,' he said. 'But I completely understand and I'm glad you shared the news with Janet and my sister.'

'I told Janet because I needed someone to talk to, and she's been such a good friend. And then I rang Fi because there were questions that I wanted to ask about what she went through. That was when she said she'd come and visit us.'

James moved his hands from her face to her shoulders and gave them a gentle squeeze.

'So, whose idea was it to tune into YouTube?'

'It was Janet's. She told me about all the breast cancer videos that are on there. But as we were watching them, I got upset.'

'I'm not surprised. But look, now that I know what you're going through, I can be there for you. And the first point I want to make is that most breast lumps turn out not to be cancerous. I know that because I researched the hell out of the subject when Fiona was diagnosed. And I'm guessing that you know it, too. So, you need to stay positive.'

'I've been trying to, for the sake of the kids,' she said. 'But it's not easy. I just can't stop thinking about what will happen to them – and to you – if the test results show that I have cancer.'

The tears broke free then and she fell against him, her whole body shaking. He didn't know what to say so he simply put his arms around her and held her tight.

After Annie stopped crying, they sat down on the sofa to talk about it.

James poured them each a glass of wine, but he left the crisps in the kitchen because he no longer had an appetite.

He could tell that Annie was relieved that she had at last

confided in him, and he was glad that she had. He felt so sorry for her, and he intended to do everything he could to help her keep her spirits up.

But he knew it wasn't going to be easy. It was as though she had already convinced herself that the outlook was grim.

She let him feel the lump in her breast and he was surprised at how large and hard it was.

'It doesn't hurt and I've no idea quite how long it's been there,' she said. 'I want to believe it's a benign tumour, but there's a good chance that it's not.

'Breast cancer is the most common cancer in the UK, and over fifty thousand women are diagnosed with it each year. At the clinic I'll be given an ultrasound, a mammogram, and perhaps a biopsy will be taken, but the wait will go on after that because the results will probably take at least a couple of weeks to come through,' she said.

It was hard for James to keep his emotions in check and as the conversation continued, he could feel the muscles knotting in his stomach.

It was almost eleven o'clock when Annie patted him on the knee and said, 'I think it's time we went to bed. I suspect the kids will be up fairly early, and you need to get back on the trail of Gordon's killer.'

'I could take the day off and spend it with you,' he replied. 'I'll tell the team that I'm not feeling—'

'No way are you doing that,' she interrupted him. 'If you allow this to distract you then it will make me feel worse than I already do.'

CHAPTER FIFTY

Neither of them got much sleep. Throughout the night they lay on their backs or in each other's arms and talked about the blow that fate had dealt them.

James continued to offer Annie words of reassurance, telling her that there was a good chance the lump in her breast was non-malignant, but it did nothing to ease the emotional burden she was under.

At 6 a.m. his alarm roused them from their slumber because he had forgotten to readjust it.

'We might as well get up,' Annie said. 'I'll make us tea.'

James told her again that he was prepared to take the day off to be with her, but she insisted that he should go to work and do what he could to find Gordon Carver's killer.

'If it's just me and the kids I won't have time to dwell on this other shit,' she said. 'But if you're here I will, and I'll also be racked with guilt. So, please don't worry about me. I'll be fine.'

She switched on the bedside lamp and he saw that her face

was lined with emotion and fatigue. As she pushed back the duvet, he put his arm around her.

'I love you, Annie.'

'I love you too, sweetheart,' she said, before kissing him on the lips. 'And I actually feel much better now that I won't have to fib to you about why I'm not myself.'

They drank their tea in the kitchen and, at Annie's request, didn't talk about her lump. Instead, she told him that she was planning to take Bella and Theo to Janet's house today so they could play with her two sons.

She then asked him about the investigation, but as soon as he started telling her how it was going their daughter came running into the room.

'Daddy, Daddy,' she screamed and rushed over to him.

He picked her up and kissed her. Her overjoyed reaction to seeing him put a smile on Annie's face and James felt his heart give a kick.

Minutes later they heard Theo cry out and James went upstairs to get him.

What followed was an hour of Monday-morning chaos as they all had breakfast together before Annie told James to get showered and dressed.

'And then you need to hit the road,' she said. 'Go and catch a killer while I keep these two little monsters occupied. And please know that I'll be okay.'

James was dreading the day ahead as he knew it was going to be hard to focus his mind on anything other than Annie's condition.

He knew from his sister's experience that the wait to find out if something is or isn't cancer is a harrowing one. He saw what it did to her, and those who loved her, and he could already see the impact it was having on his wife.

The image of her pale, anxious face kept pushing itself into his thoughts, making it difficult for him to concentrate on his driving as he headed towards Kendal. He was lucky that the weather was relatively calm; there was a light wind from the north, but it wasn't snowing.

Conditions remained the same all the way to headquarters, where he arrived just before nine, and as he entered the office, he saw that the whole team were already there and beavering away. He was determined to put his all into the job and so he had to force himself to stop thinking about Annie. It wasn't easy, but with so much going on, the case soon filled his head again.

There were emails to respond to from Superintendent Tanner and the press office. And he made a point of reading through the printed reports from his detectives.

Unfortunately, nothing new had come in overnight. Toby McGrath still hadn't been tracked down, and the latest batch of CCTV footage from in and around the town hadn't produced any surprises.

But what did come as a surprise to everyone was the coverage that they suddenly saw being given in the local media to the fact that Chloe Walsh should have been celebrating her twenty-sixth birthday today.

It dominated the *Cumbria Gazette*'s online site, along with the local BBC TV bulletins. And it was stirring up a wave of hostile comments across the internet from anonymous trolls accusing her ex-boyfriend Daniel Porter of killing her.

CHAPTER FIFTY-ONE

James paused the briefing so they could take note of how the local news outlets were marking Chloe Walsh's twenty-sixth birthday.

It was of interest because the public were now being made aware that two significant links had been established between the missing estate agent and the murder of Gordon Carver.

The *Cumbria Gazette* revealed that not only had Gordon been working on his latest Chloe story up to the day he was killed, but also that her former boyfriend, Daniel Porter, was among those who'd been questioned by detectives investigating the journalist's murder.

It was bound to encourage more media attention and would almost certainly put Porter himself firmly in their firing line because it was widely known that he had also been interviewed about Chloe's disappearance.

The main thrust of the media coverage was that Chloe was still missing eight months after disappearing while walking home from a house party in Kendal where she'd been drinking with friends.

Several photos of Chloe were shown, one instantly recognisable to James as the same picture pinned to the wall in his office to remind him that the case was still open. She was a pretty young woman with a sweep of blonde hair, full lips, and a sharp, delicate face.

Both the *Gazette* and the BBC carried an interview with her parents who described her as the light of their lives. They didn't want to believe that she was dead, but they were certain that if she was still alive then she would have found a way to let them know.

The story inevitably encouraged some anonymous internet trolls to get in on the act with a bunch of unsubstantiated claims.

Why won't the police arrest the ex-boyfriend? He bullied her when they were together and then murdered her when she left him.

What did Daniel Porter do with Chloe's body? That's what we all want to know.

Happy birthday Chloe wherever you are. And I hope your ex pays for what he did to you.

James recalled the notes that Gordon had scrawled on the whiteboard in his house. They had been very much in line with what he was seeing now.

Did Porter kill or kidnap Chloe on that day?
Where did he hide her body?
Have the police done enough to find her?

When the briefing was reconvened ten minutes later, James reminded the team that, according to Nadine Stone, Gordon had become obsessed with the Chloe Walsh story and didn't want to stop chasing it.

'He knew her because they were at university together, and he'd convinced himself that Porter killed her,' he said. 'You will all recall how closely he followed our investigation. More than once I had to tell him that there wasn't a shred of evidence that Porter had anything to do with her disappearance. But maybe he was right, and perhaps when he went to Porter's house just over a week ago he revealed that he was about to uncover something that would bring us back to Porter's door. And so Porter panicked and went and killed Gordon on the path.

'But unless we can place him at or near the scene of the murder, it's hard to see how we can move forward with Porter as a key suspect,' he said. 'It's the same problem we faced with Chloe's disappearance – he was our main suspect, but we weren't able to prove that he was in town when she left the pub and started walking home. So, it could be that both times the bastard simply managed to avoid street cameras.'

CHAPTER FIFTY-TWO

James didn't want the Chloe Walsh birthday story to become a distraction. Sure, her misper case was ongoing, but right now the focus had to be on Gordon Carver's murder.

He therefore switched the conversation back to the current lines of inquiry and stressed that they needed to up their game.

'The pace of progress is far too slow,' he said. 'It still feels to me as though we're a long way behind where we should be.'

He was about to run through the list of suspects when his phone rang. He whipped it from his pocket and saw that it was the Super calling.

'I have to answer this,' he told the team as he stepped into his office to speak to Tanner. 'I shouldn't be long, so take a coffee break.'

'I've had the press office on the phone, James,' the boss said. 'They're facing a barrage of new questions relating to the Carver case and they're not clear on how to respond. So, I need some advice on what lines we should take.'

'Am I right in assuming that it's to do with the fact that we've interviewed Daniel Porter in connection with it?' James said.

'Yes, the BBC are asking if there's a firm connection between Gordon's murder and Chloe Walsh's disappearance. It's also in the public domain now that not only is Shane O'Brien in hospital after being attacked, but also that he too is a potential suspect.'

James let his breath escape in a low whistle. 'On that first point we have to acknowledge to ourselves that there is a connection since Porter allegedly threatened Gordon. But at this stage we don't have to say why Porter was questioned or why O'Brien is also a person of interest. I suggest we confirm that they were spoken to along with several other people and leave it at that.'

'That sounds sensible to me,' Tanner said. 'I'll get back on to the press office right away. I'll also be speaking to the Chief Constable in the next half hour, so have you got any updates for me?'

'Not yet, boss. We're halfway through the morning briefing, but it seems that nothing new has come to light.'

'That's a shame. Well, let me know if and when you get a breakthrough. And should you want me to come to Kendal for any reason then just say the word and I'll be there.'

As James called the team together again to resume the briefing, DC Foley raised her hand.

'I've come across something of interest, guv,' she said. 'And it could mean we have another potential suspect.'

'Then let's hear it, Caroline,' he responded.

She stood up from her desk and referred to her notes. 'It's from the list of names that Nadine Stone gave to us of people who had complained about something that Gordon had written for the *Gazette*. I've checked them all and four of the five can be ruled out. Two of them weren't in the country on Christmas Eve, and the other two have concrete alibis. That leaves a woman named Imogen Price who is the only one of the five who lives here in Kendal.'

'So why did she have a problem with Gordon?' James asked.

'It was over her son, Darren, who used to manage a charity shop here in the town. Some of you may remember that just over a year ago the *Gazette* followed up a report that showed there had been a significant increase in the number of charity shop staff who were stealing the takings. Gordon was tasked with investigating if this was happening in Cumbria and found out that Darren, who had managed the shop for nine months, had stolen several thousand pounds to fund a gambling addiction. It was his colleagues who grassed him up apparently. Anyway, Gordon passed the information on to us, and Darren was charged with theft. He denied it, but was found guilty and Gordon took credit for it in an article he then wrote.'

'I recall the case,' DI Stevens said. 'Darren was given a suspended sentence.'

Foley nodded. 'He was also sacked from his job and his life went dramatically downhill after that. He had to be treated for depression, his marriage broke up, and then he took his own life two months ago by slitting his wrists. It wasn't brought to our attention because he moved to Blackpool six months ago.'

'I take it his mother blamed Gordon and the *Gazette* for causing his life to spiral out of control?' James said.

'She did. A month after his death she turned up at the *Gazette* office and asked to speak to Gordon. He met her in reception, and she accused him of having her son's blood on his hands. She also claimed that Darren never stole any money, and accused the other staff members and volunteers of being the guilty ones.

Security had to escort her out of the building and days later she wrote a scathing letter to Nadine criticising the *Gazette*.'

'It's certainly worth having a word with her,' James said.

'But that's not all, guv,' Foley responded. 'When I ran a check on the woman, her face was immediately familiar to me, but I couldn't place where I had seen her before. It was only in the last half hour that it struck me that I might have seen her yesterday on the security camera footage from the pub where Gordon spent the last hour or so of his life. I just checked and I was right. She was there when he met up with Michael Frost on Christmas Eve, and she left about ten minutes before Gordon did.'

CHAPTER FIFTY-THREE

'Excellent, DC Foley,' James said. 'I want you to pull together the information you've gathered on Imogen Price and present it to the team. When that's done, you and I will go and see what she's got to say for herself.'

As she set to work, he went back into his office and called Superintendent Tanner to let him know ahead of his chat with the Chief Constable that there had been a development.

'It might not come to anything,' he said after passing on what Foley had told him, 'but it could also be a game changer. I doubt the woman knew that Gordon was going to be in the pub at that time, but when she saw him there it might have triggered a blast of anger. It's possible she then went outside and waited nearby for him to leave. When he did, she followed him, and in a moment of madness attacked him on the path because of her belief that what he did caused her son's life to fall apart and end in suicide.'

'It's certainly a theory worth checking out,' Tanner said. 'And it makes you wonder just how many enemies Gordon racked up over the years.'

'Quite a few I should imagine,' James replied. 'It's becoming all too common for journalists to face harassment, threats, and physical violence for doing their jobs.'

'It's a disturbing trend, I know, and it's fuelled to a great extent by the online toxicity that's aimed at them. I know of two national newspaper reporters who left the profession in the last few years because they feared for their lives.'

By the time James rejoined the team, DC Foley was ready to share the information she'd gathered on Imogen Price. She began by circulating a photo of the woman, who had a fleshy, nondescript face and long dark hair.

'Mrs Price is a fifty-four-year-old widow,' Foley said. 'She works from home as a freelance accountant.'

Foley drew their attention to the monitors as she ran the security footage from the busy bar at The Queen's Castle.

'This is clearly her entering the pub by herself and going straight to the bar to order a glass of wine. Gordon has already been there for over half an hour at this point, and there he is to her left in the booth. He doesn't appear to notice her, but she stares at him while waiting for her drink to be served. She then takes it to the table in the far corner.'

Foley fast-forwarded the clip, which showed the woman sitting at the table for ten minutes before finishing her drink, getting up, and hurrying out of the pub.

'I'm quite sure that Gordon didn't see her,' Foley said. 'But that's not at all surprising since there are quite a few other customers between them. He gets up and leaves some ten minutes later.'

'So, we don't know where she went from there,' James said.

Foley shook her head. 'We'll have to have another trawl through street cameras in the area. She lives a short walk away from the bar, but in the opposite direction to Gordon's house.'

An adrenaline rush took hold of James's body.

'Good job, Foley. Now, it's time we dropped in on her,' he said, before instructing the rest of the team to see if they could find out where the woman went after leaving the pub.

CHAPTER FIFTY-FOUR

Imogen Price's home was located on the east side of town, across the River Kent and just off Shap Road.

The two detectives got there within minutes in the patrol car, and as they pulled up outside the terraced house, Foley noted, 'If she is our killer, it wouldn't have taken her long to walk back here from the scene of the crime.'

James nodded. 'That's true enough. With any luck, she'll have been picked up on a camera if she did.'

The driver stayed in the patrol car as they walked up to the front door. James rang the bell and, much to his relief, it was opened within seconds by the woman they had come to see.

She was wearing a thick jumper and a pair of loose-fitting jeans.

As they held up their ID cards, James said, 'Hello, Mrs Price. I'm Detective Chief Inspector Walker and my colleague is Detective Constable Foley. We need to speak to you in relation to an investigation we're carrying out. Would it be okay to come in?'

Price narrowed her eyes and turned down the corners of her mouth. 'I don't understand. What has it got to do with me?'

'It'll be much better if we can explain it to you inside,' James said. 'The investigation is into the murder of local journalist Gordon Carver. I'm sure you've heard about it.'

'Of course. It's all anyone is talking about.'

'Well, we're interviewing the people who had a serious grudge against him so that we can eliminate them from our inquiries. And it's come to our attention that you were one of them because you believe he played a part in causing your son Darren's life to spiral out of control. You even confronted him after Darren took his own life two months ago.'

Her eyebrows shot up. 'I'm now a suspect in his murder just because of that?'

'It's our job to explore every possible scenario, Mrs Price,' James said. 'And given what you—'

She held up her hand, fingers spread wide. 'Please stop there and listen to me. I had every right to confront the man and to complain to his editor. I wanted him and everyone else to know that I don't believe for a single second that my son stole from the charity shop. He was stitched up and it wasn't fair.'

Her voice was shaking with emotion now and so James said, 'There are questions we need to ask you, Mrs Price, and I really don't think we should ask them here on the doorstep.'

After a few tense beats, she expanded her chest with a deep sigh and took a step back.

'You'd better come in then,' she said. 'But I'll tell you now that I did not kill that man.'

She took them into the living room and gestured towards a long, curved sofa. When they were sitting down, she folded her arms across her chest and stood facing them, her back against a patio door.

It was a small, bright room with no Christmas decorations but lots of framed photographs of two males who James assumed were her son and late husband.

'So, what is it you want to ask me?' Price said, her voice stronger and less emotional than it was barely a minute ago.

It was Foley who responded. 'First, would you mind telling us a little about yourself, Mrs Price? All we know is that you're a widow and Darren was your only child. And you work for yourself as an accountant.'

The woman was clearly surprised by the question, and she took a few seconds to reply.

'There's not much else I can tell you. My husband died from a heart attack four years ago, and after that it was just me and Darren. Sure, my boy had his problems, but we were always close and after he got married he and his wife stayed here in Kendal. Yes, he had an issue with gambling and got into debt, but he swore to me that he did not steal money from that charity shop, and I believed him. His wife, Samantha, didn't, though, and after he got fired and then appeared in court, she gave up on him and left, which broke his heart.'

'Why did he move to Blackpool?' Foley asked.

She unfolded her arms and started playing with the lobe of her left ear. 'One of his old mates lives there and runs a small factory. He offered Darren a job. Although I missed him, I hoped he'd get his life back on track. But he didn't. Instead, he became more depressed and eventually it got too much for him, and that's when he …'

She stopped talking and tears filled her eyes.

'I can appreciate how difficult it must have been for you,' James said and felt a genuine blast of sympathy for her.

She shook her head. 'I very much doubt that. Losing both him and his dad has made me wonder if there's any point in carrying on. My life is shit and that's why I was actually glad to hear that Carver had been murdered. My son would be alive if it wasn't for him and the lying bastards who worked with Darren in the charity shop.'

'But you're saying you didn't hate the man enough to want to kill him?' James said.

She swiped the back of her hand across her eyes. 'I don't have what it takes to murder someone, detective.'

'So, when was the last time you saw Mr Carver?'

She answered without hesitation. 'It was actually on Christmas Eve and must have been shortly before he was killed. I went to the Queen's Castle pub here in town and was shocked to see him there.'

James and Foley traded glances as neither of them had expected her to mention it before they did.

'Did you confront him again?' James asked her.

Another shake of the head. 'I was tempted to, but after I sat down with a glass of wine, I realised that there'd be no point, that it wouldn't change anything. So, I quickly finished my drink and left. I'm sure he didn't even see me there.'

'Is the Queen's Castle a pub you regularly go to?' Foley asked.

'No, it isn't. I don't normally visit pubs, but it was where I first met my husband all those years ago, before it was taken over and done up. And since this was the first Christmas without both him and Darren, I decided to pop along there to reminisce.'

'Where did you go after you left the pub?' James said.

'It was snowing so I came straight home. And if you don't believe me, you can ask my neighbour, Donna, who is also a widow. After I arrived home, I opened a bottle of wine and invited her to come over and share it with me. We both got sloshed watching crap on the telly. You can speak to her now if you want to. She lives in the house on the left, and I know she's there because I heard her come back from the shops about an hour ago.'

James had to push down his disappointment that another potential suspect appeared to have fallen by the wayside.

'What you've told us is really helpful, Mrs Price,' he said. 'We will talk to your neighbour when we leave here and I'm sure we won't have to disturb you again. But before we go, can you think back to Christmas Eve in the pub? Do you recall seeing anyone acting suspiciously?'

'What do you mean?'

'Well, for instance, did you notice if any of the other customers were paying particular attention to Mr Carver?'

She aimed unblinking eyes at James as she thought about it. 'I'm afraid I didn't. The only bloke I thought was acting a bit odd was the one who picked me up outside. He was weird and even a little scary.'

James creased his brow. 'Can you explain what you mean by picked you up?'

'I'm sorry, I should have said he helped me up. You see, my head was all over the place after seeing Carver in the pub, and I wasn't paying attention to where I was going – plus, a light snow was falling. After crossing the road, I tripped over the kerb. The bloke was standing a couple of feet away and he took my arm and helped me get up.'

'Can you describe him for us?'

'No. That's why he was weird. He was wearing a hooded jacket and one of those Covid masks, so I didn't see his face. He did speak, though, to ask if I was all right. That's how I know it was a man.'

'Did you get any sense of how old he was or if he had an accent?'

'No idea about his age and there was no accent. At least I don't think there was.'

'What happened next?' James asked.

A shrug. 'I thanked him and walked away. When I looked back, he was still standing there, but I noticed that he was leaning against a tree and staring across the road at the pub.' A thought struck her then and her mouth dropped open. 'Oh, blimey. Do you think he might have been waiting for Carver to come out? And that he could be the person who killed him?'

James felt his breathing stall and it was left to Foley to tell Mrs Price that it was a line of inquiry they would follow up.

Foley then took out her notebook and added, 'But can you describe this man in a little more detail, Mrs Price? What kind of coat was he wearing, for instance, and what colour was it?'

CHAPTER FIFTY-FIVE

'He was wearing a hooded puffer jacket that stood out because it was black across the chest, shoulders, and arms, and red around the waist,' Imogen Price said.

Foley took out her phone and typed *black and red puffer jackets* into Google. Within seconds dozens of them were appearing on the screen. They were of varying designs and all quite eye-catching.

Foley handed Price the phone and asked her to let them know if the coat the man had on was among them.

'It was quite similar to that one,' Price said after about thirty seconds, indicating a coat that was being sold online for fifty pounds. 'The mask he was wearing was black. That was why I thought he looked a bit scary as well as weird,' she said.

James was well aware that many people still wore face masks to lower the risk of viral transmission following Covid, but his work had shown him many times that some also wore them to conceal their identities both before and after committing a crime. He'd seen for himself how they could create a sinister impression, especially if the wearer also had a hood up. Finding out who the man was would go to the top of their to-do list.

They asked a few more questions before James checked his watch and decided it was time to go. But just as he and Foley stood up, the doorbell rang.

As Price stepped quickly out of the room, they followed her into the hallway where she opened the door to a short, elderly woman with grey hair and a round face.

'Hi, Imogen,' the woman said. 'I saw the police car parked outside and it got me worried. I've come to check that you're okay.'

The woman turned out to be Donna, the next-door neighbour whom Price had mentioned, and after Price swiftly explained what was going on, James asked Donna about Christmas Eve. Donna confirmed Price's story about the pair of them sharing a bottle of wine while watching the television, and said they were together until about eleven o'clock.

It was enough to convince both James and Foley that Imogen Price should no longer be considered a suspect.

'But at least we can replace her with another suspect,' James said once they were back in the patrol car. 'The mystery man in the mask.'

They arrived back at the office at one o'clock. Some of the detectives were out to lunch so James asked Foley to spread the word that he would hold another briefing at two. It gave him time to grab a coffee and sandwich, check his inbox, and prepare an agenda. He also took the opportunity to call Annie.

She told him that she and the kids were at Janet's house, and he could hear children's laughter in the background.

'There's no need to keep checking on me,' she said. 'I'm fine and I'd rather you stayed focused on the job. Is there anything new you can tell me?'

'Not yet, love, but I won't be late, and we can have a chat.'

When the briefing eventually began James spent the first minute telling the team about their visit to Imogen Price's home.

'Caroline and I are pretty certain that she told us the truth,' he said. 'She has what appears to be a foolproof alibi for when Gordon was murdered, and we don't believe she made up the story of the man in the mask. So, we have to put our all into finding the guy. He was clearly acting suspiciously, which means he may well have known that Gordon was in the pub at that time and was waiting for him to come out. The question is, did he then follow him to the path and attack him? Unfortunately, the CCTV camera that's facing the pub and showed Imogen Price leaving there doesn't cover the opposite side of the road.'

Foley had arranged for the photo of the puffer jacket Price had pointed out to be uploaded to the system. As it appeared on the monitors, James said, 'We need to go back over all the CCTV we've recovered to see if we can spot the jacket or one that's similar. I'm sure it wasn't in Shane O'Brien's wardrobe when I checked it, but we'd better have another look. We should also find out if any of our other suspects own one like it. That's Daniel Porter and Elliott Stone. We'll need to apply for warrants to search their homes.'

James invited the team to tell him what progress they'd been making, but the feedback was disappointing. Officers were still searching the streets of Kendal for Gordon's phone and the murder weapon, and there were no other leads to get them excited.

That was until three o'clock when a call came through from Manchester Police to inform them that Toby McGrath, the man accused of attacking Shane O'Brien, had handed himself in.

CHAPTER FIFTY-SIX

Toby McGrath was not alone when he handed himself in. He was accompanied by his lawyer, a woman named Alison Tudor.

Arrangements were quickly made to transport McGrath from Greater Manchester Police HQ to Kendal, though Miss Tudor was going to have to make her own way. The journey would take them about ninety minutes, giving James some time to prepare for a formal interview.

He began by asking DI Stevens to remind him and the team what they knew about the guy.

Pointing to McGrath's photo on the evidence board, Stevens said, 'We know he was one of the three men on O'Brien's revenge list. And it's alleged that after he found out about it, he went after O'Brien and clobbered him with a club hammer, leaving him for dead.

'We also know that the pair used to be part of the same county lines drug gang operating here in Cumbria. O'Brien was the more senior figure and when money went missing from the gang's coffers five years ago, he blamed McGrath and turfed him out.

McGrath moved to Manchester and a year later got his own back by providing the Organised Crime Unit with info that helped get O'Brien sent down.

'McGrath is thirty-six years old and single, and he heads up one of the many organised crime mobs in Manchester, dealing primarily in drugs and people trafficking. Since setting up there, he's managed to stay one step ahead of the law.

'We also know that he's a vicious bastard who likes to carry a club hammer around with him,' Stevens concluded. 'When he was based in Penrith we managed to put him away twice – he got two years for a violent assault and six months for threatening behaviour.'

'McGrath isn't suspected of killing Gordon Carver,' James pressed home the point, 'but depending on what he tells us, we might soon be charging him with attempting to murder his old mate, Shane O'Brien.'

It was coming up to 5 p.m. when McGrath and his lawyer were shown into the interview room where James and Stevens were waiting.

The crime boss was wearing tight jeans and a scruffy black hoodie. He was a tall, heavy-set man with a broken nose and eyes that were little more than slits.

His lawyer, Alison Tudor, was half his size and smartly dressed in a black overcoat and polo sweater. She looked to be in her mid-thirties, and her oval face was framed by soft, dark hair.

Once they were seated, James introduced himself and Stevens and stated the purpose of the interview before making them aware that it would be recorded. After reading McGrath his rights, he said, 'I'll begin by telling you that I spoke to Shane O'Brien soon after he regained consciousness following the attack on him. He claimed it was you who did it, Mr McGrath, and that the weapon you used was a club hammer.'

McGrath took a deep breath before blowing out his cheeks. 'It's true, I did hit him, but it was in self-defence. The bastard punched me first and we got into a fight. I pulled out the hammer when he had me up against the wall and was yelling that he was going to kill me. I feared that if I didn't lash out then he would do it.'

James gave him a sceptical look. 'That's not how he described to us what happened. He told us that you punched him in the face soon after you arrived at his father's house, and before he could regain his balance, you struck him with the hammer.'

McGrath hissed a curse as his eyes lit up with a sudden fury.

'Well, what would you expect him to say?' he snapped. 'He wants me to take the blame for something that he brought on himself and I'm not going to let him.'

His lawyer reached over and gave his arm a squeeze. 'Just pause it there, Toby, and let me pass on to the officers your version of the events that have led to you being here today.'

She spoke in a clear, confident voice, and James wondered if she was the go-to lawyer for many of the reprobates in Manchester.

'Like everyone else, my client was surprised to learn that Shane O'Brien had been released from prison early,' she said. 'He'd been made aware weeks before that O'Brien was planning to seek revenge against him when he got out, along with several other men. He therefore thought long and hard about whether or not he should go and confront the man. He eventually decided to do so on Christmas Day because he'd spent the previous night staying with a friend in Carlisle, and he'd managed to find out from a contact in the police that O'Brien was staying with his father in Milnthorpe.

'He did not intend to harm him. He wanted him to know that he'd been told about the revenge list he'd drawn up, and to warn him that he would regret it if he came after him. However, O'Brien wasn't prepared to listen, and things quickly got out of hand. My client has admitted that he hit O'Brien with the hammer in order to protect himself, but he vehemently denies that he wanted to kill him.'

McGrath interrupted her at this point, saying, 'If I'd gone there to top him, I would have taken along a gun or knife instead of the hammer. When he fell to the floor his body went still and it seemed he'd stopped breathing, so I panicked and made off. I learned later on that night that he was still alive, and I knew he'd land me in it. So, I dropped off the radar to think it through, and then this morning decided that I had no choice but to hand myself in and tell my side of the story.'

James tightened his lips and felt his heartbeat quicken in his chest. He'd been here before: two people involved in a violent brawl giving very different accounts of what had happened. In this case they were both equally credible, and without any eyewitnesses, it was going to be difficult to get to the truth.

'My client is well aware that he made a huge mistake by confronting Shane O'Brien on Christmas Day,' Tudor said. 'And that he made things worse for himself by not going straight to the police when he thought he'd killed him.'

James worked his jaw in circles for a few moments as he thought about what he'd been told and then said to McGrath, 'When you turned up at his dad's house, were you surprised that he let you in?'

He nodded. 'I was, to be honest, but I'm sure he was more surprised to see me. When I said I wanted to speak to him he just waved me inside and I sensed it was because he was curious to know what I was going to say.'

'So, was there much of a conversation before things kicked off?'

'Not much. I followed him into the living room and as soon as we got there he asked me what I wanted. I told him I'd heard about his list and that I was on it, and he claimed he didn't know what I was talking about. He reckoned it was cobblers and when I said I didn't believe him he started shouting and screaming, just like he did when we used to work together. It set me off and I told him that I was a different man to the one I used to be and that I wasn't intimidated by him like I was back then. It sparked a total fucking slanging match and then he rushed forward and punched me in the face. That's when he said he was going to kill me for grassing him up to the police.'

'Did he tell you who else he planned to seek revenge against?'

'No, but that was one of the questions I was going to ask him. I didn't get the chance, though.'

The longer the interview went on, the more agitated McGrath became, especially when he was forced to deny that he was head of a crime gang in Manchester.

Before winding things up, James explained that he would be held in custody while charges were considered. McGrath wasn't happy, but on the advice of his lawyer he didn't bother to kick up a fuss.

CHAPTER FIFTY-SEVEN

DI Stevens escorted McGrath to the custody suite while James saw the lawyer out of the building. He then returned to the office where the team were still hard at it.

Before updating them, he went and stood in front of the evidence boards, arms crossed, absorbing the details.

The only significant addition was the photograph of the puffer jacket worn by the mystery man who'd been standing outside the Queen's Castle pub on Christmas Eve while Gordon met with Mad Dog Mike inside. But that wasn't enough to encourage James to believe they were any closer to solving the murder. There was still so much they didn't know. So many unanswered questions. It was becoming quite soul destroying, and causing the pressure to build on him and the team.

He started the final briefing of the day once Stevens returned from the custody suite, and the team listened silently, their faces pale and attentive.

'I'm now satisfied that what happened between McGrath and O'Brien was not directly linked to Gordon's murder,' he said, 'as it seems that McGrath didn't even know that Gordon was also on O'Brien's revenge list. So, my thinking is that we consider charging both of them with aggravated assault. At the same time, O'Brien remains a suspect in Gordon's murder even though we now know that he was in Penrith when it took place because we can't discount the possibility that he got someone to carry it out on his behalf – the man in the puffer jacket perhaps. After all, the guy no doubt has more than a few underworld contacts.'

'Phil, I want you to take the lead on the assault charges. That way the rest of us can stay focused on the murder. I suggest you interview O'Brien again and make him aware of what McGrath told us. I'd also like you to get him to go back over his Christmas Eve alibi. See if there's any way we can pull it apart.'

James went on to flag up where they were with the various lines of inquiry and once again expressed his disappointment that they weren't making enough progress.

He then handed out various tasks to those who'd be working through the night, including looking back through all the CCTV footage to see if they could spot someone wearing the black and red puffer jacket.

After wrapping up the briefing he put in a call to Superintendent Tanner to update him.

'Pressure from the media is continuing to mount,' the Super said. 'The Chief Constable wants us to stage another press conference and this time I'd like you to front it with me.'

'When will it be, boss?' James asked.

'It could be as early as tomorrow, and we'll do it in Kendal. I'll confirm it one way or another first thing in the morning.'

Before pocketing his phone, James checked the time and was surprised to see that it was almost seven.

Where had the bloody time gone?

He tapped out a text to Annie telling her that he would soon be making his way home and was looking forward to seeing her. She responded and let him know that she had made some soup for him.

But just as he was slipping on his jacket, one of the support officers appeared in his office doorway to inform him that Gordon Carver's parents had turned up at the station and they wanted to speak to him.

CHAPTER FIFTY-EIGHT

Ruth and Nigel Carver were brought to the interview room where James was waiting. They both looked extremely tired and wore pained expressions.

He invited them to sit down across the table from him and asked if they wanted anything to drink.

'No thank you, Detective Walker,' Nigel replied. 'We'll have one when we get home. We've been to Gordon's house to collect some of his things and thought we'd drop by to see what's happening with the investigation. Have you any idea yet who killed our son? You said you'd keep us informed, but you haven't, and we're confused by all the lines being put out by the media.'

The man stared at James, his eyes grey and watery above colourless cheeks.

'I'm really sorry that you haven't been updated,' James said meaningfully, 'but much of what's been taking place we haven't been able to share with you or anyone else. Unfortunately, we still don't know who carried out the murder, but that doesn't mean we're not making headway.'

'What about those people you've questioned whose names have been mentioned in the news reports? There's that Daniel Porter, the young man who some people believe killed his missing ex-girlfriend. And that criminal, Shane O'Brien, who was attacked after he came out of prison.'

James nodded. 'Yes, they have been spoken to, Mr Carver, because they'd previously made it known that they were not happy with what Gordon wrote about them in the *Gazette*. However, they both deny being responsible and there's no evidence to suggest that they were.'

'But surely you can't just leave it at that,' Ruth spoke up, her voice thin and wheezy. 'They might well be lying to you.'

'That's why they remain persons of interest, Mrs Carver, along with other individuals we've spoken to,' James said. 'I can assure you that we don't just believe whatever we're told. A great deal of time and effort goes into determining if something is true or not.'

'Then can you at least tell us if Gordon was killed because of his work as a journalist?' she responded. 'Or could the motive have been more personal?'

'At this stage it's impossible to know for sure. And as I explained to you before, it could even be that he was the victim of a random attack, carried out by someone who didn't know him. Someone who just happened to be there on the path as he was walking home.'

The couple glanced at each other before Nigel spoke.

'There's something else we want to ask you, detective,' he said. 'It's about the woman who spent time with our son at his house on Christmas Eve, just hours before he was killed. Will you tell us who she is? You must know by now.'

James experienced a flutter of unease. He wasn't sure that now was the right time to let them know what Gordon had been up to with his boss.

He was still trying to work out how best to respond, when Nigel followed up with, 'Perhaps if I rephrase the question, you'll find it easier to answer. Was the woman Nadine Stone, the editor of the *Cumbria Gazette*?'

James coughed into his fist before replying, 'Actually it was. I was planning to tell you after I'd discussed it with her.'

'Why hold back? Was it because they were having an affair?'

'No, Mr Carver. It was because some of what we discussed was in confidence. She did confirm that it was her who was at the house on Christmas Eve. She went there to discuss a story he was working on about the missing estate agent, Chloe Walsh.'

'But the neighbour, Erika Lynch, saw them sharing a kiss when she left.'

'Mrs Stone said it was just a friendly Christmas kiss and a hug.'

'But we spoke to Erika just over an hour ago, before we went into Gordon's house,' Nigel continued. 'We wanted to tell her and her husband that we were grateful they informed the police after they found his body in the wood. And when we asked about the woman Mrs Lynch saw leaving the house, she insisted that it was a long, passionate kiss. That suggests to us that the woman was his secret lover as well as his boss, even though she's married.'

James felt his skin prickle. 'That's something you will have to discuss with Mrs Stone.'

'We intend to. But I don't understand why you're being evasive, Detective Walker. We have a right to know what our son was up to before he died. And if he was involved with that woman in a personal capacity then perhaps her husband found out, which would surely mean he may well have decided to end it by taking Gordon's life.'

James issued a sigh as he pinched the bridge of his nose. The only way to avoid making a mess of things was to be honest.

'Very well,' he said. 'I'll tell you what Mrs Stone told me. But I would ask you to please keep it to yourself because it's not what she told her husband and their son and daughter.'

'But did he know about it?' Nigel asked. 'And if so, is he a suspect?'

'He knows now that his wife went to Gordon's house on Christmas Eve, but only because we confronted her with it. She told him it was to discuss work and assured him that they were not having an affair. But she then told me in confidence that they were, and it had been going on for several months. It seems she was very fond of your son and he of her. And for your information, we did question Mr Stone and he's accounted for his movements at the time Gordon was attacked.'

'Then it'll be okay for us to talk to Nadine and not him?' Ruth said.

'That's entirely up to you, Mrs Carver. But I'd appreciate it if you would leave it a few days at least.'

She shrugged. 'We don't have a problem with that. And we don't have a problem with her since it seems she made Gordon happy.'

James left it a beat before asking, 'How did you find out that the woman who visited your son was Nadine Stone?'

It was Nigel who answered. 'When she and her husband came to see us in Burneside on Saturday she was wearing a beige overcoat and dark red ankle boots,' he said. 'We thought nothing of it until Erika told us just now that the woman who went to Gordon's house also wore a beige overcoat and red boots. We drew the obvious conclusion and your reaction to my question confirmed our suspicions.'

*

After Mr and Mrs Carver left the station, James reflected on his decision to confirm that their son had been having an affair with Nadine Stone.

He'd been put on the spot and felt okay that he had chosen not to withhold the information or to lie to them. He agreed with Nigel that the couple had a right to know, and he doubted that it would remain a secret for long anyway. He was sure that Elliott Stone didn't believe what his wife had told him, and it could conceivably lead to the – potentially public, given Nadine's job – break-up of their marriage.

When James returned to his office, he thought about calling Nadine to let her know that Gordon's parents were now aware of her relationship with their son. But it was already half seven and so he decided it could wait. He wanted to get home to spend some time with Annie, and since the weather was being so unpredictable, he had no idea how long it would take him.

When he exited the station, the cold wind grabbed at his clothes and made him shiver. But once he was in his car and en route to Kirkby Abbey, the heater soon warmed him up.

It didn't make him feel any less uncomfortable, though, and not only because the case was playing on his mind. He was also struggling to deal with the devastating prospect that his wife might soon be given some life-changing bad news.

CHAPTER FIFTY-NINE
ANNIE

It had just turned 8.15 and Annie decided to pour herself a glass of wine. She felt she needed it.

The kids were in bed and the soup was ready to heat up if James wanted it when he arrived home.

She carried her glass into the living room and dropped onto the sofa. The day had passed slowly, but at least she'd been kept busy, and during the three hours they spent at Janet's house she'd managed to stop thinking about the threat she was facing.

But now it was back in her head and with it came another blast of anxiety. She hated feeling scared. Feeling weak. Not being in control of her own destiny.

She found no comfort in the fact that some ninety out of a hundred women in the UK are apparently alive five years after a breast cancer diagnosis because once the disease reached stage four the survival rate was much lower, and she had no idea as yet if that was what she was facing.

As she sipped her wine she felt the heat rise in her cheeks, but she was determined not to let herself cry and to put on a brave face for her husband's sake. That was despite the fact that something she'd seen on Facebook in the last hour had plunged her even deeper into that painful pit of despair. It was a post from a long-time friend informing her followers that her mother had lost her long battle against breast cancer and had died in hospital that very morning.

The news had caused the air to crash out of Annie's lungs and a wave of emotion had reduced her to tears. It came as a stark reminder that, despite the encouraging statistics, the New Year that was about to begin might well prove to be her last.

Dark thoughts were still wearing her down ten minutes later when she heard James's car pull onto the driveway. She put down her empty glass and went to answer the front door.

As soon as he entered the house, he cracked a warm smile and pulled her tight against him, kissing her head.

'I was hoping to get away sooner, but there was too much going on,' he said. 'What have you been doing?'

'Enjoying a glass of wine,' she replied as she pulled her own mouth into a smile. 'Would you like me to pour you one so that you can have it with the soup?'

'That's the best offer I've had all day,' he said.

She could tell straight away that he was stressed as his face was ashen and cords stretched the skin of his neck.

Instead of telling her what a tough day he'd had, he just wanted to know how she was coping and if the kids were okay. She told him what he wanted to hear as there was no way she was going to mention the Facebook post she'd seen. That was something she was going to keep to herself.

It wasn't until he'd finished the soup and was settled on the sofa with a glass of whisky that he spoke about the Gordon Carver murder investigation.

It made her realise why he appeared so tense. It seemed the team were not making significant progress, and it gave James even more to worry about.

'You'll get there in the end,' she told him. 'You always do.'

'I hope so,' he replied. 'We could both do with something happening that will raise our spirits.'

They talked and drank for another hour, and she told him that she'd made Janet and his sister Fiona aware that he knew about her lump. But though she did her best to assure him that she was now feeling more positive, it was obvious from his expression that he didn't believe her. And when he pulled her into his arms again, she had to gulp down a sob that threatened to engulf her.

CHAPTER SIXTY

It was another uncomfortable night during which they both struggled to sleep. At six on Tuesday morning James was ready to get up, and though he tried to persuade Annie to stay in bed, she said didn't see the point of lying there awake.

While he shaved, showered, and got dressed, she went into the kitchen and made them coffee and some toast.

When he joined her at the breakfast bar he felt another wave of guilt flush through him. He had a strong urge to call in sick so that he could spend the day with her, but he knew that she wouldn't let him. She didn't want him to know how worried she was about the lump and at the same time she desperately wanted him to find out who killed Gordon Carver.

'What have you got planned for today then?' he asked her as he munched on his toast.

She pushed back her shoulders and drew a breath. 'Tomorrow is New Year's Eve, so I need to do some shopping this morning,' she replied. 'We're short of quite a few things, including milk, tea bags, and fresh meat.'

'What about this afternoon?'

'I've already arranged with Janet to take the kids for a walk so long as the weather stays relatively calm.'

'I'm sorry I won't be able to join you.'

Annie managed a smile. 'It's not your fault and you really need to stop blaming yourself.'

James knew she was right, but he also knew that it wasn't going to be easy. Once again, the job was making it hard for him to be there for his wife and his kids, and he couldn't help feeling bad about that.

Reaching across the breakfast bar, he took her hand and said, 'Hopefully, we can do something together this coming weekend. Or maybe on New Year's Day.'

She smiled again. 'If we can that will be great, but if we can't then we'll just have to grin and bear it.'

Weather-wise, it was a fairly calm start to the day, but a fresh layer of snow had fallen overnight so James had to scrape it from the car windows.

He then drove with extra care to Kendal to avoid losing control on the ice patches that covered large sections of road.

His senses remained on high alert throughout the journey, but that did not stop thoughts about the case from crowding his mind. And he wasn't looking forward to fronting a press conference alongside the Super. It wouldn't be so bad if they had some encouraging news to impart, but they didn't, at least not as far as he was aware. He hadn't called the office to check, but he was sure he'd have been contacted if there had been a development overnight.

It was 8 a.m. when he reached headquarters and by then his brain was already aching with the effort of thinking.

Half the team had arrived before him and were prepping for the morning briefing. Before it began, he was given a quick update by the overnight crew and took a call from Tanner who told him that the press conference wouldn't be taking place until late this afternoon.

'I'll make my way to Kendal just before lunch,' the Super said, 'but let me know if anything new comes in before then.'

As soon as the rest of the team turned up James cracked on with the briefing. He began by letting everyone know about the presser and said, 'I don't want to give the journos the impression that we're not making any progress, so let's discuss how to move things forward today. We'll start with where we are with the various lines of inquiry.'

The distinctive puffer jacket worn by the man who was standing outside the Queen's Castle pub when Gordon Carver was there on Christmas Eve was the first item on the agenda, but disappointingly nothing like it had turned up on the latest batch of CCTV footage that had been recovered. The warrants to search the homes of their suspects also hadn't yet been signed off.

'This is a promising lead, and we'll continue to pursue it,' James said. 'It gives us another excuse to question Daniel Porter and Elliott Stone. We need to know if either of them possess a jacket like it.'

As the discussion continued it quickly became clear that his detectives hadn't come up with any fresh ideas. No new suspects had emerged, and they were therefore struggling to know where to go next with the case.

It was a situation that James was all too familiar with, and as always it filled him with a sense of dread.

But after an hour of knocking their heads together they received some news that dramatically boosted morale.

A man had turned up at headquarters to hand in a mobile phone that he'd found in his front garden, which was close to the murder scene.

'If it turns out to be Gordon's phone then it could be the breakthrough we've been waiting for,' James said.

CHAPTER SIXTY-ONE

James felt a rush of adrenaline as he hurried to reception to speak to the man who had found the mobile phone.

He'd given his name as Craig Anderson and had already been shown to a side room and informed that a detective would be with him shortly.

The desk sergeant told James that Mr Anderson had arrived by himself and had come straight from his home on Harvard Street, which was only a couple of hundred yards from where Gordon was murdered.

The sergeant then held up a transparent freezer bag containing the mobile phone and said, 'He assured me that he hasn't touched it with his bare hands. He put on gloves to pick it up and place it in the freezer bag.'

'Forensics have been alerted, but I don't want them to take it away until I've spoken to them,' James responded. 'First, I need to have a quick word with Mr Anderson.'

The man was standing with his arms behind his back while staring out of the window when James entered the room.

'Hello, Mr Anderson,' he said. 'I'm Detective Chief Inspector Walker.'

As the man turned James saw that he was tall and middle-aged, with cropped hair and a pencil moustache.

'Have you found out who the phone belongs to?' he asked.

James shook his head. 'Not yet, but thanks so much for bringing it to us. I know you've spoken to the duty sergeant, but before you go can you please tell me exactly how and where you found it?'

'Of course,' he replied. 'I live on Harvard Street with my wife, and like everyone else in town we were shocked by what happened to that reporter. We knew that the police have been searching for his mobile phone along with the weapon that was used to kill him – in fact, we've seen your officers looking into bins.'

'But I gather you found it in your front garden.'

Anderson nodded. 'That's right. It was this morning as I stepped out to take the dog for a walk. Before I closed the door behind me, I realised that I'd forgotten to grab the poop bags. I dropped the lead and let her run into the front garden while I went back inside to get them. When I came out, I saw that, as per usual, she'd started rummaging in the shrubs that are up against the inside of the fence. But this time the lead had got tangled on a bush and I had to go and sort it. That's when I spotted the phone on the ground. The bush had shielded it from the snow, and it occurred to me that it might have been the phone you lot were looking for. So, I went back into the house, got my gloves on, and put it into the freezer bag before bringing it here.'

James thanked him again and made a note of his address and phone number before seeing him out of the building.

When he returned to the front desk, one of the digital forensics officers was waiting for him while holding the bag containing the phone.

James explained, 'It's possible, if not likely, that it belonged to Gordon Carver. I need you to gain access to it to confirm it for us. And if there are any prints on it, I want them lifted and checked against the database.'

Back in the office, James filled the team in on what Craig Anderson had told him.

'The first thing we need to do is find out if there are any CCTV cameras in and around Harvard Street,' he said. 'If not, then check the properties for door cams. And work out the various routes the killer might have taken to get there from the murder scene.'

James couldn't stop thinking about the mobile phone, which he hoped would provide the investigation with a much-needed boost. Thankfully he only had to wait an hour for the tech team to get back to him. They had managed to access the phone and confirm that it had belonged to Gordon.

James passed this onto the team and said, 'His prints are on the screen and case, but forensics also lifted several from another individual who is not on the database. That person could well be our killer. We know that the prints could not have been left there by Shane O'Brien and Michael Frost because they both have criminal records and their prints are on file, so we need to get prints from the other two suspects – Daniel Porter and Elliott Stone. We can do it when we question them about the puffer jacket.'

'I suggest we also check to see if the prints belong to Nadine Stone,' DC Sharma said. 'It could well be that she handled the phone when she spent time with Gordon on Christmas Eve.'

'That's a good call, Ahmed,' James said.

He quickly decided that he and DS Abbott would go first to Porter's house and then to Stone's. He didn't want to miss out on seeing their reaction to the discovery of the phone and the presence of the mystery man outside the pub, and the opportunity to question them some more.

'We'll go as soon as the warrants come through,' he said. 'And while we wait, I'll update the Super.'

Tanner was already on his way to Kendal for the press conference when he answered James's call.

'There's been an encouraging development, boss,' James said. 'Gordon's mobile phone has been found in a front garden close to the murder scene. I'm willing to bet that it was dropped there by the killer.'

James told him how Craig Anderson had come across it, and that several unidentified fingerprints had already been lifted from the screen and case.

'We know they don't belong to two of our suspects because their prints are on the database and there's no match,' he said. 'But I'll soon be dropping in on the other two to check them out.'

'Does that mean you won't be free to attend the press briefing with me?' Tanner said. 'It's now scheduled for four o'clock.'

'Not necessarily. It's only just gone eleven and it depends on what we turn up.'

'Well, get back to me with whatever you've got as soon as you can.'

Ten minutes later the team learned that there were no CCTV cameras on or around Harvard Street. So, officers were dispatched to find out if the person who discarded the phone had been captured on any door cams.

Fifteen minutes after that came the news that the warrants to search the homes of their suspects had been granted.

James felt his heart take a leap as he and Abbott made their way to the patrol car that would take them to Daniel Porter's place on the Sedbergh Road.

CHAPTER SIXTY-TWO

Before heading to Porter's house James had arranged for a team of uniforms to follow him and DS Abbott in a van. From experience, he knew that it was usually wise to execute a warrant mob-handed.

Fortunately, they didn't have far to go as Porter lived only about five miles from the town.

'What do we do if he's not in, guv?' Abbott asked as soon as they set off.

'We'll contact him by phone,' James said. 'Get him to return home. If he refuses to or we can't contact him then we force our way in. There'll be plenty of prints for us to lift.'

Abbott was about to ask another question, but stopped when James's phone rang. He pulled it from his pocket and answered it without checking who was calling.

'Hello there, James,' his sister Fiona said. 'Are you free for a chat about Annie?'

He felt a flicker of unease because he didn't want to have that conversation while sitting next to Abbott.

'I can't talk now, Fi,' he said. 'I'm with some colleagues and on our way to a job. I'll call you later if that's okay.'

'Of course. I just wanted to touch base and let you know that I'm thinking about you both.'

'I appreciate it. You take care.'

'You too.'

As he slipped the phone back into his pocket, Abbott said, 'I'm assuming that was your sister, guv. How is she? I've been meaning to ask.'

James cleared his throat. 'She's doing well, thanks. I didn't get a chance to talk to her over Christmas, and she wants to catch up.'

'Bless her. Well, when you speak to her again, please pass on my regards.'

'I certainly will.'

Guilt tugged at his chest as he turned to look out of the window. He was eager to talk to his sister about Annie, but it was going to have to wait until he was by himself. No way could he risk letting his colleagues know about his wife's potential condition. It wouldn't be fair on her and it would be yet another distraction for both him and the team if they found out.

James managed to snap his attention back to the case before they arrived at Daniel Porter's house, and he was relieved to see the man's black Range Rover on the driveway when they got there.

Porter obviously saw them pull up because he opened the front door before James and Abbott reached it.

His gaze immediately flicked from the two detectives to the uniformed officers piling out of the van, and a spark of alarm distorted his features.

'What the fuck is this all about?' he shouted.

James whipped a document from his jacket pocket and held it

up. 'My colleagues and I have a warrant to search your property, Mr Porter. It's in relation to our investigation into the murder of journalist Gordon Carver.'

Parker just stood in the doorway, the hostility radiating off him.

'Well, there's no way I'm letting you in until I've consulted my lawyer,' he said. 'You can't just …'

'We can and we will force our way in without your permission,' James told him. 'So, I suggest you stand aside and let us get on with it.'

He met James's gaze and didn't flinch or look away. 'What the hell do you expect to find then? I've told you I didn't kill Carver. And there's nothing here that will link me to his murder.'

'We have to determine that for ourselves,' James responded. 'And fresh evidence has come to light that makes it necessary for us to take your fingerprints.'

Porter's eyes widened and his pupils dilated. But before he could say anything else, James signalled for the uniformed officers to push past him into the house. Porter blasted out a stream of expletives, but didn't try to stop them.

'It'll make sense for you to fully cooperate, Mr Porter,' James said. 'Once inside I'll explain in detail what exactly we're looking for and why we need to take your prints.'

Porter stared at James, his jaw pulsing, his face white with anger, but after several long seconds it finally hit him that he had no choice in the matter, and he stepped back into the hallway.

CHAPTER SIXTY-THREE

James and Abbott allowed Porter to lead them into the kitchen. At the same time, the uniforms began their search of the other rooms.

They'd been briefed to look out for a black and red puffer jacket and anything else that might link Porter to Gordon's murder.

Once in the kitchen, Porter stood with his back to the sink, shuffling from foot to foot, the tension visible in his expression.

'This is a clear fucking case of police harassment,' he seethed. 'And as soon as you're gone, I'll be making an official complaint.'

'That's your prerogative, Mr Porter,' James said as he removed his phone from his pocket. 'In the meantime, I need you to look at this.'

He brought up the photo of the puffer jacket and showed it to him.

'Can you tell me if you own a coat similar to this one?' he said.

Porter glanced at the screen through squinted eyes and shook his head.

'No, I don't. But if that's all you're looking for then why didn't you just ask me instead of invading my home?'

James ignored the question and pointed to Abbott. 'My colleague will now use a device to take your fingerprints. This is because Mr Carver's mobile phone has been found close to where he was murdered, and we believe it was discarded by his killer. Some unidentified prints have been lifted from it and we're therefore in the process of ruling out those people we've questioned.'

Porter raised his brow. 'I still don't understand why I'm a suspect. It doesn't make any sense.'

'It does to us,' James said. 'You threatened Mr Carver over something he was intending to write in the *Gazette*, and then you lied when you told us that you didn't leave here on Christmas Eve even though you drove into town.'

Abbott stepped forward then, clutching a small fingerprint scanner.

'This will be very quick,' she told Porter, 'and it won't take us long to then compare your prints with those found on the phone.'

James knew this was a critical moment. If Porter objected to providing his prints, then it would almost certainly be because he knew they would be a match. And that'd be enough to convince them that he was their killer.

But he didn't object, and James felt a twinge of disappointment.

It was a speedy process and while it was being carried out Porter kept looking towards the door, presumably waiting for one or more of the uniforms to appear.

Once the prints were taken, James asked him some more questions while Abbott carried out a quick search of the kitchen. However, she didn't find anything that would incriminate Porter, and neither did the uniforms who concluded their search half an hour later.

'Has every room been searched?' James asked the head of the team.

'Yes, guv. The garden, too.'

'What about the basement?'

'We didn't realise there was one.'

'There isn't,' Porter spoke up.

James raised his brow.

'But that's not true,' he said. 'I distinctly remember you inviting us to search it eight months ago when we were looking for Chloe Walsh.'

Porter's face changed as panic set in. 'You're mistaken. There's never been a basement. If there was, they would have found it.'

James felt the blood roar in his ears as he gave the order for the officers to search the house again, this time for a concealed entrance to the basement.

To Porter, he said, 'You're lying, and we'll soon prove it. So, I suggest you tell us where it is.'

Porter mumbled a curse and a look of feral rage appeared in his eyes.

'I'm not fucking lying,' he growled as he started walking towards the door.

'Where do you think you're going?' James asked him.

'Outside for a fag.'

James stepped forward to block his path. 'No way. You're staying here until we've—'

Porter lunged forward and pushed James with such force that he fell back against the wall.

'Get the fuck away from me,' he yelled as spit flew from his mouth.

In an instant Porter was seized by two of the uniforms. He put up a fierce but fruitless struggle before he was forced down onto a chair.

James stood in front of him and watched as the man's face crumbled and tears started falling from his eyes.

'What is it you don't want us to find?' James said. 'You might as well tell us because whatever it is we're going to find it.'

Porter didn't respond. Instead, he squeezed his eyes shut, dropped his head into his hands, and started crying like a baby.

CHAPTER SIXTY-FOUR

Porter's reaction was shocking, but it encouraged James to think that whatever secret the guy had been keeping was about to be uncovered.

He asked him again how to access the basement, but got no answer.

Turning to Abbott, he said, 'I didn't go down there myself when the place was searched before, and I can't recall where the entrance to it is, but I'm guessing it's hidden behind a fixture in the hallway or in the garage. Or perhaps under the stairs.'

James instructed the uniforms to continue holding Porter while he and Abbott left the kitchen to join the search.

James was aware that it wasn't uncommon these days for people to turn their basements into hidden gems for entertainment and relaxation. He'd seen basements that were used as wine cellars, game rooms, and even home theatres.

For many people, the idea of a concealed space created a sense of adventure and mystery. And for others it was somewhere to hide things, or even to hide themselves if they felt threatened.

Doors were usually hidden under floorboards and behind wardrobes, mirrors, and bookcases, and James didn't think it would take them long to find it.

And he was proved right when, after just fifteen minutes, an officer discovered a door behind a floor-to-ceiling shelving unit in the hallway. The door itself wasn't locked, and when pushed open it gave access to a staircase that led down into the basement.

James descended it along with two uniforms. At the bottom was another door, which had a key in the lock that they used to open it.

Beyond that was a small, narrow room with storage units along two walls. It wasn't until the light was switched on that they saw another door at the far end.

This one also had a key in the lock and when it was opened, James and the officers found themselves looking into a large open-plan kitchen/living room that was already lit up. There was a sofa, a TV, a table with two chairs, plus two closed doors leading off from the space.

As they stepped into it, James wondered why Porter had denied it existed and why the thought of them paying it a visit had caused him to have a meltdown.

But just seconds later he got the answer when one of the doors was pushed open and a young woman with shoulder-length blonde hair appeared.

She was clearly shocked to see them and a small, startled cry flew from her mouth.

At the same time every muscle and sinew in James's body froze.

'Oh, m-my lord,' he stuttered. 'You're Chloe. Chloe Walsh.'

She blinked rapidly, as if coming out of a trance, and gave a slight nod.

CHAPTER SIXTY-FIVE

James had experienced countless shocks during his career, but nothing compared to the sudden appearance of Chloe Walsh, the young woman who'd been missing for over eight months and was feared dead.

She looked thin and fragile beneath a baggy red jumper and black tracksuit bottoms.

James felt the blood stiffen in his veins as he stared at her across the room.

She stared back at him, her jaw slack, her eyes bulging in their sockets.

'Where is he?' she uttered, her voice weak. 'Does he know you're here?'

'If you mean Daniel Porter, then yes, he does know,' James replied. 'He's being held upstairs and you're safe.'

She sucked in a rasping breath before clapping a hand over her mouth.

'I'm Detective Chief Inspector Walker with Cumbria Police,' James added, as he stepped towards her. 'Would I be right to assume that your ex-boyfriend has held you down here against your will for many months?'

Her eyes moved between James and the uniformed officers before she responded with, 'Yes, he has.'

James experienced a blast of emotion; it felt like his heart was trying to punch its way out of his chest.

'Well, your ordeal is over now, Chloe,' he told her. 'And Porter will no longer pose a threat.'

She gave an anguished cry and burst into tears before rushing forward and throwing herself at James. He put his arms around her and pulled her against his chest.

As she sobbed into his shoulder, he gestured for the officers to check the other rooms.

'Are you okay health-wise?' he asked her. 'Do we need to get you to a hospital right away?'

'I'm fine,' she responded between sobs. 'Just tired, and desperate to get out of here.'

'I'll take you upstairs once we've got Porter out of the house. We can then get in touch with your parents to let them know that you're alive. They had no idea why you suddenly disappeared eight months ago, Chloe, and they feared the worst. We searched high and low, and my officers even came down here to the basement, but it was empty.'

She moved back from him and wiped her eyes with her sleeve.

'That's because he didn't bring me straight here after he grabbed me off the street,' she said. 'He took me to a cottage he rented near Penrith and locked me in a room for over a week. I was drugged and tied to a bed.'

'Has he harmed you in any way?'

'Not physically.'

James felt his stomach muscles contract.

'Well, I can assure you that he'll pay a heavy price for what he's done,' he said. 'Now, before we go upstairs, can you confirm that you've been alone down here?'

'I have, but Daniel spent time with me most days and nights. Sometimes he'd let me go and sit with him upstairs, and he even took me into the back garden to get some fresh air.'

'What's beyond those other doors?'

'A bedroom and a toilet with a shower. Daniel's parents converted the basement into a mini apartment for him before they both died. He brought me down here to see it when we were together.'

Just then the officers came out of the other rooms and gave James the thumbs up to indicate that they were both empty.

'I want you to go up and tell DC Abbott to come down here,' he told them. 'Then get forensics to send a team over right away.'

Chloe had closed her eyes and James could see that she was struggling to come to terms with what was happening. Her body was shaking and she was breathing heavily through her nose. He was anxious to get her out of the basement, but not before Porter was on his way to HQ.

'Is there anything you'd like to take with you?' he asked her.

After a couple of beats she nodded. 'I've got a few things. I can put them in a bag.'

'Then let's get it done,' he said.

He followed her into the bedroom where, in addition to a double bed and a wardrobe, there was also a running machine.

'Just take whatever you need right now,' he said. 'Anything you leave behind I'll arrange to be sent to you.'

She shook her head. 'That won't be necessary. When he brought me here all I had was my handbag and the clothes I was wearing the night he abducted me. The other stuff, including what I'm wearing, he bought for me since then and I don't want to take it with me.'

As she set about stuffing a few belongings into a plastic bag, DS Abbott walked into the room wearing an expression of incredulity.

'This is unbelievable,' she said. 'But it's also brilliant news.'

James introduced her to Chloe, who responded with a barely perceptible smile.

To Abbott, he said, 'We'll be coming up shortly so can you get Porter out of the house and take him to the station? Tell him he's going to face some serious charges. I'll then bring Chloe there and we can let her speak to her parents before I have a longer conversation with her. And pass on the news to Superintendent Tanner, who should be there by now.'

Having filled the bag with her few belongings, Chloe turned to James. He thought for a moment that she was going to break down again, but instead she drew a tremulous breath and said, 'What made you come to the house if you didn't know that I was here?'

After a brief hesitation, James decided that there was no point keeping it from her.

'Are you aware of what happened to journalist Gordon Carver, who I understand was an old friend of yours?'

She bit her bottom lip. 'Yes, I am. He was murdered on Christmas Eve. Daniel told me about it and then I saw it on the news. It really upset me. He was a good person, and we were at university together.'

'And do you also know that he believed that Porter was responsible for your disappearance? He was convinced that your ex-boyfriend murdered you and hid your body somewhere. And he made a point of telling others what he thought.'

She shook her head. 'No, I wasn't aware of that. Daniel took my phone away and he never mentioned it. In fact, he never talked about Gordon at all until Christmas Day, when his body was found.'

'Well, we discovered that Gordon was going to write another piece in the *Gazette* to mark your twenty-sixth birthday, and intended to make a point of mentioning your ex. Porter objected and made threats against Gordon just a week before the murder took place. Porter therefore became a suspect, and we came here to search for evidence.'

Her jaw went rigid and she stared at James with a look of confusion on her face.

'On the news they reported that Gordon was murdered in the evening,' she said. 'Is that true?'

James nodded. 'That's correct. We believe it was between about nine and ten. He was walking home after meeting someone in a town-centre pub.'

Chloe dragged in a long, loud breath. 'Then it couldn't have been Daniel who killed him. He was here on Christmas Eve. He went out in the afternoon to get some drinks and after he came back, he stayed with me until well after midnight. We watched television together and he made a point of giving me a set of books as a Christmas present before I went to sleep.'

CHAPTER SIXTY-SIX

James clenched his jaw and felt the bitter taste of disappointment. Chloe Walsh had just provided one of their prime suspects with what appeared to be a watertight alibi.

Because there was no way that Daniel Porter could have murdered Gordon Carver on Christmas Eve if he'd spent the entire evening with her. And James didn't doubt that she was telling the truth. Why would she lie to protect the man who had held her against her will for over eight months? And despite her horrendous ordeal she was clearly still of sound mind.

Even so, he asked her if she was sure about it and she insisted that she was.

'I want the bastard to go to prison, but not for something he didn't do,' she said. 'If he got blamed for it then whoever did kill Gordon would not face justice.'

She was right, of course, and James had to push his disappointment aside in order to deal with this new case that had suddenly been thrust upon him.

A case that was going to stir up a tsunami of public interest and force Gordon Carver's murder into the background.

Porter had been careful to ensure that everything linked to Chloe had been kept in the basement, including her coat and shoes.

Once she had put them on, she said to James, 'I'm ready.'

Her voice was husky with emotion and her face swollen from crying. But it occurred to James that she looked remarkably well considering what she'd been through.

She was thinner than she was in all the photos he'd seen, but she wasn't emaciated, so Porter must have ensured that she was regularly fed. However, her face was pale and taut, and there was a fearful glint in her eyes.

James felt a lump rise in his throat when he thought how lucky she was to have been discovered. He was well aware of the shocking cases of other women who had been held captive in basements for much longer, including that of Elisabeth Fritzl, who was locked away by her own father for some twenty-four years.

He held out his hand for Chloe and she took it.

'Porter will no longer be in the house, so you won't have to see him,' he told her. 'I'll be taking you to our headquarters and we'll contact your parents from there. You'll need to brace yourself, Chloe. Everyone is going to be so excited to see you.'

A bunch of uniformed officers were waiting in the hallway when she emerged from the basement. The atmosphere was electric and James could feel the sparks.

'So glad you're okay,' one of the officers called out.

'We're all rooting for you, Chloe,' another remarked.

Chloe was clearly overwhelmed, but she managed to treat them to a hesitant smile as James led her out of the house and into a waiting patrol car.

CHAPTER SIXTY-SEVEN

Chloe didn't speak during the short drive into town, and James left her to her thoughts as she stared out of the window at the passing scenery.

It felt surreal sitting next to the young woman he never believed he would ever get to meet. The woman he had come to strongly suspect had been murdered by her ex-boyfriend. Now he knew that Daniel Porter took her but didn't kill her. And neither did he kill Gordon Carver on Christmas Eve.

So, who the hell did?

James's mind was racing with more questions and a wave of unease swelled in his chest.

Finding Chloe was a huge result, and he would never forget that moment when she stepped out of that room in the basement, but he couldn't allow it to distract him entirely from the murder investigation.

Porter being ruled out as a suspect was a major setback, and would increase the pressure on James and the rest of the team. At the same time, he was finding it hard to wrap his head around what had happened in the last few hours. And that was causing his cheeks to heat up and his pulse to spike like crazy.

Just as they were approaching headquarters Chloe suddenly spoke up without turning away from the window. 'Have you any idea why Gordon was murdered?'

'Not yet,' James answered. 'Daniel Porter was one of several suspects because we believed he had a strong motive. But when I questioned him, he insisted that he didn't do it and was at home when it happened.'

'I know for a fact that he's a liar, but he's not lying about that,' she said. 'He made a big thing of Christmas Eve. Claimed he wanted it to be special for me. We spent most of the evening on the sofa with him telling me how much he loved me and how he really believed that one day I would love him back and we'd move to another country and be a couple again.'

'How did you feel about that?' James asked her.

'It was what he kept telling me and every time I heard it I wanted to vomit. There was no way I could ever forgive him for what he'd done to me. I broke up with him because he was controlling and abusive, but then he showed himself to be a complete monster, and I came to hate every bone in his body.

'I told him there was no going back to how it once was between us, but he refused to accept it. If you hadn't found me then I dread to think how long he would have kept me in the basement. And I do wonder if he would have eventually gone on to kill me.'

Her face crumpled then and her body appeared to collapse in on itself. Tears gushed from her eyes and James reached out to put a hand on her shoulder.

'It's all over now,' he told her. 'You'll be able to get on with your life and that man won't be a part of it.'

*

Chloe was given a warm welcome at headquarters. Among those who were waiting to greet her in reception were Superintendent Tanner and detectives Isaac, Abbott, and Sharma. There was also a doctor on hand from the Constabulary's Occupational Health Unit who had a brief conversation with her about her condition.

After telling the female doctor that she didn't have any health problems, Chloe was taken to an interview room where she was offered a hot drink and something to eat. She opted for a coffee but didn't want any food.

DS Abbott joined her and James in the room, and informed her that a unit had just arrived at her parents' home and had broken the good news to them that she'd been found.

'Your mum and dad will be brought here shortly, but they've been told to expect a call from you before then,' Abbott said as she handed Chloe a mobile. 'I've tapped in their home number, so you just have to press the green button.'

It was a short and highly emotional conversation between Chloe and her parents. She told them that she was safe and well and couldn't wait to see them, but she didn't speak about her ordeal. When the call ended James slipped out of the room, leaving Abbott with Chloe.

He hurried to the office where he got the rest of the team together, along with the Super, and told them what Chloe had revealed about what had happened to her, concluding with, 'She also told me that Porter could not have killed Gordon because he was with her when the murder took place.'

'Well, that's not the only thing that works in Porter's favour,' DC Isaac pointed out. 'We've had it confirmed that the unidentified prints on Gordon's mobile phone don't belong to him.'

'There's also the fact that we didn't find a red and black puffer jacket in his home,' James said. 'He may not be a suspect in Gordon's murder anymore, but we'll make sure that he'll go down for kidnapping and various other offences.'

'Porter has been placed in a cell and a duty solicitor is on standby to represent him,' DC Sharma said.

'I intend to question him after I've spoken in more detail to Chloe,' James said. 'After that, I'll leave it to one of you to formally charge Porter so that I can return my attention to our murder investigation.'

Tanner then reminded everyone about the press conference that was scheduled to take place at four o'clock.

'Before then we'll need to issue a statement about Chloe,' he said. 'I expect it will mean that most of the questions at the conference will now be about her and how we found her, and not about the hunt for Gordon's killer. I'll liaise with the press office and pull something together.'

James wrapped things up then and returned to the interview room.

CHAPTER SIXTY-EIGHT

James could have got another member of the team to carry out the interview, but he knew he needed to hear first-hand about Chloe Walsh's ordeal at the hands of Daniel Porter.

He began by asking her what happened the night she went missing and she described how Porter pounced as she was walking along a deserted road after leaving her friend's party.

She was passing a parked car when the front door was thrown open and he jumped out, grabbed her, and injected her in the neck with something that knocked her out. The next thing she remembered was waking up tied to the bed in the cottage he'd rented.

He told her that he wasn't prepared to live without her and that she belonged to him.

'He said he would move me to his house after the police had searched it,' she carried on. 'And before he did, he prepared the basement for me. There was food in the fridge, some new clothes, and even a running machine so that I could stay fit.'

'Did he force you to have sex from the start?' Abbott asked her.

Chloe closed her eyes and nodded. 'At first, I tried to resist, but he would tie me up and sometimes even drug me. Thankfully I didn't have to worry about getting pregnant because I had a contraceptive implant inserted while we were dating, and it's supposed to last for three years.'

During those first few weeks in the basement she tried desperately to come up with ways to escape, but wasn't able to. So, she eventually gave up and accepted that she'd never be free unless he decided to let her go.

James ended the interview after forty-five minutes when DC Sharma came to let them know that Chloe's parents had arrived.

James didn't want Chloe's parents to be reunited with their daughter until he'd spoken to them first, so he left the interview room and hurried to the office where they'd been taken.

Superintendent Tanner was talking to them when he got there and the joy and relief on their faces was evident.

Dean and Sylvia Walsh were both in their mid-fifties and it had been several months since James had last seen them. Back then they were grief-stricken and desperate to know what had happened to their only child. Now their nightmare had come to a sudden end and Sylvia showed her gratitude by embracing James and thanking him for finding Chloe.

'We didn't think this day would ever come,' she said. 'We tried to accept that we would never see her again.'

'Before I take you to her there are some things you should know,' James said.

They hadn't been provided with details about how and where Chloe was found so he filled them in, telling them that what many people had suspected – that her ex-boyfriend was responsible for her disappearance eight months ago – was true.

'She was kept in the basement of his home, and we found her there purely by chance,' he said. 'And you need to know that she has suffered traumatic sexual abuse and will likely need counselling and a lot of support,

It was a lot for them to take in and it brought tears to their eyes, but at least they weren't going to have to ask Chloe too many difficult questions straight away.

James didn't keep them waiting long before he took them to the interview room, and when the family came together, he felt his heart swell and his throat tighten.

It was such an emotional moment that even DS Abbott lost it and started sobbing into her cupped hands.

CHAPTER SIXTY-NINE

James stayed in the interview room for only a few more minutes.

Before leaving, he explained to Chloe and her parents how he expected the rest of the day to pan out.

'I'm going to arrange for you to go to hospital so that you can be checked over,' he said to Chloe. 'A family liaison officer will be appointed to go with you and your parents. And you should know that later this afternoon there's going to be a press conference to inform the media that you've been found, and reporters will undoubtedly be scrambling to interview you. If you're happy to speak to them, then that's fine, but if not, it isn't a problem and we can help you navigate that. One suggestion would be to consider releasing a photo of your family back together, as that can be an effective means of appeasing the press and buying yourself some breathing space.'

'What about Porter?' Chloe's father asked. 'Where is he and what's going to happen to him?'

'He's locked up in a cell and I'll be questioning him shortly,' James said. 'He will then be charged with various offences, including kidnapping, and I can assure you he's going to face years in prison.'

'The bastard should be locked up for the rest of his life,' Chloe's mother said. 'He's evil.'

James returned to the office and every nerve in his body was buzzing as he handed out instructions to the team. He wanted Chloe's hospital visit arranged and a FLO assigned to her. He also asked DC Isaac to go and stay with Chloe and her parents in the interview room, relieving DS Abbott so she could return to the office.

He was then told that a forensics team had arrived at Porter's house along with DC Hall, who would be overseeing the search.

Superintendent Tanner informed him that a statement had just been released to the press about Chloe being found, but it did not mention that she'd been kept in Porter's basement.

'We will, of course, have to provide more details at the presser,' he said. 'And by then we should be able to say that her ex-boyfriend has been arrested and charged.'

Before ending the meeting James asked if there had been any developments in the Gordon Carver murder investigation. But there hadn't been, which prompted him to say, 'We have to acknowledge that what happened today has knocked us off course. It's understandably a major distraction, but Gordon's killer is still out there, so let's make sure that by tomorrow we're back to putting our all into finding the scumbag.'

As soon as DS Abbott returned to the office, James tasked her with arranging for Porter to be taken to an interview room along with the duty solicitor.

'I want you to sit in on it with me,' he told her.

Before going there himself, he grabbed a coffee from the vending machine and took it to his office from where he called

Annie. He wanted to let her know about Chloe and find out how she was.

'That's fantastic news,' she said. 'I can't believe it. The poor girl must have been through hell.'

'I couldn't believe it either when she walked out of the bedroom in the basement,' James said. 'She's now with her parents and I'm about to interview Porter.'

'Well, give him a bloody hard time.'

'You can count on it. Meanwhile, what are you up to?'

'I'm getting the kids ready for our walk. Janet will be here any minute.'

'And how are you feeling?'

'I feel good actually, and I'm looking forward to getting out of the house for a bit.'

'Enjoy yourselves then and stay safe.'

'I will. And thanks for letting me know about Chloe. That's really made my day.'

CHAPTER SEVENTY

DS Abbott was waiting in the interview room with Daniel Porter when James got there.

He was immediately reminded that just days ago the man had sat on the same chair while being asked if he had murdered Gordon Carver, represented by the same brief, duty solicitor Graham Bond.

Porter looked different this time, James noted. His face was drained of colour and his eyes were as bleak as the weather.

James felt the acid churn in his stomach as he sat down and faced him across the table.

He began the interview by reading out the standard police caution, after which the solicitor said, 'I've had a brief conversation with Mr Porter, and he wants you to know that he's prepared to fully cooperate with you, Detective Walker.'

'I suppose that's because he knows that he really doesn't have much of a choice,' James responded. Turning to Porter, he went on, 'You've been caught bang to rights, Mr Porter. There's indisputable evidence that you kidnapped your ex-partner,

Chloe Walsh, and held her against her will in your basement for no fewer than eight months. And that you acted with depraved indifference to your victim. As a result of what you put her through, Chloe will be mentally scarred for the rest of her life, and I fear that if we hadn't found her today then you would have gone on to kill her.'

Porter stiffened suddenly and his expression became dark and hostile.

'You're talking rubbish,' he fumed. 'I would never have killed her. I love her and I always will.'

'Then why did you do such a terrible thing to her?'

'I was confused and fucked up,' he replied. 'I wanted to punish her for breaking up with me like she did. But I also wanted to convince her that we were meant to be together. And the only way to do that was to keep her close to me.'

James swallowed hard and took a moment before continuing in order to keep his irritation in check.

'I'd like you to confirm some of what Chloe has already told us,' he said. 'Is it true that you insisted on having sex with her without her consent throughout the time you held her captive?'

By now, fine beads of sweat had gathered above Porter's top lip and his eyes appeared to be unfocused.

He nodded and seemed resigned to the fact that there was no point denying anything.

James continued to ask him questions and when Porter responded he spoke rapidly, nervously.

He admitted that one of the reasons he did what he did was because he feared that if they stayed apart after she broke up with him then she would soon hook up with someone else.

'I couldn't risk that happening,' Porter said. 'It would have destroyed me.'

James asked him again what he did on Christmas Eve, and this time he said he spent it in the basement with Chloe.

'I know you've got it into your head that I killed Gordon Carver, but I didn't,' he added. 'I was with Chloe the whole time. We were sat watching television when he was killed. Ask her and she'll tell you.'

'She's already told us that,' James said. 'And it means that you're no longer on our list of suspects. But that's the only light in the darkness for you, Mr Porter.'

James questioned the man for almost an hour, by which time his insides were feeling as tight as a clenched fist, and it was coming up to half three when James informed Porter that he was going to be formally charged with several offences, beginning with kidnapping and false imprisonment, and held in custody.

He then left it to DS Abbott to oversee the process and went back to the office.

Several hours had passed since Chloe had been found, but the team were still pumped up with excitement. The recovery dominated conversations and most of the calls that were coming in were about it.

After James updated them on his interview with Porter, he reminded them again that it was time to turn their attention back to the murder investigation.

'Thankfully, Daniel Porter is now going to suffer the consequences of his actions,' he said. 'But I want to ensure there's justice for Gordon and his family, too. We therefore have to redouble our efforts, especially now that we've lost one of our prime suspects.'

He was about to ask for some ideas on how to take things

forward when Superintendent Tanner came into the room to tell him that reporters and camera crews had begun to arrive for the press conference.

'At least we've got some positive news to pass on to them,' Tanner said. 'And hopefully it will mean the hacks won't focus on our lack of progress with the Carver case.'

CHAPTER SEVENTY-ONE

The media mob had turned up in force and there were at least twenty people – reporters, photographers, and TV camera operators – present.

James recognised some of the faces, including that of *Cumbria Gazette* journalist Duncan Bishop, who had been covering the Carver case since the start.

As James and Tanner took their seats behind a table facing the audience, the anticipation was palpable.

The Super kicked off the briefing by reading out a short statement he'd prepared.

'I'd like to begin by thanking everyone for coming here today,' he said. 'The intention was to update you on the investigation into the murder of journalist Gordon Carver, and we'll be happy to answer any questions you have relating to that in a moment, but first I'd like to say how delighted we are that local estate agent Chloe Walsh, who has been missing for over eight months, was this morning found safe and well by my colleague here, Detective Chief Inspector James Walker.'

He went on to reveal how and where she was found and that her ex-boyfriend Daniel Porter was in the process of being charged with kidnap and false imprisonment.

'I'm pleased to say that she has already been reunited with her parents,' he said.

Tanner went on to invite questions and the first came from a BBC reporter who asked if it was true that police went to Porter's house because he was suspected of murdering Gordon Carver.

Tanner said that it was, but Porter was no longer a suspect in the killing of Gordon Carver. He then gave James space to explain how they found Chloe while searching the house.

Questions came thick and fast, and both James and Tanner were careful not to give so much away as to jeopardise future court proceedings, but it wasn't long before attention turned to the Carver case and James let it be known that a number of people had been questioned.

'Unfortunately, we still don't know who killed Mr Carver and why,' he said. 'But we are making progress and you'll be provided with updates on all future developments.'

He had already decided to delay drawing attention to the red and black puffer jacket worn by the mystery man who was seen standing outside the Queen's Castle pub just before Gordon was killed. He was concerned that the individual would almost certainly get rid of the jacket before the police could identify and approach him.

After that the questions dried up and Tanner closed proceedings by reaffirming his commitment to keeping the media informed of developments relating to the Carver murder investigation and the Chloe Walsh kidnapping.

James was just glad it was over, and a wave of relief surged through him as he stood up and left the room.

It was generally accepted that the press conference went pretty well. There were no awkward moments, and the hacks appeared satisfied with what they were told.

No one doubted that the Chloe Walsh story would make headlines for days to come. She was going to be very much in demand, and teams of journalists would undoubtedly try to find out as much as they could about Daniel Porter.

They would also want to know how he had managed to get away with what he did for so long, as Chloe's terrible ordeal was the stuff of nightmares, the kind of thing that might eventually be made into a TV documentary or even a movie.

The team were still discussing what had happened when James received an update from DC Hall, who was at Porter's house overseeing the forensic search.

'There's plenty of evidence here that supports what Miss Walsh told us,' he said. 'We've found her mobile phone and there's also a drawer filled with knockout drugs including ketamine and Rohypnol.'

Hanging up the phone, James came to the decision to get DS Abbott to take the lead on pulling together the case against Porter, and went to speak to her.

'I'll still work closely with you, Jess,' he told her. 'But it means I can concentrate on finding Gordon's killer.'

He then brought the working day to a close, and told the team to be in bright and early in the morning, before heading to the canteen to get something to eat before leaving for home. On the way he received a call from Nadine Stone.

'So, it turns out that Gordon was right all along about Porter,' she said. 'The bastard was responsible for Chloe's disappearance.

It's such a shame that the truth didn't come out while Gordon was alive.'

'I totally agree,' James replied. 'Did you watch the press conference?'

'Of course. And congratulations on finding the poor girl. I've told the team to devote the next edition of the *Gazette* to the story. And we're hoping to be the first to interview her.'

'Well, good luck with that.'

'Thank you. And what about Gordon's murder? Where are you with it now that Porter has been ruled out as a suspect?'

'We're pressing on and you'll be informed as and when there are any developments.'

He decided to end the conversation there, choosing not to tell her that her husband remained on the list of suspects, and that they would soon be asking for his fingerprints.

CHAPTER SEVENTY-TWO
ANNIE

Annie's phone buzzed with a message just minutes after she'd put the kids to bed. It was from James, wanting her to know that he would soon be on his way home.

She sent a short reply.

Drive carefully, my love. Do you want me to make you some dinner? xx

He responded immediately.

I've just picked up a sandwich from the canteen so no thank you. I will be in need of a drink, though xx

She could only imagine what kind of day he'd had. Finding Chloe Walsh would have had a huge impact on him.

Annie had returned from her walk with Janet in time to see James front the press conference on TV with his boss, and his face had been pinched and tense.

It was also obvious to her that he was feeling the pressure of not having solved Gordon Carver's murder. He hadn't sounded at all convincing when he'd told the journalists that his team were making progress with the investigation.

It was because she didn't want to add to the stress that he was under that she had decided not to tell him that her breast lump had grown slightly bigger and was now painful, too. He didn't need to know just yet, and telling him wouldn't make her feel any less worried.

It was surely enough that he now knew about her condition, and was clinging to the hope that it wouldn't get any worse and that when she eventually got tested their worst fears wouldn't be realised.

She would, of course, have been more open with him if this Christmas had been crime free and he'd been able to take some time off. But circumstances were such that James was feeling the pressure of a burdensome workload and there was only so much that even a man as tenacious and determined as he could be expected to cope with at any one time.

It was almost eight o'clock by the time he arrived home, and he gave her a long, lingering kiss on the mouth before taking off his coat.

'Before you ask, the kids had a good day and are tucked up in bed,' she said. 'And I want you to know that I'm really proud of you for finding that young woman. Her parents must be so happy.'

'They are, but it was a stroke of luck,' he replied. 'Porter tried to convince us that the house didn't have a basement, but I remembered from a previous search eight months ago that it did. Turned out he'd concealed the entrance in the hallway behind a shelving unit.'

'Well, you need to tell me all about it. I'm dying to know more.'

'First I want you to tell me how you are.'

She rolled her eyes at him. 'I'm good and trying not to think about myself. So, let's put my little problem to one side for now while you fill me in on what has been a momentous day for you.'

They settled in the living room, he with a large whisky and she with a glass of wine.

She could see that the events of the day had taken their toll on him. There were tired shadows beneath his eyes, and the rest of his face was grey, the skin tight.

'Before we chat, I need to make two calls,' he said. 'The first is to Fiona. She rang me today, but I was on my way to Porter's house and couldn't talk to her.'

The conversation with his sister was short and sweet, and he put it on speaker so that Annie could join in. Fi wanted to know that they were both okay and to remind them that she was still keen to pay them a visit next week.

After the call, James rang the office and asked for an update on Chloe Walsh. He was told that she'd been seen by a doctor at a private medical facility and no health issues had been detected. She was now on her way to a Constabulary safe house where she'd be spending the night so as not to be pestered by news hounds.

James poured them each another drink and then told Annie about his day. But she could tell that his heart wasn't in it, especially when he spoke about the Carver murder case. He made it clear that he was frustrated by the lack of progress and couldn't help feeling guilty.

'Well, tomorrow is a new day,' she told him. 'So, I suggest you come to bed now and try to get a good night's sleep. Then hopefully you'll be back to firing on all cylinders in the morning.'

CHAPTER SEVENTY-THREE
NEW YEAR'S EVE

James was surprised when he woke up on Wednesday morning and saw that it was half five. It meant he'd had a full six hours of unbroken sleep.

And not only that. He couldn't recall having any dreams or nightmares, which was pretty unusual in itself.

After switching off the alarm, he managed to slip out of bed without disturbing Annie and went downstairs to get ready. She was still spark out when he came back up, but he didn't want to leave the house without telling her, so he gave her a nudge.

'I'm sorry, hon, but I thought you should know that I'm off to work,' he said. 'Is there anything I can get you before I go?'

Her eyes flickered open and her face creased up. 'What time is it?'

'Almost six. I've got a busy day so I thought I should get going. I can make you a tea if you want.'

'No thanks. With luck I'll drop off again and sleep for another hour before the little monsters start to stir.'

He leaned over and kissed her forehead. 'Have you got anything planned for today?'

'We're going to Janet's for lunch. And if you're back early enough then I'll make you, me, and the kids something special to mark New Year's Eve.'

'That'd be great,' he said. 'I'll let you know when I can get away.'

He covered her shoulders with the duvet and stepped out of the room without telling her that he'd completely forgotten it was New Year's Eve.

It was another dark and dismal morning across Cumbria. No fresh snow had fallen, but the wind was brutal during the drive to Kendal.

Trees swayed and snatched at the sky, and some of the broken branches that were blown across the road struck the side of James's car, making it even more difficult for him to concentrate on the day ahead.

He needed to get the team back on track with the Gordon Carver murder investigation. They had lost a prime suspect in Daniel Porter and no new leads had emerged. Plus, several lines of inquiry that were supposed to have been followed up yesterday got put on hold because Chloe Walsh's sudden reappearance derailed everything.

But James was confident that it wouldn't take them long to pick up where they had left off. And a priority would be to identify the fingerprints on Gordon's mobile phone.

They'd established that they didn't belong to Porter or Shane O'Brien, so perhaps they did belong to Elliott Stone. They hadn't been able to place him at the murder scene on Christmas Eve, but his wife's affair with Gordon provided him with a hellishly strong motive.

It was James's intention to visit the Stone home today to get his prints and check to see if he owned a black and red puffer jacket. But if the result proved negative on both counts, then they'd lose yet another suspect.

When he arrived at headquarters just before seven, he went straight to the canteen and got himself a coffee and a bacon sandwich. He stayed there to eat it while he checked the morning newspapers on his phone.

It came as no surprise that the Chloe Walsh story filled most of the front pages with headlines such as: FREE AT LAST AFTER EIGHT MONTHS IN A CELLAR and POLICE FIND MISSING CHLOE IN HER EX'S BASEMENT.

There were photographs of Chloe and Porter, plus quotes from yesterday's press conference. And most of the reports gave James full credit for finding her.

He left the canteen after fifteen minutes and went straight to the office where some team members were already at their desks, including DS Abbott, and he asked her for an update on Chloe Walsh.

'She apparently had a good night's sleep, guv, and is still at the safe house with her parents,' she said. 'I'll be joining her there soon along with the appointed family liaison officer. The papers are clamouring for an interview, so I'll see if she's up for it. Meanwhile, Porter is languishing in a prison cell, and I'll let you know if I think we should bring more charges against him.'

James switched his attention to the Carver case and noted that the team were busy checking through the latest batch of CCTV footage that had come in from Christmas Eve, and reviewing all the information that had already been gathered.

As expected, there had been no overnight developments to give James any reason to feel optimistic, so when he eventually called the team together for the briefing, he stressed the need for them to come up with some fresh ideas.

'Yesterday we got distracted, but we now have to move things on as quickly as possible before any potential evidence that's out there dries up,' he said.

'I'll shortly be paying another visit to Elliott Stone's house as we need to find out if the unidentified prints on Gordon's phone belong to him or perhaps even his wife. If not, then we need to discover who the hell they do belong to.'

When he concluded the briefing shortly thereafter, he went into his office to check his emails and call Superintendent Tanner. But just as he sat down behind his desk, DC Sharma appeared at his door.

'We've come across a CCTV clip that you'll want to see, boss,' he said. 'It's quite possible it actually shows Gordon being followed by his killer.'

CHAPTER SEVENTY-FOUR

The CCTV clip ran for only seven seconds, and the time stamp was 21.15 on Christmas Eve.

It showed Gordon Carver crossing a road that was situated between the Queen's Castle pub and the spot close to his home where he was murdered. He had his hands in his pockets and was walking at a fast pace.

As he stepped out of sight onto the kerb, another figure came into view heading in the same direction.

James's breath lurched in his gut when he saw that the person had on a red and black puffer jacket that was very similar to the one in the photo Imogen Price had identified.

'This provides clear evidence that when Gordon set off home after meeting with Michael Frost, he was followed. The problem is we can't see the man's bloody face,' he said. 'But it could well be Elliott Stone.'

The guy had his jacket hood up and didn't turn towards the camera as he hurried across the road about twenty yards behind

Gordon. It didn't help that it was a slightly blurred image because a light snow had been falling at the time.

'I've just been told that it's a very short distance between that spot and the scene of the murder,' Sharma said. 'And there are no other street cameras along the way.'

James was disappointed, but also excited. Granted, they couldn't identify the man in the puffer jacket, but the clip meant it was now reasonable to assume that he could be their killer.

It was a shame that Imogen Price hadn't been able to provide them with a fuller description because of the mask the man wore.

'I think it's time we went public with a description of the jacket. We'll release the clip at the same time,' James said when he got the team back together. 'I know it's a risky move because if the perp sees it, he'll almost certainly dump the jacket, but I think it's a risk worth taking at this stage in the game because of the pressure we're under. We won't go with it straight away, though. First, we need to ascertain whether Elliott Stone owns a jacket like it.'

James took DC Isaac with him in a patrol car to Elliott and Nadine Stone's house in Oxenholme, and he got three uniforms to follow in another car so they could search the place.

On the way he phoned the Super to update him and to tell him about the latest CCTV clip that had been recovered.

'Do you know for certain that Mr Stone will be in?' Tanner asked him.

'We don't, but I didn't want to alert him. And given that it's New Year's Eve, I think there's a good chance that someone will be.'

And he was right. There were two vehicles on the couple's driveway when they got there – Nadine's Volkswagen and her husband's Peugeot van.

'Well, it looks as though it's not going to be a wasted journey,'

Isaac said. 'How likely do you think it is that Elliott Stone is the killer? After all, he claims he didn't know that his wife was having an affair with Gordon until you put her on the spot and she admitted she'd spent time at his house.'

James shrugged. 'I'm not entirely convinced that he told us the truth about that. And I don't think we should believe that he went straight home after leaving the Majestic Hotel following the confrontation with Nadine. There's too much at stake to rule him out just yet.'

'Well, you could be right, guv. Hopefully, we'll soon find out.'

It was Nadine who answered the front door to them when they arrived at the small, detached property. She looked tired, her shoulders hunched and her eyes heavy. But when she glanced beyond the two detectives, the sight of the uniformed officers made her gasp as if a punch had taken her breath away.

'What the hell is going on?' she said in a voice stretched with tension.

'We're here as a result of some developments in our investigation into Gordon's murder,' James told her. 'We've obtained a warrant to search your house, and we've got some more questions for your husband.'

Nadine stared at him aghast. 'You can't possibly be serious. You've already spoken to Elliott, and what on earth are you going to be looking for?'

Just then her husband stepped up behind her, his face pale and unshaven.

Eyes blazing, he jabbed a finger at James. 'This family has got enough problems without having you lot raid our home like we're a bunch of gangsters. It's totally over the top and you must know it. And how many times have I got to tell you that I did not kill Gordon Carver?'

'We can't just take your word for it, Mr Stone,' James said. 'That's not how it works, I'm afraid. Because of the new evidence that's emerged, we had no choice but to return here with a search warrant and ask you both to provide us with your fingerprints.'

Elliott shook his head. 'For god's sake, why do you want our fucking prints?'

It was more or less the same reaction they'd got from Daniel Porter when they turned up at his house the day before, and James gave a similar response.

'I'll provide you with a full explanation inside. I'd ask you to do yourselves a favour and cooperate with us since we won't be leaving here until we've done what we came to do.'

That was all it took to get Nadine to step back inside and to gesture for her husband to do the same. He did so, but continued to stare at James with frost in his eyes.

'Is anyone else in the house?' James asked them.

'Charlotte is in the living room,' Nadine said. 'She wasn't feeling well this morning, so she didn't go to work.'

'What about your son?'

'Ryan's at his own place. His partner arrived back this morning after spending Christmas with her parents in Scotland.'

'Then let's go into the living room and warn your daughter what's about to happen.'

James followed the couple along the hallway while Isaac held the front door open for the uniforms to enter.

Charlotte was slumped on the sofa in a dressing gown watching television, and she looked up at James with a quizzical expression on her face.

Nadine grabbed the remote control from the coffee table and muted the TV.

'Don't be alarmed, sweetheart,' she said to her daughter. 'The police have come to look around the house and to speak to us again. They won't be here very long.'

Charlotte's body stiffened and she sat up straight. 'Does that mean they still think that Dad is a murderer?'

James was suddenly reminded that Charlotte was inclined to speak with blunt honesty, without considering the social implications of her words. And he recalled how, when they were last here, she was admonished by her brother for revealing that her parents had fallen out.

'That's absolutely not what the police believe,' her mother said in answer to her question. 'It's just that …'

'It's just that they've made a huge fucking mistake and they're about to realise that,' Elliott fumed.

Charlotte shook her head in response and said, 'Well, I don't think you're a murderer, Dad. You get angry sometimes, and you swear a lot, but you definitely wouldn't kill anyone.'

James spoke up then before either parent could respond.

'Can I suggest you both sit down so I can tell you what has brought us here?' he said. 'And while I do that, our officers will check the other rooms as quickly as possible. I can assure you that they won't make a mess of things.'

'But what are they looking for?' Nadine said as she lowered herself onto the sofa between Elliott and her daughter.

'I'll come to that in a moment, Mrs Stone,' James told her. 'First, let me explain why we need to take your prints. You see, we've found Gordon's mobile phone, and we believe it was discarded by his killer. There are some prints on it that we have yet to identify, and we need to take yours for elimination purposes.'

'Well, I can tell you now they're not mine,' Elliott insisted, his voice loud. 'I never touched his phone.'

'Me neither,' Nadine said.

'And if that's true then we won't have to bother you again,' James responded. 'My colleague here has a mobile fingerprint scanner, and the process will take just seconds.'

'And what if I refuse to let you do it?' Elliott replied.

It was Charlotte who reacted to this, by saying, 'Oh, just let them get on with it, Dad. I'm keen to see how it's done. It should be interesting.'

Elliott gave her a sharp look and blew out a breath before turning back to James. 'Okay, you can do it. But first tell us why you came here with a bloody search team. What is it you think we've got hidden away?'

James took out his phone and brought up the photo of the black and red puffer jacket.

'We want to determine if anyone who knew Gordon owns a jacket similar to the one that I'm about to show you,' he said. 'You're among several people we're approaching and whose homes have been subjected to a search warrant.'

'But what's so special about it?' Elliott asked.

'We believe that the killer was wearing the same coat, or something very similar, when he attacked Gordon,' James said.

He then stepped closer to the sofa and held up the phone in front of Elliott, who leaned forward to stare at it. James immediately noticed that the look on the man's face was clearly one of shock.

'Do I take it from your reaction that you recognise the jacket?' James said.

Elliott hesitated for a second before shaking his head. 'No, I don't. And I can assure you that I've never owned a coat like that.'

James wasn't convinced he was telling the truth and was about to show the photo to Nadine when Charlotte reached out and grabbed his arm with her hand, moving it so that she could see the phone's screen.

The second she laid eyes on the photo, she turned to her dad and said, 'I know that you don't have a jacket that looks anything like that one, Dad. But surely you haven't forgotten that you and Mum bought one just like it for Ryan for his birthday this year. Remember? I told you that I didn't like it because it's too flash.'

Nadine responded by grabbing the phone from James's hand.

As soon as she saw the photo she gasped aloud and said in a faltering voice, 'This is not the same as your brother's jacket. His has got a different pattern on it. I'm sure of it. And there's no way that …'

The words froze in her throat, and when she looked at James, he could see the alarm raging in her eyes.

CHAPTER SEVENTY-FIVE

The sudden silence that followed was electrifying. Nadine and Elliott turned to each other, their mouths open, their features taut. It was as though the shock had hit the couple like a falling wall.

'Are you kidding me?' their daughter said as she switched her gaze between both parents. 'You're now worried that Ryan might have blood on his hands? Come off it. Lots of blokes must have coats like that one. And my stupid brother wouldn't know how to kill anyone.'

'I'm sure you're right, Charlotte,' James said. 'But we will need to speak to him as soon as possible.'

His words prompted a sharp reaction from Elliott, who raised his hands in the air, his face on fire. 'You can't be bloody serious. First me and now my son. It's crazy.'

'Why did you pretend that you didn't recognise the jacket, Mr Stone?' James asked. 'It was obvious from your face that you did the moment you saw the photograph.'

Elliott drew a hand across his face and through his hair before letting a long, loud breath out through his teeth.

'I was just confused, that's all,' he said. 'It didn't register with me. There was too much going on in my head.'

James didn't believe him, but chose not to press him on it. Instead, he turned to Nadine, who was clearly both confused and anxious.

'I'm now going to show you why this quite distinctive puffer jacket has become so crucial to the investigation,' he said.

He pulled up the relevant CCTV clip on his phone and asked Elliott to sit back down so that all three of them could see it.

After pressing play, he said, 'This shows Gordon crossing a road shortly after leaving the Queen's Castle pub on Christmas Eve. He's on his way home, and as he walks out of shot this other man in a red and black puffer jacket can be seen following him. We now know that the same man had been waiting outside the pub while Gordon was inside.'

'But that could be anyone,' Nadine said. 'You can't see his face.'

'That's why it's necessary for us to speak to Ryan now that we know he has a coat just like it. As I recall, you told us that he didn't arrive here until Christmas morning. So I'd like him to tell us where he was on Christmas Eve.'

She shook her head. 'But our son hardly knew Gordon. He wouldn't have had a reason for wanting him dead.'

James saw no point in prolonging the conversation. He completely understood why they didn't want to accept that Ryan might have killed Gordon.

But at the same time, it was a lead that had to be followed up as a matter of urgency.

Just as he was about to speak again, one of the uniforms entered the room and made it known that they hadn't found a red and black puffer jacket in the house.

Turning back to the family, James said, 'I have to ask you not to contact Ryan until I've spoken to him. I intend to go to his home now while DC Isaac remains here with you as we still need to obtain both your sets of fingerprints. I promise to get back to you as quickly as I can.'

Both Nadine and Elliott wore looks of desperation, but they just sat there in frozen silence as James turned and walked out of the room.

Their daughter reacted differently, though, and James heard her tell them not to worry. That everything was going to be all right.

CHAPTER SEVENTY-SIX

James instructed two of the uniforms to stay with DC Isaac and the other two to accompany him in the patrol car to Ryan Stone's apartment back in the town.

As he walked out of the house the adrenaline dropped like a bomb into his bloodstream. His copper's instinct was telling him that this was a significant development.

Before now Ryan Stone had been a highly unlikely suspect. James had known that he worked as a local tour guide and lived with his girlfriend, but it appeared he had no reason to want Gordon Carver dead. But now they had to take into consideration that he was also the son of the woman who Gordon was having an affair with. Plus, he lived within walking distance of the crime scene, and he owned a black and red puffer jacket.

James also recalled how when he last met Ryan he'd leapt to his father's defence and made a point of saying that it wouldn't have surprised him if Daniel Porter had murdered Gordon. He'd also claimed that two of his mates had described Porter as a bad apple, perhaps in an attempt to divert attention away from himself.

These thoughts and more were filling James's head as the patrol car moved at speed towards Ryan's address, which was only a few streets away from headquarters.

It was almost one o'clock already and the wind still hadn't let up, but luckily the snow that was forecast was holding off.

After just a couple of minutes he was tempted to call Isaac to make sure that Ryan's parents were okay. He'd left them in a highly emotional state and felt guilty about that. But he quickly decided that his DC was more than capable of handling the situation, however difficult it became. He needed to concentrate on what lay ahead. On how to elicit information from a young man who might be desperate not to reveal the truth about where he was and what he got up to on Christmas Eve.

Ryan's address turned out to be an apartment in a small, modern block off the Burneside Road. After the patrol car parked up, James approached the building with the uniformed officers.

There was a video doorbell panel on the wall next to the communal entrance and he pressed the button for apartment five.

Within seconds the small blue light came on to indicate that the camera had been triggered and a female voice said, 'Hello. Can I help you?'

'I'm Detective Chief Inspector Walker, with Cumbria Police,' James said as he held up his warrant card. 'I'm here with my colleagues to speak to Mr Ryan Stone. Is he in?'

After a brief pause, she gave a hesitant response. 'Er, yes, he is. I'm Naomi. Ryan's my boyfriend. We share this apartment. Does he know what it's about?'

'When you mention my name, he will. I met him a couple of days ago at his parents' home.'

'Oh, I see. You're investigating the murder of that journalist.'

'That's right.'

'Ryan told me about it. I'll go and get him. He's in the bathroom.'

Another few seconds passed before Ryan's voice came through.

'Good afternoon, Detective Walker,' he said. 'I wasn't expecting to see you today. What's up?'

'I'd like to come in and have a word,' James replied. 'There've been developments in the Gordon Carver murder investigation, and I need to ask you some questions.'

'I can't think why. All I know about it is what you told me and what I've seen on the news.'

'That may well be the case, but I still want to speak to you.'

'Do my parents know you're here?'

'They do. I've just come from their house and told them what I'm about to tell you.'

A short pause followed before Ryan said, 'You'd better come in then. We're on the first floor.'

A bell rang and the front door was unlocked. James and the officers mounted the stairs to the first floor and as soon as they reached it, they saw Ryan standing in his apartment doorway wearing jeans and a grey sweatshirt.

His face was set in a scowl, his jaw rigid, and it struck James that he looked nervous, perhaps too nervous for someone with nothing to hide.

'I'm sorry we've turned up unexpectedly, but there was no time to pre-warn you,' James said.

Ryan didn't respond, just stood back and waved them inside.

As soon as James entered the hallway, he saw something that caused his heart to skip a beat. There were several coats on hooks attached to the wall on his right. And one of them was a red and black puffer jacket, identical to the one worn by the man caught on CCTV following Gordon Carver as he walked home from the pub on Christmas Eve.

CHAPTER SEVENTY-SEVEN

James chose not to draw attention to the puffer jacket straight away, and instead simply followed Ryan into the living room where his girlfriend Naomi was waiting. She was standing with her back to the balcony door and looked about the same age as Ryan. She had on a short denim skirt and white blouse, her long, dark hair was loose around her shoulders, and she wore a deep frown on her thin, pale face.

Ryan introduced her to James and the two officers before crossing the small room to stand beside her, arms crossed.

'So, what is it you want to tell me, Detective Walker?' he said, his voice low, flat, his anxiety tangible.

James felt the blood move to his face, warming it.

'I want you to know that two pieces of evidence have surfaced that we believe are going to help us establish the identity of Gordon's killer,' he said. 'One is the discovery of Gordon's mobile phone, which was dumped in a garden close to where he was murdered. There are unidentified fingerprints on it that were almost certainly left by the killer. The other is a clip of CCTV footage that shows a man following Gordon just minutes before the attack on him took place.'

Ryan just stood there, clearly shocked, not moving.

'We're therefore in the process of collecting the fingerprints of people who knew Gordon, and your father's prints are being taken as we speak,' James continued. 'We've so far ascertained that the prints on the phone do not belong to Daniel Porter, and we've officially ruled him out as a suspect in the murder since he was elsewhere when it happened.'

Ryan was still rooted to the spot and the blood had retreated from his face. James's approach was working. If Ryan Stone was indeed the killer, then it was beginning to dawn on him that the walls were rapidly closing in.

'Since you're among those who knew Gordon, Ryan, I'd like you to provide us with your prints for elimination purposes,' James went on. 'But that can wait until after I've shown you the CCTV clip. I just want to see if you recognise the man who followed Gordon that evening from the pub where he'd been drinking.'

James took out his phone, brought up the footage and held it out for both Ryan and Naomi to see.

'You'll notice that the man is wearing a distinctive red and black puffer jacket,' James said. After a pause, he added, 'And as you can see, Ryan, it's the same as the one hanging up in your hallway. The one your parents bought you for your birthday. I therefore have to ask you if that's you we're looking at on the screen, and if the prints on Gordon's phone will be a match for yours? Because if they are, then I'll be arresting you on suspicion of murder.'

It was Naomi who reacted first, the air gushing out of her like a punctured balloon.

'Tell him it isn't you, Ryan,' she said, her eyes pleading. 'Please, tell him.'

The fact that he hesitated, if just for a split second, was enough to convince James that he was their man.

'Of course they're not my prints,' Ryan eventually managed to utter. 'I didn't kill him. Honestly. I had no reason to.'

His breaths were coming in rasping gasps now and he suddenly looked petrified as his eyes danced between James and the two officers.

'I simply don't believe you, Ryan,' James said, opting to continue applying pressure. 'And I'm sure that your parents won't either when they're confronted with the evidence. By then, of course, there'll be more of it from other CCTV cameras and from forensic analysis of your clothes.'

James knew that there was always a point at which a person who denied wrongdoing suddenly realised that it wasn't worth continuing to do so if the evidence was so firmly stacked against them. And he felt sure that Ryan Stone had already reached that point, having been caught off guard and made aware of the serious mistakes he'd made. His body was shaking like jelly and there was now a vacant look in his eyes.

It was as though he had suddenly disappeared within himself, terrified of what was going to come next.

'Before we take you to the station to be formally interviewed under caution, I want to ask you again about the prints on Gordon's phone,' James said. 'And this time I'll expect an honest answer. Will they turn out to be a match for yours?'

Ryan closed his eyes tightly and expelled a loud breath. Then he covered his face with his hands and spoke through his fingers.

'Yes, they will,' he said in a voice that was barely above a whisper. 'I didn't think to clean the phone before I dropped it over the fence.'

'Then it was you who killed Gordon.'

This time he didn't answer. Just nodded.

CHAPTER SEVENTY-EIGHT

James wasn't entirely surprised that Ryan Stone had caved so quickly, but from the desperate look in his eyes, James wasn't actually convinced that he realised what he'd done.

But Naomi did and she stared at her boyfriend with open-mouthed incredulity as tears coursed down her cheeks.

'You can't mean it, Ryan,' she said to him. 'You would never have done something like that. I know you too well.'

He turned to her and spoke through trembling lips. 'I thought I knew me too, my love. But I obviously don't. Why else would I have fucked up my life, and yours?'

Ryan moved towards Naomi, but she pushed him away and let out a cry of anguish before dropping her face into her hands.

'I'm so sorry,' Ryan said to her, but she didn't respond, just sobbed noisily, which prompted James to signal for one of the officers to escort her out of the room.

His mind was now spinning with questions he wanted Ryan to answer, but he didn't want to ask them here in the apartment. The station was only minutes away and it made more sense to grill him there. The guy was in a fragile, unpredictable state, and the sooner he was in a secure environment the better.

'In view of what you've told me I have no option other than to arrest you on suspicion of murder, Ryan,' he said. 'You'll now be taken into custody where you'll be expected to provide us with a full statement and be formally questioned.'

'Can you tell my parents what's happening?' Ryan replied. 'I need to talk to them. To explain why I did what I did.'

'They'll be informed, of course, as will the parents of the man you killed.'

Only then did his emotions rise to the surface, and he dissolved into tears.

James wasted no time getting him out of the flat. He was cuffed and taken to the patrol car by the driver. Before following them, James asked Naomi if there was anyone that they could contact who'd be able to come and be with her.

She still hadn't regained her composure, and her face was screwed up as though in pain, but she managed to tell him that her best friend lived nearby and she would call her.

'My parents need to know about this as well, but I'll have to phone them as they live in Scotland,' she said.

'Officer Cullen will stay with you,' James said. 'I'll also have to arrange for a forensics team to come here and examine Ryan's belongings.'

Just four minutes after driving away from the apartment they arrived at headquarters.

James was fired up and anxious to let the team know about Ryan Stone's arrest. But first he needed to get the custody officer to sign Ryan in and go through the usual process of taking his prints and a DNA sample, and reading him his rights.

While this was happening, James arranged for a duty solicitor to be put on standby. He then went to the office, which was a hive of activity, and felt a quiet sense of satisfaction as he broke the news to the team.

A cheer went up, but there were also a lot of shocked faces in the room. The question they all wanted answered was: What was Ryan's murder motive?

'The working assumption has to be that he went to confront Gordon to try to stop his parents from splitting up,' he told them. 'We should find out soon enough if we're right. I don't think he intends to hold anything back.'

James went on to list tasks he wanted carried out, including sending a forensics team to the apartment.

He then asked DC Sharma to go to Burneside to inform Gordon's parents before they heard about it from someone else.

'Meanwhile, Dawn is still with Ryan's parents in Oxenholme, so I'll call her and tell her she can break the news,' he said. 'I'll also speak to the Super and let him liaise with the press office.'

The first call he made was to DC Isaac who told him that Elliott and Nadine Stone had been waiting anxiously for news.

'Tell them I'll want to speak to them again at some point,' James said, 'and explain that it'll be a while before they can see their son.'

Before he ended the call, she told him that she had taken the couple's fingerprints and found they were not a match for those found on Gordon's mobile phone.

'But I expect that it'll be confirmed shortly that they are a match for those of their son's,' James said.

Next, he called Superintendent Tanner, who was delighted with the update.

'We won't go public with it until you've charged him,' he said. 'So, let me know as soon as you have.'

CHAPTER SEVENTY-NINE

It was coming up to three o'clock when the interview got underway.

James had asked Detective Constable Foley to join him, and they sat across the table from Ryan and the duty solicitor, who on this day was a brief named Louise Ritchie.

By then they'd had confirmation that the unidentified prints found on Gordon's phone did indeed belong to Ryan. And James revealed this after Ryan was informed of his rights and told that the interview was being recorded.

'I want you to talk us through what happened on Christmas Eve,' James said. 'But can you start by telling us what motivated you to murder Mr Carver?'

Ryan looked a mess. His face was white and blood vessels bulged out of his temples. When he spoke, his voice was flat and lifeless.

'Seven weeks ago, I found out by accident that my mum was having an affair with Carver,' he said. 'She was in our living room and speaking to him on the phone when Dad was away. She didn't realise that I was in the hall and could hear her, so I chose not to say anything in case I'd got it wrong. Instead, I kept an eye on her – my apartment is close to her office at the *Gazette*, so it was easy for me – and it wasn't long before I realised that what was going on between them was pretty serious. She went to his house quite often and then lied to us about where she'd been.'

'Did you confront her?' James asked.

He shook his head. 'I didn't dare. I feared that if I did then she might decide to leave Dad to be with him. And I couldn't bear the thought of that.'

'So, what did you do?'

'I thought long and hard about it and got worried that the longer it went on the less likely it would be that they'd stop. Then I convinced myself that I had a stark choice, which was to let the bastard destroy our family, or take him out of the picture so that Mum would stay with Dad.'

'Did you tell your girlfriend about your mum's affair and how you felt about it?'

'Of course not. I didn't want anyone to know what was going on.'

'What led to you going after Mr Carver on Christmas Eve specifically?'

Ryan's forehead was now beaded with perspiration and his eyes were glistening with unshed tears.

He suddenly took a long, quivering breath, and balled his hands into fists on the table.

'I was at home alone that day because Naomi had gone to spend time with her parents over Christmas,' he said. 'I spent the morning by myself thinking about what to do, and then my dad called to tell me he'd soon be driving home from Preston where he'd been working on a job. He asked me if I knew where Mum was because she wasn't answering her phone and her office said she'd left work early.

'I told him that I didn't know where she was, but as soon as the call ended, I decided to go and see if she was at Carver's place. And when I got there, I saw her car parked outside. I watched from across the road for about ten minutes before she came out, and she and Carver kissed each other before she drove off. It made me feel sick and I went back home to get half pissed on beers.

'I then came to the decision that it was time I needed to act before it was too late. So, I headed back to his house even though I wasn't sure what I was going to do when I got there. But I did know that I had to be careful not to let him see me, so I put on one of the Covid masks I'd kept in a drawer.'

'What happened when you arrived at his house?' James asked him.

'That's the thing. I didn't make it there because on the way I happened to be walking past the Queen's Castle when I saw Carver cross the road and go inside.'

'And so you decided to wait for him to come back out.'

He nodded. 'I had nothing else to do and he was in there for less than an hour.'

'We spoke to the woman who fell over the kerb close to you. She told us that you helped her to her feet.'

He shrugged. 'What else could I do?'

He squeezed his eyes shut then and pushed out a loud moan. The solicitor put a hand on his shoulder and asked him if he needed a break.

His eyes sprang open. 'No. Let's get it done.'

'Can you describe what happened when Gordon left the pub?' James pressed.

'I knew he'd be heading home and so I followed him,' he answered. 'Believe it or not, I still wasn't sure even then what I was going to do. When he started walking along the path through the wood I knew he would probably turn around and see me if I got too close, but it also struck me that it would be a good place to attack him because there was no one around. After that, things happened really quickly. I lost control. It was like some fucking monster that'd been living inside me had forced its way out.

'I spotted a rock and picked it up and then ran towards him. As I got close, I saw that he was calling someone on his phone and thought it might have been Mum. He must have heard me closing in as he moved to turn around, but before he could, I clobbered him over the head and he went down. I was going to hit him again to make sure he was dead, but I didn't think I needed to because I couldn't see him breathing. I then picked up his phone to see if it was Mum he'd been calling, but it wasn't. I didn't recognise the number.'

'What did you do with the rock?' James asked.

'I wiped it on the snow and threw it into the wood. But as I've already told you, I didn't think to do the same to the phone before I lobbed it into that garden.'

And so there it was. A full and frank confession from a young man who had destroyed his own life and ended that of a highly respected journalist.

CHAPTER EIGHTY

Ryan Stone was taken back to the custody officer, and he let out a strangled sob when he was formally charged with murder.

As James watched him being led off to a holding cell, he felt his jaw clench and his cheeks heat up.

This was the first case he had worked on where a man had been murdered by the son of the woman he was having an affair with. It was bound to divide public opinion, with some people no doubt taking the view that Gordon Carver got what he deserved, and that Ryan did what he did in a desperate bid to hold his family together.

It had been a challenging case for James and the team, and no one had expected it to end this way.

Back in the office, there was relief and jubilation among his detectives and also expressions of surprise as to the motive behind the murder.

James was given various updates when he got them together. He was told that Gordon's parents had been informed that Ryan had been charged with killing their son, and also why he did it.

'It won't be long before it's out there, so Nadine needs to be warned that she's likely to become the target of abuse,' he said.

He told DC Hall to go to Ryan's flat to work with the forensics team who'd arrived there, and then updated Tanner, who said a press release would be put out.

The next two hours were spent dealing with an avalanche of paperwork and James also made a point of asking DS Abbott how things were progressing with the Chloe Walsh case. He was told that it was all coming together and that Chloe was doing well. She had even agreed to give an interview to the Press Association so that it could be shared with newspapers and the broadcast media.

By seven o'clock James was feeling the pull of sleep. He was drained of energy and his eyes felt dry and sore.

He called Annie to let her know that he'd soon be on his way home and to say sorry for not telling her earlier that he'd be late.

'There's absolutely no need to apologise,' she said. 'I just saw on the news that Gordon's murderer is in custody and that it's down to you. So, well done, James, for solving two cases in two days. You deserve a medal.'

Annie had a stew prepared for him when he got home, along with a large glass of wine. 'I know it's New Year's Eve, but I don't think I'll be able to stay up until midnight,' she said.

James grinned. 'Me neither. Early to bed and early to rise, I reckon.'

The kids were in bed and so Annie sat with him as he filled his stomach. While doing so, he told her about his day and how shocked he was that Ryan Stone had turned out to be the killer.

'I feel so sorry for his family,' he said. 'First, Nadine's affair with Gordon comes to light, and now this. It's hard to imagine how they'll ever be able to move forward.'

It was just after nine when they climbed into bed and as they did so, James asked Annie if there had been any changes to her condition. She said there hadn't and he could only hope that she was telling the truth and not keeping anything from him.

CHAPTER EIGHTY-ONE
NEW YEAR'S DAY

Gordon Carver's murder may have been solved, but it didn't mean that James could take the day off. There was still a lot to be done.

After getting up, he promised Annie that he'd be home early so that he could celebrate the New Year with her and the kids.

'And after today you'll have my full attention,' he told her before setting off.

For a change the sky was clear, a perfect blue, and the wind had dropped. It was therefore an easy drive to Kendal.

Along the way he listened to the news on the radio, and sure enough the arrest of Ryan Stone was making the headlines. The Chloe Walsh story also remained high up the running orders, and there was even a sound bite from Cumbria's Chief Constable, who praised the efforts of DCI Walker and his team.

James got to the office just before eight and spent the first hour dealing with paperwork and responding to emails.

When the morning briefing got underway, the team were still on a high and keen to crack on. It was obvious that they weren't concerned about missing out on a Bank Holiday, and for that James was grateful.

There were a few updates, including one from DI Stevens, who said that he had charged both Toby McGrath and Shane O'Brien with aggravated assault following the violent confrontation that took place in the latter's father's home. And O'Brien had also been charged with threatening behaviour as a result of the list he'd drawn up.

Another update came from DC Hall, who said that the forensic search of Ryan's apartment hadn't turned up anything of interest, but his puffer jacket and some of his other belongings were now undergoing forensic analysis.

After the briefing, James felt it necessary to visit the parents of both Gordon Carver and Ryan Stone.

Each encounter proved extremely emotional, and he learned that Nadine had decided to resign as editor of the *Cumbria Gazette*.

'My own son murdered the paper's most popular journalist because of what I did, so there's no way I can stay on there,' she said as tears cascaded down her face.

After leaving the Stone's house in Oxenholme, James decided not to return to the office. By then it was almost four o'clock and he was determined to keep his promise to Annie and get home early.

He was glad he did because he was able to spend some precious time with Bella and Theo. He'd missed them and they'd missed him.

It was also good to be with Annie without being distracted by the job. He could tell that she was becoming increasingly anxious about the tests that were soon to be carried out on her breast.

He wanted to be there for her and to assure her that even if they faced an uncertain future, they faced it together.

EPILOGUE
THREE WEEKS LATER

It had been an eventful start to the New Year for James, beginning with a fierce blizzard that raged across Cumbria and caused him to be stuck in traffic for four hours on the road between Kirkby Abbey and Kendal.

Then came Annie's visit to the breast clinic, where the tests carried out on her lump included an ultrasound, repeat mammograms, and a biopsy. Afterwards she had revealed to him that the lump had grown and become tender, which made him worry even more about seeing the results.

Days later he attended Gordon's funeral, which really tugged at his heartstrings. There was a huge turnout and among the mourners were Chloe Walsh and Mad Dog Mike. Unsurprisingly, Nadine didn't attend.

It was now six days on from the funeral and at last James had something to smile about.

Just seconds ago they'd been told over the phone that the tests on Annie's breast lump had shown that it was a solid, but non-cancerous, tumour.

The news brought tears to James's eyes, and when he wrapped his arms around his wife he felt the hot rush of relief through his veins.

'Our prayers have been answered, my love,' he told her.

They were informed that such lumps are quite common, and sometimes can cause pain and discomfort, but there was nothing for Annie to worry about and a simple procedure would be carried out to remove it.

This was news they wanted to share, and the first person they let know was James's sister, Fiona, followed by Annie's best friend, Janet.

'Time now to put the kids to bed,' Annie said after coming off the phone. 'Then we can open a bottle of wine and discuss between ourselves how to make the most of the future we can once again look forward to.'

Overwhelmed by emotion, James pulled her into another hug, and this time he held her against his chest for a full minute as hot tears rolled down his cheeks.

THE END

ACKNOWLEDGEMENTS

Another big thank you to the team at Avon/HarperCollins for sticking with this series and helping me to bring each book to life. I'm especially grateful to my editor, Amy Mae Baxter, who provides me with so much support and guidance.

If you've enjoyed *Cold Blooded Killer*,
then why not head back to DCI
James Walker's first case?

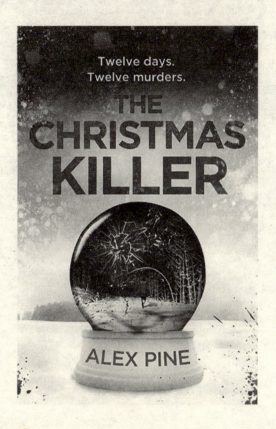

A serial killer is on the loose in Kirkby Abbey.
And as the snow falls, the body count climbs …

One farmhouse. Two murder cases.
Three bodies.

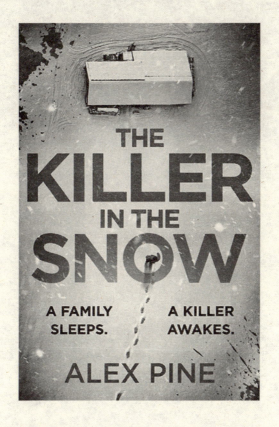

THE
KILLER
IN THE
SNOW

**A FAMILY
SLEEPS.**

**A KILLER
AWAKES.**

ALEX PINE

DI James Walker knows that to catch
this killer, he needs to solve a case
long since gone cold …

**Christmas has arrived in Cumbria,
and wedding bells are ringing.
But an ice-cold killer is waiting in the fells …**

Something old, something new.
One guest is a killer.
The question is: who?

This Christmas, the hunters become the hunted …

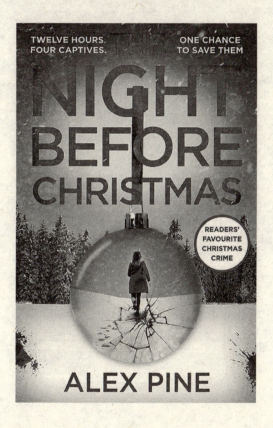

TWELVE HOURS.
FOUR CAPTIVES.

ONE CHANCE
TO SAVE THEM

NIGHT BEFORE CHRISTMAS

READERS'
FAVOURITE
CHRISTMAS
CRIME

ALEX PINE

As a snowstorm descends, three lives hang in the balance. But can the killer be caught before the trail goes cold?

Chilling truths are buried in this snow …

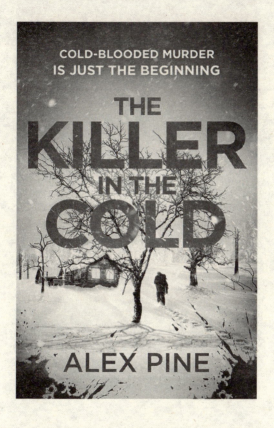

Time is ticking as DCI James Walker races to
uncover a killer's next victim. But can he find
them before the snow washes away the evidence?